MW00324370

Gift

Gift

a novel

Johnny Bloodworth

For Sue
Enjoy
Johnny Bloodworth
listen to the children

Copyright © 2017—Johnny Bloodworth

ALL RIGHTS RESERVED—No part of this book may be reproduced in any form or by any electronic or mechanical means, including information storage and retrieval systems, without permission in writing from the authors, except by a reviewer who may quote brief passages in a review.

Published by Deeds Publishing in Athens, GA
www.deedspublishing.com

Printed in The United States of America

Cover design by Mark Babcock

Library of Congress Cataloging-in-Publications data is available upon request.

ISBN 978-1-947309-06-7

Books are available in quantity for promotional or premium use. For information, email info@deedspublishing.com.

First Edition, 2017

10 9 8 7 6 5 4 3 2 1

To Sandra, who saw me typing away at the computer for many mornings and didn't ask what I was doing. When she finally did ask, and I told her I was writing a book, she didn't laugh. She read what I had written, and again she didn't laugh.

… and to Aunt Mary

Author's Note

Gift is a work of fiction. The setting is based on the real town of Greensboro, Georgia and its environs. Greensboro, Georgia was my grandparents' home. During the fifties and early sixties, I spent much time in town with them, and with an aunt, uncle, and cousins out "in the country." When I was in the fifth grade, 1955, we lived in Greensboro for a time and I attended school there until Christmas.

Although I have taken literary license to change or adjust a few places and create others to suit my story, I hope a reader who knows or remembers Greensboro will recognize it. For other readers, I hope that I have created a real place.

Except for an occasional reference to a public figure, all the characters in my story are creations of my imagination. I have given some of my characters names that may evoke a memory and perhaps a smile. But as they say, "Any similarity to a person living or dead is purely coincidental."

— Johnny Bloodworth, October 2017

1

"Deputy William Brown, please come in. I have something to discuss with you that you will find very interesting." Sheriff De-Witt pushed back his chair and turned it to face the small room that was the Greene County Sheriff's Department. He called out, "Bill," a short pause, "Bill!" With his voice going up an octave, "Oh, Deputy Brown, Deputy Bill Brown!" This call was answered by the flush of the toilet, and Deputy Bill Brown walking into the office. He was holding his pants up with his left hand and his revolver and belt with his right.

"Damn it, Bill, get dressed. Looks like we've got a dead body."

"A body?" answered Bill as he smoothed his shirt into his khakis and strapped on his holster.

"Yeah, Joe Godfrey called from his store. A colored boy walking up the road saw a body off the side near Indian Rock. He ran to the store and told Joe, said it looked like a white woman. You get up there and see what's what. If there is a body, don't move it. Mostly don't move anything and keep folks away. You know how to use our camera?"

"I think. I had some photography during MP school. I can make it work."

"Good. Now get on up there and don't let anybody mess with the body or the area, but take some pictures. From what Joe said it's about halfway between the DuBose place and the road to Mt. Nebo Church, across from Indian Rock. As soon as you get there let me know what's going on. I might call GBI and get somebody down here to help us. I guess I ought to call doc and the funeral home, too. This ain't no way to start a week. I'll leave here as soon as Diane gets here and I make the calls. Turn on the radio in the car."

"Yes, Sir," Bill said as he pulled the camera case off the shelf and opened it. "Sheriff, I know how to use this. We have three rolls of film and I think each will make twelve pictures. That ought to be enough, but if Hunter's is open you might pick up a few more rolls. Get 120."

The Sheriff grunted an affirmation followed by "Turn on the radio."

"You, too."

The sheriff looked at the black metal box taking up nearly all the table by the door. The dials were dark and there was no sound coming from it. He stepped over and flipped the switch on the front and there was a pop from the speaker followed by some static and the dials showing some light. Inside he saw the tubes glowing red-orange and the whole thing settled into a low hum. He picked up the big microphone and squeezed the lever. "Bill, you there?" No reply. "Bill, can you hear me?" Still no reply. "Damn thing ain't working," he said as he put the microphone down.

As soon as the microphone hit the table, Bill's voice came through the speaker. "I can hear you, sheriff. And everything seems to be working. Remember, you have to let go of the mike switch to hear me."

"Yeah, I forgot." He remembered and squeezed the lever and repeated, "Yeah, I forgot. Call me when you find the place and remember to turn off the radio when you get out of the car. The damn thing will run down the battery quick." He picked up the handset to the phone and clicked the button a couple of times until he heard the operator answer. "This is the sheriff, get me doc."

Bill turned left from Broad Street at Mr. Phelps' store onto Laurel Avenue and right at the corner of Elm Street, he passed the dirt road on the left going to Eatonton. In another quarter mile, he turned left onto the dirt road everyone called Godfrey's Store Road.

It was early November but there hadn't been a good frost until the last two nights. The ditch banks beside the road were grown up. The growth was dull green except frost burn showed up on the tender tops. Burned or still green, everything was covered with the red-orange dust of Georgia clay. In 1946, most dirt roads in rural Georgia were shared by wagons and only a few cars and trucks. In Greene County, the wagons were still in the majority and their steel wheels and the hooves of the mules and horses cut the clods of clay to dust. The wider tires and speed of the cars and trucks stirred it up. The dust covered everything.

"What we need is a good rain to clean things up. But if I have to look at a body today, I guess I'm glad we have had the cold weather,"Bill thought.

In a moment, the DuBose house was on his right. It was white, two-story, and sat away from the road on a little hill. It was by far the most impressive house on this side of town. Every time he went by, the same thing went through his head, how did DuBose get away with stealing from the railroad? He couldn't think about that now.

The DuBose house disappeared behind him, and ahead he saw two wagons. One was in the road pointed toward him, and the other was headed up the road toward Godfrey's Store. Several men, white and colored, were standing by the wagons and looking left. He glimpsed a movement in the direction they were looking, and he realized there was somebody there.

Damn it, one white man is going to mess up my investigation. He sped up a little and considered turning on the siren and red lights. Calm down, boy. I don't need to go in there all riled up. Hell, they don't know any better. He stopped the car in the middle of the road and was reaching for his hat when the radio crackled.

The sheriff asked, "Bill, you there yet?" He picked up the handset, held it to his ear and keyed the microphone button.

"Just drove up and there's eight or ten people here."

In his ear he heard, "Get them out of there unless they know something."

"I will. Are you on your way?"

"I'm going to find doc. Should be there in twenty minutes. Now get those folks out of there. I called GBI. They are coming unless we call them back. You call me if we don't need them."

"Yes sir, out." Bill turned off the car and the radio.

Everyone had turned toward his car, including the man who was off the road. He started to make his way back. Bill recognized him and called out trying not reveal his frustration.

"Charles, how about you stay where you are for a minute. I want to talk to you."

Charles stopped where he was and Bill covered the distance to the edge of the road. "Is the body there? Is she dead?"

"Yes, sir. Just there," Charles said pointing at a pale arm and hand Bill could now see. "She's dead."

Charles Dalton was twice Bill's age, so the "sir" in his answer let Bill know, for now, he had some control of the situation. Crafting the next question, he asked, "I see her. Did you get close enough to touch her or move her?"

"No, I weren't going to touch her. I wanted to see if I knew who it was. Oh no, I wouldn't touch her. No, sir."

"Do you know who she is?"

"I can't tell for sure, but she looks like Annie Mattox. Looks like blood on her dress, too."

Charles' response brought murmurs from the white men standing by the road.

Bill didn't know the name Annie Mattox and asked, "Did she live around here?"

Charles continued, "Yes, sir. Her daddy had a little cabin down behind Mt. Nebo Church. But I ain't positive it is her. He died last spring, her momma's been gone a long time. Deputy, can I come out of here?"

"Yes, come on out, but try and come out the same way you went in. GBI is coming and they don't want things disturbed."

Bill walked over to the group of white men. He knew three by name and recognized the other. He didn't know if invoking the Georgia Bureau of Investigation would get more or less information out of them, but he did know he would have their attention. "Mack," he said, looking at the only one without a hat, "Do you know the Mattox girl? Do you think you could identify her?"

"I do. A while back her daddy used to work for my daddy some. I'd see her when we would pick him up. Two years ago, that'd be the last time I talked to her," he said, scratching his bare head. "I seen her on the road some since he passed. I suspect I could say if it were her, but I wouldn't care to go look."

"It wouldn't be now. We can't go to her until GBI gets through. It would be after they took her to the funeral home."

"I reckon I could do that," Mack replied.

An older man said, "I used to see her with her daddy some. But since he passed I only seen her walking on the road. I gave her a ride about two months ago. She didn't say much except she was helping Mr. Brunson's wife with housework."

"Mr. Brunson?" Bill questioned.

The man replied, "His place is up the road past Richland Creek. He milks a few cows and sells butter and eggs. His wife had a stroke or something a while ago and can't do much."

"I know who you are talking about. Anybody else know anything about the Mattox girl?" No one offered anything more. Bill took a little tablet and pencil from his pocket and wrote down everyone's name and where they lived.

He went over to the coloreds' wagon and asked. Mostly the answers were "No, suhs" and head shakes. The man driving the wagon climbed down when Bill approached and stood silently through his questions.

He stepped closer to Bill and said something in a hushed voice. Bill looked up and over his patrol car to the road toward town, and replied to the man who nodded his head. The colored man took his seat, called to the others and they all climbed into the wagon. He shook the reins and popped them lightly on the mule's back and the wagon creaked up the road.

Mack called to Bill and pointed down the road toward town, "Car's coming."

"That'd be the sheriff and the doctor. Unless y'all got something to say to him or GBI you didn't tell me you might as well go on. GBI will be here soon."

Charles and two men climbed in their wagon and started toward town. Mack started walking up the road toward Godfrey's. Bill took the camera out of the car as the sheriff stopped behind Bill's car.

The sheriff was alone and when he was closer he said, "Doc's not coming. He was waiting on a baby. A live one is more important to him than a dead one. Have you seen the body?"

"No, sheriff, only the hand and arm there. I finished talking to the bunch that was here. You want me to tell you what I found out from them or do you want to go see the body?" Bill said as he pulled out his tablet.

"Tell me, and take some pictures before GBI gets here."

Bill went over everything he found out. The sheriff didn't know Annie Mattox, but he did remember the Mattox man dying last spring. He told Bill to go see Mr. Brunson as soon as GBI arrived.

Bill said the coloreds didn't know anything or if they did, they weren't saying. The sheriff just grunted in response. Bill neglected to mention the short conversation with the wagon driver.

"Show me what you have," said the sheriff.

The first thirty feet or so was low, growing with a few briars. When Bill neared the body, he looked where Charles pointed and saw a pale foot and leg disappearing into blue cloth and underbrush. After another two steps, he made out the other arm, equally pale, pointing into the woods. A step closer the blue cloth became black and took on the shape of an upper body. He still couldn't see a head or face. "Hold it, sheriff. I'm going to take a couple of pictures."

For the first time since he arrived, Bill stopped doing and started thinking about what he was seeing. Thinking out loud, he included the sheriff. "It doesn't make sense that she died here. If she did, she wouldn't be all laid out straight like she is, and she'd likely be laying on top of the grass instead of in it. Same if she'd run in here and died trying to get away from somebody. I think she was killed somewhere else and dragged in here. Dragged by the hands the way they're pointing over her head. If she'd been pulled by the feet her clothes would be all pushed up. There isn't a shoe on the foot I can see. If she had shoes maybe we can find them."

"Makes sense, Bill. But before you go looking for shoes, get closer and get some more pictures."

Bill pushed through a low bush and there she was in front of him. Her face was toward him, but he couldn't tell if her eyes were open for the flies and ants. Her skin was pale and blue, almost the color of the top of the dress she wore. Her left side from her breast down was covered in dark dried blood. The dress was still buttoned to the top, but he saw a cut in it at the top of her left breast. The arm and leg he couldn't see originally were laid out the same, the arm above her head and the leg straight out with no shoe. He took more pictures. He finished the first roll, reloaded and decided to get some closeups of her face. After taking six more pictures, he called to the sheriff, "I'm coming out and I think I was right about her being dragged by the hands. Her other shoe is gone. I think I'll go back the way it looks like she came in and see if I can tell anything. Okay?"

"Yeah, go ahead," the sheriff said.

Bill looked at the girl's legs and picked about a six-foot path she might have come through to get to where she ended up. The straw and leaves may have been disturbed a little, but there was nothing proving she had come in that way. He kept working backwards. First finding a possible path and looking to see if anything showed. On the third section, he found a small black shoe. He called out to the sheriff, "I think I found a shoe. It hasn't been here long either. It's small, has to be a woman's, left foot."

"Better leave it for the GBI boys."

"I will, but I'm going to take a picture." Bill kept working along parallel to the road and when he had gone a little further, he came to a small open place where there was a mark in the bare ground, curving to the road. The heel of her shoe could have made that. From there he saw a route to the road and the granite boulder everybody called Indian Rock. Bill skirted along the route and crossed to the rock. The rock had nothing to do with Indians, but it did serve as a landmark and meeting place. A little path was worn around it. Two or three feet into the underbrush, he saw the right shoe. He poked the camera through the leaves and snapped the last picture on the roll. Bill made a small flag of a stick and page of his tablet and stuck it in the ground next to the shoe. A strap had been gnawed pretty good. A rat or skunk. And there were some spots he was sure were dried blood. As he walked out, a black Ford panel truck came speeding up the road. He knew immediately it was GBI. Bill waved them to a stop behind the sheriff's car.

The sheriff walked to meet them. The GBI agents came out of the truck ready to go.

The driver said to Bill, "Where's the body?"

Before Bill could answer, Sheriff DeWitt said, "You made good time, thanks." As he walked up to them he continued, "I'm Sheriff Ben DeWitt and this is my chief deputy, Bill Brown. Let us tell you what we've found so far."

As the only deputy, Bill was not particularly surprised to be the chief deputy, and he graciously accepted the battlefield promotion, probably without a pay increase. He nodded to the agents.

The driver appeared to be in charge and said, "Sheriff, we like to make our own findings first, if we want anything else we will ask. Show us the body so we can start.

"Fellows, I'm sorry. I didn't get your names. We'll need them for all of our paper work."

"I'm Detective Hancock, Johnny Hancock, and my partner is Agent Jesse Ray."

"Good to meet you Johnny, Jesse. Come on over here and Bill will get you up to speed and show you the victim. Go ahead, Bill."

Bill pointed toward the arm and hand they could see from the road and explained, "There she is. She appears to have been killed by a stab wound to her chest. And her shoes are missing. We think she was killed elsewhere and…"

Cutting Bill off, Hancock said, "That's what we determine, deputy. We will get started now. Jesse, get your kit, and I'll go in and take some pictures. Sheriff, we'll be about an hour. When we are done, you can have the body taken to a funeral home where we will continue our investigation." He started through the briars to the body.

Sheriff DeWitt walked over to his car, motioning Bill to follow. At the car, he looked at Bill and said, "Well, I guess that's how the experts do it. I'll stay here and watch, and maybe I can learn something. I want you gone so you don't learn any bad habits from these state boys. Put your camera up. I don't want them trying to get any pictures you've taken. See if you can talk to Brunson and find out if he has seen the Mattox girl. Call Diane and tell her I will be out here a while longer and to get a hold of Fred Thompson to come pick up the body in an hour."

"I'm on my way. Oh, sheriff you might give this to Dick Tracy and Sam Catchem when they come out of the woods." Bill held up the right shoe. "It's the mate to the left shoe I found near the body. I think she was killed over behind the rock and dragged to where she is now. I marked the spot where I found this. But, we'll let the GBI boys tell us. Hope they find the left shoe."

"Good job, Bill. I'll make sure they find the other shoe. Now get on."

In his car, Bill looked to where the body was and saw a pop of light from a flash bulb and the GBI boys moving the body. I'm sorry she's dead, but right now I'm glad she doesn't have to put up with those two.

"Bill to Diane, Bill to Diane, over."

In a couple seconds he heard, "This is Diane, go ahead."

He told Diane what was going on, and he gave her the sheriff's instructions. Bill asked, "Diane, please call over to the school and see if they have a record for Annie Mattox. I'd say she was about twenty now so they ought to go back a few years." As he passed by it on the left he said, "Oh yes, she might have lived on Mt. Nebo Church Road."

"You think Annie Mattox is the dead girl?" Diane asked.

"Maybe, but we don't know anything now. I guess this is all over town."

"Not yet, but me asking questions at the school might get things started."

"Just tell them we are trying to eliminate possibilities. I'll check in before I head back. Anything else going on?"

"Shit, in Greene County?"

For Diane, "shit" was neither vulgar or profane, and it was always at least three syllables. "Diane, I've told you about your language on the radio."

"Yes sir, Major Deputy Brown, sir. Over and out."

"Roger." Ahead he saw Mack Poole walking along the side of the road hunched over against the chill of the morning. "Get in, Mack, I'll give you a ride." As Mack got in the car, Bill flipped the switch to turn the radio off.

"Thanks, I'll take it. Did GBI get there?"

"Yeah, and they are all over the place. I guess they know what they're doing. Anyway, there's something else I want to ask you about."

"What's that?"

"Do you know the DuBose woman?"

"Yes, sir I know who that is." Mack replied.

"I mean do you know anything about her?" Bill continued.

"Well, there's talk, mostly with the coloreds, that she's got the gift. You know she can talk to spirits, dead people. Some of them say she is a conjure woman and knows hoodoo and all. Some go to her to talk to dead kin."

"Any whites go to her? How about you, Mack? Have you?"

"Oh yeah, she gets some whites. Some go right regular. From what I hear Miss Mary does have the gift. I ain't never been to her. I thought about it after my Pap passed to see if he had something hidden on the place, money or something. She charges pretty high, too. Anyway, I found Pap's hiding place, and all that was there was a two-dollar bill and half a bottle of Jack Daniels. I drank the whiskey sitting where I found it, passed out, woke up, and went home in the dark. I ain't studied no more about Miss Mary after that."

Mack paused a minute, "If Annie died close to her house, Miss Mary might have felt something. You know Annie's spirit might become a plat-eye, and Miss Mary would help calm her. I sure don't want no plat-eye on my road, specially as much as I'm on it."

Bill thought Mack's "Miss Mary" implied he had "studied" more about her than he was letting on. And, Mack may have more to tell. "Mack," he said, "do you have time to show me the Mattox cabin? I'll get you home after we go there."

"Yes sir, I'll show you. It ain't far past the church back yonder, but the way up to the cabin's so growed over I doubt you can drive up. You'll have to walk, but it ain't far."

They rounded the curve just before Godfrey's Store. By now the road was only a wide path of red clay and the store was right up to it. Very few cars or trucks ever came this way because the road really didn't go anywhere. Joe's store was in a grove of pecan trees. The store itself was a big box made of never painted heart pine, except there was a big and faded red Coca-Cola sign on the side, the rest of the store was the soft brown-black patina heart pine becomes. A shed roof held up by two short brick columns and cedar posts covered the front door.

As Bill stopped he said, "Joe called us this morning about the body and I'm going to tell him what we've found out. Besides, I want something to drink. Come on in and I'll buy you a dope."

The inside was comfortably dim, only the windows on the front and two bare bulbs on cords hanging from the ceiling lighted the store. A potbellied stove near the counter hissed with a fresh charge of wood. Joe Godfrey looked up when Bill opened the door and added light to the room.

"Deputy," Joe called out, "did you find a body?"

"Yes, the sheriff and GBI are working there now. It appears it was a young white girl. Do you know Annie Mattox?"

"Yes, I do, of course I do. She lives down the way behind Mt. Nebo Church. Was that who it was? She was a sweet girl, but she had it tough."

"We aren't sure yet and there was nothing with the body to say who it was. When was the last time you saw her?"

Joe paused and looked up at the light and said, "Friday evening, right before I went home. She walked in and bought a spool of blue thread. Paid for it with a case half dollar. I remember because I had to open my cash box to make change. She came in, bought the thread, and started down the road. She didn't say a word hardly. That's how she was sometimes." Joe took notice of

Mack who was standing near the door. "Mack, you would've seen her." Looking at Bill, he continued, "Mack came by in his wagon going her way. Couldn't been five minutes."

Mack walked toward Joe and Bill, "I seen her, I did, and I gave her a ride, but just to her road. She jumped off the wagon and started walking down toward her cabin. She didn't say much, hardly even a thanks when she jumped down. But, like you say, that's the way she was sometimes."

Bill walked over to the red Coca-Cola box and opened the lid. There were a couple of dozen bottles of several flavors of soft drinks standing in a bath of icy water. He pulled out a little green bottle of Coca-Cola opened it on the side of the box and said to Mack, "Get you something; it's on me."

Mack picked a Nehi Grape and opened it as Bill fished a dime out of his pocket and started for the door. "Let's go, Mack. Joe, I'll drop the bottles off later."

Bill turned the car around and headed to Mt. Nebo Church Road. Both nursed their drinks until Mack said, "Yonder's the road."

"This where you let her off on Friday?" asked Bill.

"Well, she really jumped off while I was moving."

"She didn't say anything while y'all were riding?"

"No."

"You say anything to her?"

"I tried to talk a little at first, but she sat looking down and wouldn't say nothing so I quit. Deputy Brown, I were a little scared when Charles said it were Annie. I reckon that's why I said I ain't talked to her in years."

"I understand. But you have talked to her since her daddy

died?" Bill asked as he turned the patrol car down toward Mt. Nebo Church and the cabin.

"Yes, sir."

"I suspect a good bit, y'all living so close and all."

"Yes, sir."

They drove on in silence past the church where the one lane road became two tracks with some brown growth in the middle. From the shallow ruts, Bill knew only wagons used this part of the road. "Anybody live down here?" he asked.

"Moses Jackson and his boy, Travis," Mack answered as they came to an opening in the brush and trees growing close to the road. "They got two cabins and a little farm plot. The road ends at his place. Here's Annie's place."

"How far is the cabin?" Bill asked. He could tell the way into the woods was wide enough for a wagon and maybe a car, but with little use the growth was close to the path. Waiting for Mack's answer, Bill got out and walked around to the right side of the car.

"It ain't far."

Bill adjusted his hat and started toward the path. He called to Mack still sitting in the car. "Come on."

Without answering, Mack followed Bill and caught up with him as the path turned. The cabin sat in the middle of a patch of bare red dirt. There was nothing to make it look like anyone had lived there for a long time. A small porch had been on the front, but the floor had long since fallen away. What little roof remained was propped up by two cedar posts and faith. The butt of a big pine log had been moved to the door to make a step. The door was part way open, and the inside of the cabin was dark.

Bill stopped short of the porch and called out, "Annie, Annie Mattox," Mack gasped and jumped. "What's the matter, Mack?"

"I thought you seen her."

Bill walked to the door and put one foot on the log step. He called "Annie" again, and he stepped into the little cabin. It was dark in the single room. The only light came from the door and one window on the front and one on the back. He moved away from the door and, as his eyes adjusted, he saw an oil lamp on a wire hanging from a log rafter. Shuttered openings were at each end of the cabin. Bill stepped to the right and lifted the latch on the shutter and pushed it open. He could see pretty well. "Mack, you coming in?"

"I'll stay out here, if that's all right."

"Suit yourself."

Bill continued to look. On one side was a small table. A very old Franklin stove was in the hearth. On the other side of the room was a wooden bed frame with a new looking quilt spread on it. Everything seemed to be in its place. A girl's place – clean and tidy.

Near the foot of the bed sat a sewing machine. It was an old one but a Singer, and it had the treadle table. A spool of blue thread sat on the spindle. Three scraps of cloth, a half empty paper of pins, and a page cut from a magazine with a drawing of a dress on it lay on the machine's table. That drawing and this cloth look like the dress on the body. Annie's body? This cloth will pretty well prove it is Annie. Bill took the page and a piece of the cloth and folded them in his back pocket.

Bill called out the door, "Mack, there's a sewing machine in here. Do you know anything about it?"

"Yes, sir, it were her momma's own. But, Annie, she sewed on it and sewed pretty good. After he passed, she gave me a shirt she made for her pap."

On the floor near the sewing machine was something he didn't recognize. It had a ruler, he figured, because it was marked in inches, stuck into a metal base so the ruler stood straight up. There was a little vessel which moved up and down on the ruler. The vessel had a rubber tube attached to it and at the other end was a rubber bulb. Bill squeezed the bulb and a puff of white came out of the narrow opening at the top of the vessel. The puff settled to the floor, leaving a small white spot. Bill dragged his fingers through the spot and rubbed them together. Nothing in particular about the way it felt. He smelled his fingers and couldn't tell anything. He started to pick it up by the ruler but it slipped out of the base. He pushed the ruler in and picked up the whole thing by the base and walked to the door with it. "Mack, do you know what this is? Have you ever seen it before?"

"Yes, sir," said Mack somewhat proudly, "that there is a sewing marker. You put chalk dust in the little box there. And set the box on the stick where you want the dress to end and squeeze the ball and it blows a little chalk mark on the dress. Go around in a circle and it gets marked all around."

"Would Annie use this?"

"Oh, yes, sir."

Bill set the marker back and closed the house as best as it could be. "I reckon that's all we can find out here. It doesn't look like anybody has been here for a day or two. I need to get up to see Brunson. Where I can I take you?"

"Just get me up to the road by my path and I'll walk the rest of the way. It ain't far and it's kinda rough for a car. Who do you think killed Annie?"

Bill decided on, "We still don't know if it is Annie" for his response. "Do you know any reason why someone would want to kill her?"

Mack walked along silently until they came to the car. "I surely don't."

Bill worked a bit to turn the car around in the narrow road and started out to Godfrey's Store Road. "You think it would take somebody pretty mean to hurt her?"

"Yes, sir, I reckon," Mack said.

"I'll come tomorrow, I guess, and talk to Moses Jackson and his boy. Don't tell them I'm coming if you see them."

"Yes, sir, but I hardly ever see them."

Bill stopped the car in the middle of the road when Mack said it was his path. As Mack reached for the door handle, Bill put his hand on Mack's shoulder, and he recoiled. Appearing not to notice Bill said, "Mack, thank you for your time today. It has been a big help. If the GBI boys haven't figured out who our victim is I may need to come get you to help with identification. Mean time we'll pray it wasn't Annie."

"Yes, sir, I surely will."

Bill added, "Maybe she is staying with the Brunsons," but Mack was already hurrying down his path.

The Brunson farm was only about two miles more up the road, across Richland Creek. When he pulled in the yard, Mr. Brunson saw him and started toward the car. "I know Ben De-Witt good, deputy, but I don't know you," said Mr. Brunson as he continued toward the patrol car.

"I'm Bill Brown, Mr. Brunson. Sheriff DeWitt hired me after I got out of the Army Air Corps. My daddy had a dairy farm near White Plains."

"Brown, you say. I knew your daddy, he passed a year or two ago. You have a sister, too? You here about the dead woman?" Brunson asked.

"Yes, sir, he passed while I was overseas and I have a sister. I am here about the body we found. We don't know who she is for sure, but Charles Dalton said she looked like Annie Mattox. Somebody else said Annie had been working for you since your wife's been sick. Does Annie work for you?"

"I guess, but we ain't seen her since Friday evening. She wasn't supposed to come Saturday, but she wasn't here yesterday either. We ain't seen her at all since Friday. I need her, too. My wife's in bad need of her help. Do you think she's the one?"

"Yes, sir. Now I do. Since she's not here and not at her place, I'm afraid it is most likely her that was killed. Can I help you with your wife?"

In more of a moan than words, Mr. Brunson said, "Oh no, it's sad about Annie. She was so good to Addie. I don't know what I'm gonna do now. It's bad, real bad. I need a woman to help; you can't do nothing."

"Is there anybody around here I can go get? A neighbor? A relative? Anybody, Mr. Brunson? I'll go and bring them."

With his head in his hands, Mr. Brunson continued, "No, nobody. I'll take care of her. It's hard, so hard. I'll do it."

"Mr. Brunson, do you know anybody who would want to hurt Annie?"

"No, Annie is nice. She takes good care of my Addie. She

was going to move to Athens, but she said she would stay with us 'til the new year. I don't know what to do." Mr. Brunson cried in his hands.

Bill walked over to Mr. Brunson and put his hand on his shoulder. Not used to the touch of another, especially a grown man, Mr. Brunson pulled away and again let his face fall into his hands and sobbed.

Bill patted Mr. Brunson's shoulders and said, "Unless there is something I can help you with right now, I'm going to town to make a report to the sheriff. I'm going to get the nurse from the health department to come out here tomorrow to check on you and Miss Addie. Okay?"

A cow lowed and Mr. Brunson and Bill looked up to the barn. Mr. Brunson said matter-of-factly, "I've got work, deputy. We'll be all right; it will all be over soon. Sorry, so sorry about Annie."

"I'll send the nurse tomorrow."

Mr. Brunson never responded as he headed toward the cow. Bill was on the road to town by the time Mr. Brunson reached the barn. Instead of opening the door to the little milking barn, he opened the gate to the pasture and walked to the house.

In their bedroom, full of the foul smells of soil and illness, he scooped up his Addie and the soggy feather mattress and carried her to her garden. He lay her on the bench he had made for them from the big cedar tree struck by lightning the first year they lived in the house. The bolt split the trunk perfectly in half and he used a six-foot section sitting on rocks for the bench. It was polished smooth from all the time they sat there watching the garden and talking. He didn't know if she could see or not, but he made sure Addie was facing her flower garden. At the house, he picked up his Stevens double and four number 6 shells. He loaded the twelve-gauge as he walked to the garden.

2

Travis Jackson clicked his tongue and shook the reins over his mule's back. "Major," he said, "put a bit of life in your step, and we'll be home early this evening."

Major knew he was heading home; he didn't need encouragement.

"There go the deputy out of Mr. Brunson's place. I reckon he be in a hurry too, kicking up dust like that. Maybe Mrs. Brunson passed, bad sick as she been." Travis turned and saw Mr. Brunson moving toward the house. He raised his hand and called, but not loudly, "Mr. Brunson."

Mr. Brunson never noticed.

Travis was not sure whether he heard the sound first or felt the lurch when Major broke into a trot. "I don't know, Major," he said. "It sounded like it was behind us, but I don't know how far. I'd say it was a shotgun, but it sounded funny." Travis was okay with Major adding some distance.

He knew he heard the second explosion. "Git on, Major," he said and popped the reins, but Major had already quickened his trot. He kept looking behind, but no one came. In a few minutes, the only sound was the creaking of his wagon and the quick clop of Major's hooves on the dirt. When no third sound came, he pulled on the reins and called, "Easy, Major, easy. I don't think there's anybody coming."

Major puffed, blew and slowed, but to a quicker walk than his usual. Major was not so sure everything was over.

Bill stopped at Godfrey's Store and grabbed the two empty drink bottles and walked in. Joe was at his usual place, and Bill placed the bottles on the counter. "Mr. Godfrey," he said, "when you saw Mack come by last Friday, didn't you say he was driving his wagon?"

"Yes, he was in his wagon with his poor old mule."

"He was on foot today. You got any idea why?"

"No, that old mule's right ornery sometimes and his wagon has a bad wheel, but 'til he came in here with you, I hadn't seen him since he drove by last Friday."

Shifting to another concern, Bill asked, "Do you know a woman who could help the Brunsons? Taking care of his wife is way beyond what he can do. He didn't want me to come in the house."

"What about Annie Mattox? I thought she was helping," Joe said.

"Mr. Brunson hasn't seen her since Friday," Bill answered.

"Oh, that's not good. You do think it was Annie that was killed?" Joe asked.

"Yes. But, right now Mr. Brunson needs some help."

"I don't know nobody right off, but I'll ask my wife. Maybe she and some others can go by and see about her."

"That'd be good, I'm going to get the nurse at the health department to come out, too. Thanks again, Mr. Godfrey."

Back in his car and for the first time since he picked up Mack, Bill remembered about the radio. He flipped it on and keyed the microphone.

In a second, Diane's voice crackled, "Where the hell have you been? I've tried to get you half a dozen times."

"I've been out of the car a lot, and for a time had someone with me. What's up? I came past the scene, and nobody is there."

"Fred brought the body to the funeral home about an hour ago. The two GBI agents came, too. What a pair they are. Anyway, they left to go to Atlanta. They said she died from the stab wound sometime on Saturday. The sheriff is out but said he would be back in a little while, and for me to find out where you were and what you were doing. Over."

"I've been investigating, and now I'm returning to base with evidence. Did anyone come up with anything more on the victim's name?"

"Okay, Mr. Detective. I found out there was an Annie Mattox who went to school, but she didn't come any more after sixth grade when her mother died. She was apparently pretty smart because she made good grades, but didn't come much. She'd be twenty now, and she did live off Godfrey's Store Road."

"Diane, do you know anything about *McCall's* magazine?"

"Why do you want to know about *McCall's*.

"I found a page from it at Annie's cabin, next to her sewing machine. On it was a drawing of a woman in a dress."

"*McCall's* is a magazine for women, mostly fashions, you know, dresses and patterns. And there are paper dolls and clothes to cut out. You might like it. Did you say she had a sewing machine?"

"Yes, an old Singer."

"I wouldn't have thought somebody like her would have had a sewing machine. You think she could use it?"

"Yes, and she had been sewing recently. There were scraps of cloth about. Joe Godfrey said he had sold her blue thread on Friday, and there was blue thread on the machine. I think the drawing looks like the dress on the body. I have a piece of cloth to compare to the dress. I'm pretty sure it is the same. When we get done, call Fred and see if they have the dress, or if the GBI boys took it. I'll be there in a few minutes."

"Okay, I'll call, and I see the sheriff driving up now."

Bill saw the DuBose house coming up on the left. I sure would like to talk with her. I guess she's close enough to the road to ask if she saw anything suspicious on Saturday. Maybe she knew Annie Mattox. Annie would have had to come by here going back and forth to town. I'll come out here tomorrow.

He hit the pavement and made the couple of turns through town and pulled up at the office, and he remembered to turn off the radio. Inside, the sheriff was sitting in his chair and Diane in hers.

Sheriff DeWitt looked at Bill and said, "Well?"

Bill told the sheriff and Diane everything that happened after he left the scene, except he didn't say anything about Mary DuBose.

When Bill was finished, Sheriff DeWitt said, "If the cloth scrap you have matches the dress, I think we've got an identification. You think Mack Poole is our guy?"

Diane quickly added, "The dress is still at the funeral home. I told them to put it up and leave it be."

"Thanks, Diane," Bill said. Turning to the sheriff, "Mack knows way more than he let on at first. And he had seen Annie recently. Joe saw them together on Friday evening. Yeah, I think Mack might be our man."

Sheriff DeWitt asked, "Why didn't you bring him in? If he did it, I suspect we could get it out of him pretty quick. You already caught him in a couple of lies. His type goes down quick when the pressure is turned up."

"I don't think he'll go anywhere. I didn't let on I suspected him; he thinks he's helping. Besides, I figured the GBI boys would have this all wrapped up by the time I got here. What did they tell you?"

"They wrapped it up all right and headed to Atlanta about twenty minutes ago so they wouldn't be late for supper. I guess we will get a report, but there won't be anything in it we didn't figure out, or Dr. Parker couldn't have told us."

"Did they say where she died?" Bill asked.

"Hancock said she was stabbed where we found her and died there. When I showed them the shoe you found by the rock, he just mumbled. I told them about the other shoe, but they either didn't look or didn't find it. I picked it up when Fred came for the body. They are both in the car."

"I don't buy that. Somebody dragged her to where we found her," Bill said.

"I agree. When doc looked at her at Fred's, he said there was only one wound on her chest. It looked like it was real deep and it's what killed her. He believes it was made with a long blade knife like a dagger, and she bled to death. He said her death may have been slow without much blood on the outside. He thinks she was stabbed first somewhere else, too. There were scratches on the back of her legs like she was pulled through those briars. Go on down to Fred's and see if the cloth matches and those shoes fit her."

"On my way, sheriff. Can Diane come with me? I want her to look at the dress to see if it looks like something Annie could have made."

"You okay with that, Diane?"

"I guess. It's part of the job."

"You are right as usual, Diane. Bill, when you're done at Fred's, take the film over to Greene Pointe to Mr. Ben and get him to develop it. Those pictures are no job for a drug store. Get him to make big pictures, eight by ten or something."

There were several wagons and a pickup truck at Godfrey's, and Travis moved past the store quickly. In twenty minutes, he turned onto Mt. Nebo Church Road and in another twenty minutes he had the mule unhitched, watered and fed. He wondered why Clara had not come out to meet him as she usually did. No matter, he was glad to be home a little early.

When they came to the white, two-story colonial house that served as a funeral home, Bill drove around back and parked beside the shed for the family cars, hearse and the ambulance. Pete had the black Cadillac hearse out in front of its spot. Even in the evening cool, he was washing the red dust off. Pete Moss was in his mid-thirties now and had lived at the funeral home for fifteen years or more. It was his job to answer calls at night and on the weekends. "Evening, Pete," Bill said, as he and Diane walked to the steps of the porch.

"Evening, Diane, Bill," came Pete's reply. "I think Fred is upstairs. Go on in. The door is open."

As Bill and Diane entered, Fred came up from the basement. "Bill, did you find out who she is? Oh, hello, Diane." Fred paused, "She's a mess right now, I started to clean her up after GBI left."

"I don't need to see her right now, but if we could get the dress she had on. I might be able to make a pretty good guess as to who she is." Holding up the shoes, he said, "Oh yeah, I want to see if these shoes fit her."

"Come on down to the work room with me. The dress is in there. Diane, the girl is on the embalming table in another room," Fred said, as he started down the stairs.

The dress, along with her underwear lay on a work table. Without looking at the scrap of cloth he picked up at Annie's cabin, Bill knew they were the same. He took the scrap from his pocket and handed it to Diane. "Tell me what you think, Diane."

Holding the scrap and looking at the dress, Diane confirmed, "Yes, this is exactly the same material."

"Fred, would you take the dress out of the bag and spread it out so we can look at it?"

"Sure."

Bill said to Diane, "Tell me what you can about this dress."

"It's made out of a cotton print, sort of navy flower shapes on a lighter blue. This style is called a shirtwaist because the top looks like a shirt. And, it is short sleeved. The skirt part looks too long though, too long to be stylish. Hold the bottom up please, Fred. The bottom is not finished. There is no hem. See, the very bottom should be turned up and sewn to the dress. That's a hem."

Bill walked over and looked closely at the bottom of the dress and pointed to a place above the bottom and asked, "Is this about the right place?"

"Yes, that looks right. How did you know?" asked Diane.

"Come closer and I'll show you." Bill pointed to a series of short, faint, white lines. "Do you know what these are?"

Diane came closer and looked at the marks, she took a tissue from her pocket and rubbed one lightly and it disappeared. "These are chalk marks made with a hem marker. A hem marker is thing with has a ruler..."

"Diane, believe it or not, I know what a hem marker is. Annie had one at her place, and Mack explained it to me. Look at this." Bill took out the *McCall's* page and showed it to Diane. It was a drawing of a shirtwaist, short sleeved dress.

"This picture is that dress," Diane said pointing to the dress on the table. "Annie's dress is plainer, but they are the same. See, the one in the picture has breast pockets. Wait a second."

Diane looked at the piece of cloth Bill had given her and held it up for him. She said, "She had cut out this piece to be a pocket. See, it's straight across the top and at the bottom it goes to a point like the pocket in the picture. For it to look right on the dress, the print pattern would have to line up perfectly. If she could make her dress from only seeing this picture, she was quite good. She could have made a good living sewing. What a shame."

"How about these shoes? Could you check to see if they fit her?" asked Bill.

"I will but not today," answered Fred. "One foot is all swelled up because of the blood pooled in it, and the other is shrunk because of all the blood drained out. Let me wait until tomorrow when we've embalmed her. But with the cloth and hem marker, you are sure this is Annie Mattox, aren't you?"

"Yes," Bill answered.

The telephone rang upstairs and Pete called down, "It's the sheriff. He wants to talk to Bill."

"I'm coming, Pete." and all of them started up the stairs. In the office, Bill told Sheriff DeWitt what they had figured out. The sheriff said to tell Fred she was still officially unidentified. Bill relayed those messages to Fred who waved and headed downstairs.

Sheriff DeWitt said, "Tomorrow I want you to go get Mack Poole and Charles Dalton and bring them in to identify our victim. We might want to work Poole a little, too. We'll talk about that first thing in the morning. Meanwhile bring Diane here so I can go. I have a tip to check on. You are done for the day when you get the film over to Greene Pointe. Good work today, Bill. Really good work."

Bill hung up the phone. "Come on Diane, sheriff said to take you to the office before I go to Mr. Ben's. When you get back, please call over to the health department and see if Cornelia or the other nurse can go up to the Brunson's farm and check on Mrs. Brunson."

As Travis walked into his cabin, Clara was sitting in the rocking chair crying quietly. "Clara, what's the matter?"

"Annie is dead," she said. "Somebody done stabbed her and left her by the road up near Indian Rock. Rollo's boy saw her this morning and ran to Mr. Godfrey's, and he called the sheriff. Rollo say the deputy and the sheriff came to where Annie was. Then the sheriff called GBI and they came. Before dinner time, I saw the deputy come down to Annie's cabin with somebody. I think it was the Poole man, but they left."

"The deputy pulled out in front of me up at Mr. Brunson's place, and he looked like he was in a hurry to come down the road. When was she killed?"

"Don't know, And Travis, your daddy said she was wearing her blue dress."

"Her blue dress?"

"You remember, I told you about it. How she copied it out of the magazine and made it. It was pretty and a real lady's dress. Travis Jackson, what's the matter with you. You look plum sick."

"Oh shit, shit, shit, we need to go see Daddy right now."

Walking to the door, Clara said, "Sick or no, mind your tongue, Travis Jackson. If your daddy won't whip you for that kind of talk around me, I will. Now, what's the matter."

"When we were coming home Saturday night, you remember the lantern went out, and I didn't light it again because we were about to turn onto our road?"

"Yes?"

"And, remember we saw a wagon come out of our road going fast and turn to town? And I said it looked like Mack Poole's wagon."

In the moment, Clara understood, "Oh shit, Travis, what are we going to do? Mr. Poole must have had Annie in the wagon. He must have killed her. Oh, shit."

Moses looked up as Travis and Clara came in. "I see Clara's done told you about Annie Mattox."

"Yes, sir. But we've got something to tell you." Travis told his daddy about seeing the wagon leaving their road.

"What time was it?"

Travis looked at Clara and asked, "A little bit after nine?" Clara nodded in agreement.

"You sure it was Poole?"

"I never saw his face, but it looked like his little old mule and his wagon, and you could see the bad left wheel going back and forth. The driver was bareheaded like Poole always is. Daddy, it was him, I know it was."

Clara added, "And he killed her, Mr. Jackson. We better tell the law."

"Clara, we might best let the white folks work on this a while. They'll likely take care of it. If Poole did it, and I reckon he did, he ain't smart enough to get away with it. Yes, we'll let this be for a while. Don't fret, Clara, Annie will get her justice. I won't let it get by."

3

Bill rolled over and squinted at the clock. There was enough light coming in from the window for him to tell the hands of the alarm clock were almost straight up and down. If I get my feet on the floor now, I can push the lever on the clock and not have to listen to the god-awful buzz. Do it. Get up.

The events of yesterday rapidly tumbled through his mind and brought him to his feet. The tasks for today, namely Poole and Dalton, woke him completely. He picked up the electric alarm clock and pushed in the lever. Standing in the narrow space between his bed and the two-windows, Bill slid the curtains open. The street light illuminated the driveway beside the McLean's house and to his garage apartment. The driveway was wet, even to the point the low places had their usual puddles. Looking at the street light, he could tell there was a steady drizzle. Good, this rain will clean up things.

He realized he was cold, not a little chilled but cold. His apartment was heated with a small oil heater. He lit it for the first time on Sunday morning, and while he dressed on Monday. When he went light it, he had already run out of oil in the heater and in the can. Oil will have to wait until this afternoon. A hot shower and breakfast will solve my problem for now.

He flipped on the light in the small bathroom and turned on the water and stood at the toilet. Timing was important to get a hot shower. The heater got the water plenty hot, but it was small. It took a little time to get the hot water up from the garage. When it reached the shower, he had only a few minutes before the hot ran out. It usually took a little longer to get hot water than it did for him to pee. When he finished at the toilet, he checked the water – not quite yet. He couldn't flush. Flushing messed up everything.

After another minute, the water was just right and his timing was good this morning. The water still hot when he finished his shower, so he knew he would get a good shave. Today as always, he put on clean underwear, but today, it would be yesterday's uniform. Whatever he wore would be a mess by the end of this day. He tossed his boxers into the laundry bag and sat it by the door. He would drop it by Caldwell's this morning and pick it up this afternoon or tomorrow. Bill finished dressing. He did like wearing a uniform. He made his bed even though he had enough of that in the Army. Some of it must have stuck.

The breakfast customers at Geer's Cafe came in two kinds, the everyday regulars, and the ones who came regularly, but not every day. Bill was an everyday regular. In addition to being regular customers, everybody knew everybody else. It didn't matter where you sat, everyone was part of a conversation which moved around the room.

Yesterday the conversation was all about Georgia's 14-0 whipping of Alabama and how good this year's team could be. Six and 0 and only Tech at the end of the year was going to be a tough game. He liked it when they worried about Tech.

Today it looked to Bill like all the regulars showed up in addition to the everyday regulars. Why did they all show up in this weather? Some of those guys are not even going to work today. They all want to know about the dead girl, and I'm the one with information.

He considered not going in, but he was hungry and needed coffee. And everyone had seen him drive up. What can I tell them and what won't I tell? I can put a bunch of not telling off on GBI. Maybe, too, I can find out more about Annie Mattox, everybody already knows that name. Mack Poole, maybe I can find out a little about Mack. But before I get involved in any conversations, I'm going to have my coffee.

As he walked through the door everyone turned toward him and stopped eating. In singles and small groups, they greeted him by name or title. Bill decided to take charge and said to everyone, "Morning, let me get a cup of coffee down," he looked at Mazie behind the counter and nodded, "I'll tell you what I can. Maybe, I'll have a question or two for you."

He settled on to one of the two open stools and his coffee was waiting for him. "Thanks, Mazie. I'm going to wait a minute to order, but I'll have my usual." He didn't gulp, but the coffee went down quickly, and he nodded to Mazie for a refill.

She was close by and wouldn't get too far away because she wanted to hear, too. He turned on the stool to face his assembly. "Yes, we think the dead woman was Annie Mattox, but right now we have no positive identification." He added a few of the other things most everyone knew or had guessed. He ended with, "No, we don't have a suspect." He turned to Mazie, "Please fix my breakfast," and to the group, "If anyone does have any information for me, let me eat my breakfast and we'll talk." He looked across the room face by face and no one said anything, so he turned to the counter and sipped on his second cup and ate in peace.

When he finished his breakfast, Bill paid and walked out with no more information than when he walked in. A man he didn't know stood by his car. He looked to be thirty or more and was wearing dirty jeans or overalls under an oilcloth duster and a well-worn felt hat which was shedding the drizzle onto the duster.

"Deputy, I'm Tommy Coles. I heared you think the one what was killed was Annie Mattox. I used to live out past Godfrey's Store, and would work some with her daddy. He were a mean sort, especially to his wife and her. I ain't seen her since right before he died, but I think I would know her."

"Thanks, Tommy. Do you think you could identify her now?"

"Yes, sir, I do."

"Would you go with me to the funeral home and have a look. They may have her in a coffin by now."

"Yes, sir."

Bill moved toward the car door and pointed to the other side. Trying to sound very casual, Bill asked, "Did you ever know a fellow out your way named Mack Poole?"

Coles chuckled, "Him and his daddy. His daddy was harmless. After his woman passed, he got too lazy to raise his voice. Mack is right trifling and lazy, too, but he has a mean streak. Such a one as him weren't no good to be around when he was riled."

"When was the last time you saw Mack?"

"A couple of weeks ago on a Saturday night over to a dance at Siloam. He allowed how he had a girl and was getting hitched, but he wouldn't say who. I didn't take much stock in it as much lying as he done."

Tommy pulled a pack of Beech Nut chewing tobacco from a canvas satchel hanging from his shoulder. He started working together a chew. He paused, held up the pack, looked at Bill and asked, "You mind?"

"I'd mind a lot if you messed up my car, and Mr. Thompson would mind if you spit at his place."

"No, sir. I don't spit. At least not much. I wouldn't spit in your car or at Mr. Thompson's. I'll be special careful."

"Be careful or you'll have me and the sheriff to worry about."

Tommy loaded his chew. Bill drove for a block and asked, "Poole say anything else about who he was going to marry?"

"No, I didn't stay around him. Like I said, I don't like him much. You think he had something to do with this?"

Not wanting to answer, Bill said, "Hold on a second." He switched on the radio and put the handset to his ear. He didn't think there would be anyone to answer, but he could buy time. "Bill to base, Bill to base," he said into the mouthpiece.

A click and the sheriff's voice came through, "Bill, where are you?"

Bill answered, "I'm heading to Mr. Thompson's. I have Tommy Coles with me. He knew Annie Mattox. I'm going to see if he can make an identification."

"Good, but as soon as you get done, come on in here."

As he turned the car into the funeral home he answered, "Yes, sir."

There were no lights on in the back of the big house. Out of the car, both walked quickly toward the steps and the landing at the back door. On the way, Tommy took a quick detour to a patch of grass to spit. As he walked away, Bill noticed his overalls once had been too long, but he had walked some of the length off, leaving a fringe around his boots with a little extra notch at the heel.

Pete must have been up because he came to the back door as soon as Bill rang. "Did Fred finish with the girl?" Bill asked. "Is she okay for us to take a look at?"

"Fred cleaned her up and embalmed her. She isn't in a coffin, but she's laid out downstairs. I can show her to you there."

"Pete, this Tommy Coles, he might be able to identify her."

Pete said, "Pleased" and Tommy nodded.

The shape under the white cloth hardly seemed big enough to be a woman's body and when Pete pulled the white cloth from the head down to the chest the notion of a woman was gone completely. The three of them looked at a child.

Tommy swore softy under his breath and said, "Yep, she's Annie Mattox all right. Deputy you need to find who done this. There ain't no sense. It could have been Poole, or them coloreds what live down below her cabin."

Bill followed up with, "Tommy, you are sure this is Annie Mattox?"

"Oh yes. It's Annie. Damn, damn, damn, somebody needs to swing for this."

"Thanks, Pete, that's all I need. Tommy, let's go. I need to get to the sheriff. Where can I take you?"

"Court house," Tommy answered.

Calling after Bill, Pete said, "Fred says the shoes fit." Bill waved his hand in acknowledgment.

Bill dropped Coles at the court house and rounded the corner to the sheriff's office. Before he could close the door, the sheriff asked, "What did Coles say?"

"He said it was Annie. I asked him if he knew Mack Poole, and he told me he did, and Mack had a mean streak. He also said Mack told him he had a girlfriend and was going to get married. Mack didn't tell me anything like that yesterday. Do you know Coles?"

Sheriff DeWitt answered, "Known of him most of his life, but I don't know if we've ever had a conversation. He never has been in any trouble, at least nothing serious. He moves around the county a lot and never had a steady job. He'll stay in the woods when he can. Warden Copelan made a case or two against him for hunting out of season, but hell, he was just trying to eat."

Bill asked, "Can we believe him?"

"Mostly, I reckon," the sheriff continued, "The Army turned him down when he tried to join. I don't think he can read or write much. Now, I want you to go get Mack and bring him back here so he can look at the girl. I want to be there when he does so call me on the radio when you're headed back."

"How about Dalton?"

"No, we don't need him. Between Coles and the dress, we know it's Mattox. I want to get an idea about Poole. And be careful, he may be a sorry lot, but you heard what Coles said about him. Keep him thinking he is helping. He'll be around his place on a day like today."

Yesterday, Godfrey's Store Road was a dusty red path. Last night's rain turned the dust into a four-inch layer of pure slick.

When the 1940 Ford De Luxe patrol car rolled off the pavement, Bill could feel the rear wheels lose traction. He backed off the gas. The car and its big Mercury motor Ford put into the police model had been well maintained throughout the war years. It was made to chase moonshine runners, and it still ran good. It was faster than anything in the surrounding counties. But, all the power didn't mean much on this curvy and muddy road. Anything faster than twenty was foolish when it was dry but when the tires were spinning, fifteen was too fast. Bill relaxed. No one will go anywhere in a hurry today.

No matter how this Mack Poole thing works out, I'm going to come out here and talk to Mary DuBose. She might have seen something but if she didn't I'd still like to talk to her and find out about her. And, I want to see the inside of the house. And, there was the house. As he looked he saw a light come on in an upstairs room. Damn, it's an electric light. How the hell does the DuBose house have lights. There are no poles on this road and nobody else has lights. It can't be the EMC. They ran a line to Godfrey's Store before the war, but it came through the woods three miles from the Atlanta highway. Rayle EMC hasn't done anything since the war was over. Yeah, Godfrey's Store is the only place on this road with lights. I'll bet she has a telephone, too. Godfrey got the telephone co-op to run a line on the electric poles. The line must come from town. What the hell did Jefferson DuBose do to get what he has?

When he reached the spot where Annie's body was found, his thoughts returned to Mack Poole. He passed the store and shortly came up to the turn to Mack's place. The path had looked okay yesterday. It was overgrown but the grass and weeds were better than the mud. *I'll take a chance.* There was a little drop off from the road to the path. Coming out I'll have to get a start and never stop at the road.

After about a quarter mile the path opened to a clearing with a house. It had once been painted, and someone had kept up the yard. But both had been neglected for a long while. Since Mack's mother passed. The porch floor was mostly there, the windows had tattered curtains pulled closed behind them and there was a hint of smoke drifting out of the chimney.

Bill rolled up opposite the front door and stopped. In a minute, I'll see if the horn will rouse Mack. But for now, he looked. In back was most of a shed, most likely for the mule. The place simply looked like nobody cared at all.

Bill leaned on the horn and the sound split the silence. A hound bayed, looked at the car, slunk from the porch, and crawled under it. Bill hit the horn again, this time a little longer and he was rewarded with a longer response from the hound. The mule poked his head out of the shed and ambled to the fence. Bill got out of the car, and reached in for a third blast of the horn. Again, he had accompaniment from the dog.

Bill called out, "Mack Poole, this is Bill Brown. Come out." He could see one of the curtains open an inch or two. In a moment, the door cracked open and the head of a rough looking Mack Poole filled the space.

A disembodied and frail voice called to Bill, "Deputy, what you want with me?"

Bill called, "Like we talked about yesterday. I need your help. I need you to see if you can identify the body. If you'll come with me now, the county will buy you breakfast at the cafe."

"Deputy, give me a minute or two and I will be ready to go. Wait out there, my place ain't presentable.

"Okay, but don't take too long."

As he was getting in the car, he noticed Mack's wagon. The left rear wheel was canted out like the hub was busted. That's what has him on foot.

Bill looked up to see Mack stepping across the yard to the outhouse. In a few minutes, Mack reappeared and walked into the cabin and emerged in a few more minutes. Bill pulled the Ford in gear and rolled up to where Mack would be and stopped.

Mack was rank. The smells of body odor, wood smoke, and moonshine filled Bill's car.

Mack said, "Breakfast sounds mighty good, I didn't get much supper last night."

"We'll stop at the cafe before we go to the funeral home."

As he neared the place where the path to Mack's cabin rose to the road, Bill slowed nearly to a stop, and looked up and down the road. He couldn't see very far, but the most likely vehicle coming would be a wagon, and he could see far enough for those. He had never gotten out of first gear so he gave the V8 some gas. He could feel the rear wheels spinning a little as he raced up the incline. At the top, he turned hard left and gave it a little more gas. The rear of the Ford cleared the rise and swung across to the right side of the muddy road in a slide that threw dirt twenty feet off the road, a little more gas and a turn to the right had the back wheels digging in and fishtailed the car to the left. After a couple of more little waves back and forth, they were moving down the road with no problem.

When Bill turned on to Broad Street, he called the sheriff

and let him know they were headed for the cafe. It was quarter past ten, and breakfast was over, but he knew he could get Mack eggs, grits, and bacon, Geer's would likely be empty, and given Mack's condition, that was good.

In the cafe, there was one customer at the counter who looked up and nodded to Bill. Bill, nodded and said to Mack, "Let's take the table in the back and I will go and give Mazie our order. How do you want your eggs, bacon okay?"

"Scrambled and bacon's okay, but if they got ham, I want ham," said Mack as he sat at the table.

When Bill came back and sat down, he said, "They have ham."

Mack squirmed in the seat, "I've need to go to the…privy."

"The bathroom is that door," Bill said pointing to a door down a short hall behind Mack. "Go ahead, and maybe wash up. Don't leave it in a mess, either."

"Yes, sir."

When Mack came out, he looked a little better and maybe his aroma was down a notch or two. Looking at Bill, he said, "You ain't gonna eat anything?"

"I ate early this morning. This coffee is all I want now." Bill was going to say, "Dig in," but he was way too late for that invitation. This isn't going to take long at all. And it didn't, although Mazie had emptied the grits pot and added the last two biscuits in the place.

Mack sopped up the ham gravy with the last half biscuit. In favor of his sleeve over the undisturbed paper napkin, Mack wiped his mouth and said, "Let's go."

Bill looked at Mazie as he placed a dime under his saucer and said, "Put this on the county tab, Mazie. Thanks."

"Who's that?" Mack asked when he saw the sheriff's black Ford parked behind the funeral home.

"It's the sheriff. He had to sign some papers for Fred, and I guess he wanted to know if you could identify the body."

"I don't much like this," whined Mack as they walked to the steps of the back door. "I mean looking at dead folks and all."

Bill said, "Me neither, Mack, especially someone so young. You know you might have been the last person to have seen her alive."

Mack didn't answer.

When they entered, the sheriff was standing near the door and Bill said, "Sheriff DeWitt, this is Mack Poole. He may be able to make an identification."

"Oh, I know Mack. We go back a ways. Thank you for coming in. Let's go downstairs," and the sheriff put his hand on Mack's shoulder and turned him to the stairs.

Bill stepped in behind Mack and they started down the stairs. Mack had no choice but to lead them. Pete was already in the embalming room standing beside the table. Bill and the sheriff guided Mack to the head of the table and the sheriff asked, "Ready?"

Mack didn't reply, but with a glance from the sheriff, Pete pulled the sheet down from Annie's head to her chest far enough to expose her wound. Mack gasped and turned away. By now both Bill and the sheriff had a firm grip on Mack's arms.

Bill said calmly, "Mack, is this Annie Mattox? Can you identify her? Take a good look and be sure. Tell us and we can go."

Mack sucked in a breath, let it out and turned to the table. He opened his eyes and closed them quickly, and dropped his head to his chest. "Yes, sir. That be Annie Mattox. I'm sure. I'm sure. Let me out of here," and he turned hard against the sheriff's hold.

"Easy, Mack. We can go. Pete, cover her up," the sheriff said as he turned Mack toward the stairs. "Thank you, Mack. I know it was hard."

Mack responded with a sound and they heard the telephone ring upstairs. Pete came by quickly and headed up the steps two at a time saying he was the only one there and he had to answer it. With his hand still firmly holding Mack's arm, they paused and the sheriff asked, "Now, Mack, when did you tell Bill was the last time you saw Annie?"

The sheriff felt Mack's arm tense as he looked first at Bill and at the sheriff. "I ain't sure right now, I mean I ain't remembering real good now after seeing Annie."

Pete's voice came from the top of the stairs, "Sheriff."

Sheriff DeWitt looked up, annoyed at the interruption.

Pete continued, "Diane's on the phone and she says she has to talk to you right now. It is an emergency."

"Bill, Mack, y'all wait right here. Let me see what has Diane in such a state."

Up the stairs, the sheriff picked up the phone and turned to the wall, "Go ahead, Diane." He listened for a moment. In another moment, the sheriff turned and yelled, "Bill come here right now."

Like Pete, Bill took two steps at a time and was quickly beside the sheriff.

Mack stood at the bottom of the stairs and decided he wanted to be upstairs too, and walked up and stood by the door.

Bill stood by Sheriff DeWitt as he covered the receiver with his hand, and asked Bill in almost a whisper. "What time did you leave Brunson's place yesterday?"

Also in a whisper, Bill replied, "It was shortly after one o'clock. A cow had come up to the barn, and he acted like he wanted to check on her. He was upset about his wife and having no help for her, but when the cow started bawling, he snapped out of it and said they'd be all right. No, he said everything was going to be over soon. Actually, he said both. Why?"

"Godfrey called in and said his wife and her sister went by there this morning to see about Mrs. Brunson and found both of them dead laying out by the garden. Joe says it must have been pretty bad, because they've been carrying on awful since they got back."

Bill felt like he had been kicked in the gut, "Dead? Son of a bitch, I don't understand."

"I don't either, but Bill, get up there as fast as you can. Do you still have the camera?"

"Yes, did you buy more film?" Bill asked the sheriff.

"Yeah, it's still in the car, in the back seat. Get it, and take lots of pictures."

"What about Poole? How about I drop him at his place on my way? He isn't going anywhere."

"Do that, now get going."

4

"Come on, Mack, get in. I've have something to take care of right away." Bill ran down the steps and to the sheriff's car, and retrieved the bag of film. Mack was still only half way to Bill when he started it. "Hurry, Mack!" he called. Mack hurried a little and Bill settled into the seat. After a quick start and turn out of the parking lot, Bill calmed. There is no need racing through town and getting folks wondering now. There's going to be a mess of curiosity soon enough, and I don't want to spook Mack.

"What's going on, deputy?" Mack asked.

"It's probably nothing, and I probably shouldn't tell you. Somebody came into Godfrey's and told him there were some hobos making a camp close to the paved road. The sheriff wants me to check on them, and get them moving on."

"You reckon they could have anything to do with Annie?" Mack asked.

"I doubt it. Seems they just showed up, and it's a long walk from where they are to where we found Annie. But, it is possible." Neither spoke as Bill passed the DuBose house, Indian Rock, and the crime scene. Bill tried another question. "Mack, Mr. Brunson said Annie might be moving. Do you know anything about her moving? Did she ever say anything to you?"

Mack took a long time to answer, and scratched his head, "I might have heard something about it, but I don't remember who told me. It weren't Annie."

"Could it have been Mr. Brunson who told you?"

Mack answered quickly, "No, it weren't Brunson. He don't like me, and I don't ever go up toward his place. I ain't got no need to go his way."

Satisfied with the information he was getting and keeping Mack off guard a little, Bill tried one more. "Do you know Tommy Coles?"

"Yeah, I know him, but I don't like him," Mack replied quickly. "He's bad, real bad. Why? Did he say something about me? It'd be a lie, probably."

"He said he saw you over at Siloam, and he said you told him you were going to get married. You remember?"

"Yeah, I remember, and he didn't lie on me. I told him, except I was lying to him. What woman would have me? Weren't no good woman what would have him neither."

Godfrey's Store came into view, and Bill didn't slow down as he passed. The rain had stopped, and it was getting colder. Continuing to pick for information, Bill said, "Lying about getting married is a funny thing to lie about."

"When he stayed up here, Coles would always be digging on me about how I couldn't get no woman. He ain't got no woman neither. Now, he's the one who had an eye for Annie. I'd watch him when he was around her. Yes sir, I think he surely did like Annie," Mack said. "Coles was mean, too. Mean as he was, he were bad scared of Annie's daddy."

"I heard Annie's daddy was pretty mean."

"He were, he were mean to her, her mammy and to every-body. I know he beat Annie's mammy bad. After her mammy passed, he wouldn't let Annie go away from their cabin, not even to school. That's why she wanted to move so bad. Like I said, Coles were mean too, especially if he'd been in the 'shine. He'd go off in a minute and want to hurt somebody if things didn't go his way. Man or woman, it weren't no matter to him."

Bill weighed his next question for a minute and decided to try it. "You didn't want her to move away, did you?"

"No," a pause and Mack continued scratching his head, "I mean I didn't have no say in it. It weren't nothing to me if she moved or stayed."

Neither of them spoke again until they were nearly at the path to Mack's cabin. As they came closer, Bill could see the ruts and rises he had made coming out of Mack's path had been washed flat by the rain and cut through by a couple of wagons this morning. He was afraid if he stopped he might get stuck. With his eyes on the slop in front of him he said to Mack, "I'm going to drive by your path a little way before I stop. I'm afraid of getting stuck. You are going to have to walk in. Sorry."

"Ain't no problem, the rain's stopped."

Bill lost traction in the mud as he passed by Mack's path, but he didn't stop moving until he was about fifty yards past, and the road felt firmer. He stopped in the middle of the road, looked at Mack and said, "Thanks again for your help this morning."

"Deputy, what's gonna happen to Annie?"

"If we can't find a relative, the county will bury her."

"Ain't no relatives," were Mack's last words as he started down the road to his path.

Bill turned into the Brunson place and parked where he had the day before. Four cows were outside the fence and milling around the barn, but they started bawling and moving toward him and the car. The cows started the two fox hounds in their pen howling. Bill knew the cows hadn't been milked or fed this morning. He looked over to the garden and saw the Brunsons' bodies.

A bucket was a few feet ahead on the path to the barn. He picked it up and banged his hand on the side calling "soo, soo," and walked toward the barn. He knew milk cows would follow a man with a bucket and calling out. It meant feed and a milking. They followed him past the gate which he closed. In the barn, he found half a sack of sweet feed by the door. He had to push his way past the cows at the door to get in the yard. He poured the feed out on the ground and the cows started on it. He stepped through the gate and went to the car for the camera. I'll take a quick look around, take some pictures and radio the sheriff.

The split log cedar bench, shiny from the rain, sat under a big dogwood tree still holding about half of its rusty red leaves. Directly behind it was Mr. Brunson. He was flat on his back, and a double-barreled shotgun lay across his legs. Mr. Brunson no longer had a neck except for a ragged strip of skin tethering his head to his body. His head was turned, one ear was where his nose should have been. His still open eyes seemed to be staring up to the barn.

Beyond the bench and in front of some untended rose bushes lay a wet, white and pink pile of bedding barely holding onto a head of gray hair matted with dried blood the rain had turned to black goo.

Without moving he took two pictures of Mr. Brunson and

two more of the bench and the bedding beyond. He walked carefully around the bench to the bedding. The woman's head with its wispy white hair was holding onto its body by a bit of throat. Bill took a couple of pictures and moved closer. With his nightstick, he pushed the bedclothes away from the shoulders of the nearly headless body. There, below the ripped skin where her neck should have been, were black marks on her shoulders. Powder burns from the gun held close to her neck. He took the last two pictures on the roll of the powder burns.

When he looked up from the camera he saw two spent shotgun shells lying beside the bench. He knelt by Mr. Brunson's body and pushed his shirt open where his neck had been and on the skin and shirt were more of the powder burn marks. He picked up the gun and broke it and two more spent shells ejected. Both barrels at once for her and for him. Bill stood and looked over the scene, and Mr. Brunson's exact words came to him, "I've got work, deputy. We'll be all right, it will all be over soon. Sorry, so sorry about Annie."

Bill walked slowly to the car, started it and radioed. "Sheriff," he said, "we will have to call it a murder and a suicide, but the truth is life just passed beyond Mr. Brunson. Are you going to call GBI?"

"After yesterday I don't see the use of them. What do you think, Bill?"

"When you get here, we will go through the house. If we don't find anything to make us think somebody else is involved. We let it be what it is."

"I'll call Fred and Dr. Parker and get them up there. Anything else?"

"There are four cows in need of milking and feeding, and there's a bunch of chickens, but they're okay. I guess his hounds need feeding, too."

"I'll call Neal over at the Extension office and see if he knows somebody who'll come get the stock, else I'll call the Mason's and they'll have a barbecue and pancake supper."

Bill's answer was, "While I'm waiting, I'm going to take some more pictures."

"Good, take a bunch, especially if we aren't going to have GBI in here. By the way, Ben brought over the pictures you took yesterday. They were good. He said you had the exposure right."

"Here comes somebody. It's the old Studebaker pickup from the Health Department Carl Foxx drives. I'll bet he drove Cornelia out here. Yeah, there's two in the truck. Won't be anything for Cornelia to do now. I'll send them back. Anything else?" With nothing more from the sheriff, Bill turned off the radio and the car and walked over to the pickup. He told Carl and Cornelia the Brunson's were dead. And now it was a matter for the sheriff. Both wanted to ask questions, but he sent them back to town with no more information.

Bill used one more roll of film taking pictures of the bodies from all angles, including more close-ups of what he thought were the powder burns. He collected the shells, two from the ground and the two from the gun. They were all #6 shot. He knew Fred would find some pellets in the bodies and if they were #6's they would be more proof of the murder-suicide. As he walked to his car, he saw the sheriff's car followed by Fred Thompson's hearse and Dr. Parker's car. The sheriff and Dr. Parker were alone in their cars, but Fred had brought Pete. Everyone met at Bill's car and acknowledged one another. The sheriff took a couple steps up toward the bodies and called to the group.

With the five of them standing there, the sheriff said, "All right, Bill show us what you've found."

Bill explained, pointed, and demonstrated what he worked out had happened. The others looked, nodded, knelt, stood, and walked around. They asked questions of each other and Bill and in about fifteen minutes they walked toward the cars and stopped. Pete covered the bodies.

The sheriff looked at Fred and asked, "What do you think, Fred?"

"I think Bill is right. I remember Billy Dobson shot his daddy's head off from less than two feet. He used a double ten-gauge goose gun. Two barrels from a twelve gauge would do about the same. And those marks, powder burns, look like what was on the Dobson man's body."

"How did Dobson's head look?" Dr. Parker asked.

Fred continued, "We about didn't find his head. Old Dobson was leaning over the front of their little boat when Billy shot him. Billy said he had to reload to blow away the last bit of meat holding his head on. The head fell in the river and drifted about half a mile. It finally bumped into the back of a traveling preacher standing in the river baptizing his converts. The way they tell it, he reached around to see what hit him, and he pulled Dobson's head up by the hair. All of them walked on the water out of the river."

"Fred, be serious."

"I was serious, Ben."

"Doc, what do you think?" Sheriff DeWitt asked.

"Mrs. Brunson was shot from behind. There's no doubt. It

looks like Mr. Brunson jammed both barrels under his jaw and fired them at one time. I agree both barrels of a twelve gauge that close could about take off a head."

Sheriff DeWitt gave instructions, "Bill, you and me need to go through the house and make sure these bodies weren't a result of a robbery. Doc, if you have enough for signing the death certificates, you're done here. Fred, take these poor souls to the funeral home. The paperwork for this one is gonna be mean. Bill, call Diane and get her started trying to find next of kin then meet me at the house."

At the door to the house, the sheriff said to Bill, "You did good again today, but I'd just as soon we quit having to fool with dead bodies and get back to moonshiners and busting up stills. Let's see what's in here, and I hope it's nothing."

The back door was unlocked and they walked into a mess in the kitchen. As bad as it was, it only showed signs of an inept old man trying to feed himself and his helpless wife. Nothing seemed to be disturbed in the parlor or the hall. The bedroom was in as bad a state as the kitchen, except it smelled more of urine, soiled clothes, and sickness.

Bill looked around the room and said to the sheriff, "Nobody except Mr. Brunson has been in this house since the last time Annie Mattox was here."

"Right," the sheriff agreed, "maybe Godfrey's wife can get some women from the church to get their maids to come up here and clean up. I know she won't come back after seeing what she found. Neal said he could get somebody to come and get the stock. This is a murder-suicide, but it for sure wasn't a crime, nor was it a sin." Looking at Bill, "What about Mack Poole?"

"I let him off on the road at his place. He keeps letting out little bits. I'll come get him in the morning. I think if you question him hard and show him all the lies we've already caught him in, he'll confess. He is none too bright."

"Him, nor his daddy before him. Yeah, tomorrow will be okay. He's not going anywhere. Go on and take the film over to Mr. Ben's."

"I will, I need to get some oil. I woke up to no heat and I know my place will be cold sure enough by now."

"Yeah, go on, get your heat going. It's nearly four o'clock, no need for you to come to the office if you go to Greene Pointe. But in the morning come by my house and we'll talk. Gwen will feed you a good breakfast, not what you get at Geer's. In the meantime, I'll go see Carey and make sure he gets this right for the paper."

"Yes sir, and thank you. I'd just as soon not be the center of attention another morning at Geer's."

5

When Bill reached Mr. Ben's store in Greene Pointe it was a little before five. He felt he needed to warn Joda Ben about how gruesome the pictures were going to be. Joda said he had probably seen worse in Germany before the war. And, he was talkative and wanted to discuss photography.

Bill begged off and started to Greensboro. He knew he could get oil at O'Neal's until six o'clock and Jim would lend him something to get it home in. He was hungry. He hadn't eaten anything since breakfast, his refrigerator was empty, and all three of the cafes in town closed by three o'clock. He was down two choices. One, he could beg a meal from Diane or, two, he could try Mrs. Littlejohn's.

Mrs. Littlejohn had a big house and rented rooms to young ladies. There were two teachers there, a girl who worked at the court house and a new girl that started working in the bank. Mrs. Littlejohn had let him stay a week when he first came to Greensboro, but she didn't much like "having a rooster in the hen house" as she put it but she wanted the money and he need-ed a place. While he was there he had been charming, helpful, and paid her a lot of attention. He was pretty sure she would feed him. The biggest reason he didn't want to go there was he had taken out one of the teachers a couple of times after he got his own place.

Their first date was to a supper and dance at the Masonic Lodge near Siloam. Bill had used the last of his Army money to buy a pickup truck, a 1941 Chevy. He picked her up at Mrs. Littlejohn's and drove out to the lodge. It was a simple evening, barbecue chicken dinner and a four-piece country band that could play a little swing, but only a little. Being the lodge, they had beer and some hard stuff in the backroom, but being the new deputy and on a first date, he let it be. They had a pleasant enough time and the food was good. They danced a few times and he liked being able to hold her, and she didn't seem to mind. Later in the evening they played some slow music and they danced some more. But by ten o'clock people were leaving, and they did, too.

It was a twenty-minute ride to town and they talked all the way, mostly about the people they met. Bill asked about what the men did. She asked him about the war and flying airplanes, but didn't seem too interested. They got to Mrs. Littlejohn's sooner than either of them wanted, and walked up on the big front porch. There was a light over the front door Mrs. Littlejohn kept on all night long. Standing in the light she said she had had a nice time. He said the same, and he would call again if was all right. She said it was, and she guided him away from the door to the dark corner where the front room came out. There she kissed him. She had to stand on tiptoe to reach his mouth. It was a closed mouth kiss at first, then open and some tongue touching, but she never let her hands move from her side and he never put his hands on her. She stood down, turned and went in the door, leaving only a whispered "good night" behind. Bill turned and walked slowly to his truck and drove home wondering.

They talked from time to time during the next two weeks and went out again. This time a big date to Athens for supper and a movie. She sat close on the ride over and held his hand during the movie. On the ride to Greensboro, she sat even closer and talked through a plan for their future together with references to marriage and children. Bill didn't call on her again. He had heard she and the new Methodist minister had gone out a time or two.

Mrs. Littlejohn was the better cook; he chose her; got his oil, and drove over.

When he lived there he usually came and went through the back door which was unlocked during the day. He parked on the street behind the house and walked into the hall. Mrs. Littlejohn was in the kitchen and didn't hear him until he called from the door, "What's the best-looking cook in Greene County got for supper?"

"Nothing for the likes of you," she said with a smile, and Bill knew he would eat well.

He knew he could pay for it with a bit of information about the murdered girl, and buy dessert with a little of the sad story about the Brunsons, though with Carl and Cornelia back and Joe Godfrey's telephone, the Brunsons might be old news by now.

Mrs. Littlejohn said her girls would eat at six-fifteen, and he could wait, or she would fix him a plate now and they could talk. The latter offer appealed to both. Fortunately for Bill, the Brunson news had not spread so he doled out a few meager spoonsful of Brunsons, and she repaid with a few spoonsful of her banana pudding. Bill felt he got the better of the deal. He explained about his heating problem; thanked her profusely, and promised to stop by soon.

In the time before the girls were to eat, Mrs. Littlejohn had a chance to decide exactly how to tell her version of the story.

His apartment was cold when he walked in, and it took him about twenty minutes to get the oil heater cleaned up and lit. Once it got going it put out plenty of heat and warmed his little place nicely. Most nights he turned it off before he went to bed, and re-lit it in the morning. As the room warmed, he took his half bottle of Johnnie Walker Red from the cabinet along with the one cut crystal old fashioned glass he owned and poured in two fingers of the amber liquid. From the tap, he added a few drops of water and swirled the glass. At his lips, he inhaled the smoky sweetness and felt the warmth in his mouth and down his throat. It wasn't eight o'clock, but he realized he was dead tired, and dirty.

He undressed and let his clothes lay where they fell. In the bathroom, he turned on the shower and waited until the water got hot, finishing his drink as he waited. He needed to wash this day off. He got in and scrubbed hard and quickly, and stood letting the stream hit his head, his shoulders, his back until he felt the water starting to cool. When he got out, the bathroom was steamy and his apartment was warm. He dried himself, turned off the heater and lights, pulled out the alarm button on his clock and piled into the bed. He lay down thinking about Mack Poole and closed his eyes, and opened them as the alarm buzzed.

Up now, he looked at the clock on the stove and it read four-twenty-five, but it always read four-twenty-five. He sat on the bed and worked through Monday and Tuesday. It's only Wednesday. Now, what the hell am I supposed to do today? Go get Poole. But first, I get to eat breakfast with the sheriff at his house. I think I'll take another shower.

The shower cleared his head, and improved his attitude. When he counted-up that he had slept nearly ten hours, he began to feel pretty good. Clean underwear and a clean uniform helped, too. He tidied up his place a little, washed his glass. As he dried the glass, he remembered the RAF pilot, a Scot from St. Andrews who taught him to drink whisky during pilot's training. "'Tis nae Scotch; 'tis whisky!"

By a quarter to seven he was headed to O'Neal's to fill the patrol car and return Jim's oil can. He drove on to Sheriff De-Witt's home for breakfast.

The Sheriff stood on the stoop at the side door and waved to Bill. He had on his usual white shirt but no tie yet. Bill had only seen him in uniform twice since he started. He ushered Bill in and put him at the kitchen table set for two. In a minute, Mrs. DeWitt came in, and both made their manners. She offered to pour Bill a cup of coffee which he was glad to accept. She busied herself at the stove. The sheriff sat down and said to Bill, "I want you to go first thing and get Mack Poole. Bring him in. I think if we question him hard, he'll break. He might know something about the Brunsons."

Bill replied, "I think he'll break, too. I've already caught him in a bunch of mistakes. He doesn't know how to lie. If he did it, he will tell us. But I would be surprised if he knew anything about the Brunsons."

"Brunsons or not, I want to get the Annie Mattox case wrapped up before the GBI boys try and stick their noses in our business. Do you want any help when you go get Poole?"

"No, he thinks he is still helping us, and I won't let on any different until we get him in. I may bribe him with another breakfast. It didn't look like he had anything to eat in his cabin."

"Okay, but don't feed him before you bring him to the office."

Mrs. DeWitt brought two plates with pancakes and sausage patties and set them before Bill and the Sheriff. She turned to the stove and returned to the table with a bowl of scrambled eggs and a pitcher of warm sorghum syrup. "I've got some blackberry jam if you'd rather have it for your cakes."

"The syrup will be fine, thank you," Bill said over the sheriff's mumbling. Bill understood in time to add, "Amen" when the sheriff stopped. Gwen DeWitt left them alone in the kitchen.

They both worked intently at their plates for a few minutes. Mrs. DeWitt returned, poured them both another cup of coffee, asked if they needed anything and when she was satisfied they didn't, she returned to the front room.

"Sheriff," Bill asked, "do you know anything about Mary Du-Bose? Anything about her being a conjure woman who can talk to the dead?"

"Who told you about her, Bill?"

"I did grow up in this county, and we always heard things. But, there was a colored man at the scene on Monday, I've got his name in my book, and he told me she is a hoodoo lady and she might know something because the body was so close to her house. Mack Poole said he was scared the dead girl would become a plat-eye and haunt the road."

"A plat-eye? Poole may have more to worry about than some big-eyed haunt on the road. I've known about Mary Greene Du-Bose since she came to Greensboro. Me and her husband were friends before they married, and after. There are a lot of folks believe she has the gift and can talk to spirits. I know she has sessions, "seances," in a special room in her house for those who want to talk to their dead relatives. She has a healthy business from what I can tell. Lots of folks, whites too, that believe in that stuff. I don't, but she is different from most mediums. She charges good money, but I don't know why. Jefferson Davis DuBose had more money than God with what he got from the railroad cars."

"I've heard he stole from the railroad, but they couldn't prove anything," Bill said.

"No, he didn't steal from the railroad. They never would have put up with him if they even thought he was stealing. They wouldn't have needed to prove anything. I don't know exactly how all of this worked. He never took anything from a railroad. In the Twenties when the Florida land boom got going, the railroads built lines down to Tampa and other places. A bunch of Yankees started buying building materials and furniture and other stuff and shipped to Florida. They even shipped whole houses. That house of his came down in boxcars, so did this one."

"How did he make money from that?" asked Bill.

"The way I heard is when the rail cars got to Florida, there wasn't anybody to take delivery or even to unload some of them. They started stacking up on every siding between here and Tampa. Up north, the railroads ran out of empty cars. DuBose and a couple of other fellows started unloading the cars and sending them back up north. The sent them either empty or with a Florida load. The railroads were happy, they got paid for hauling the stuff down to Florida, and maybe for a return load. At least they got back their car and it was empty."

"That sounds pretty clever, I guess it was legal," said Bill.

The sheriff continued, "Word is DuBose and the others bought some cotton warehouses to store stuff in until they could sell it. One or two of the fellows he was working with must have had some money to pay for the unloading and warehouses. They must have made a little money in the twenties, but during the depression they didn't make a dime. When the war started, they were able sell stuff to the government and cleaned up."

"He didn't steal?"

"No. DuBose took stuff out of rail cars and sent them back. He put the freight up for safe keeping. When nobody claimed it, he sold it." The sheriff chuckled, "If he didn't tell Mary Greene where everything was before he died, maybe he did after. There still may be a bunch of stuff still sitting in a cotton warehouse somewhere. There's been talk of that since DuBose died."

"Doing all that and he still kept his job as the depot agent?"

"Why not? During the depression, he needed the job to live. During the war, the railroad needed him because of his experience. Why don't you talk to her and see if she knows anything? She might have known Annie Mattox, anyway."

"Yes, I'd like to, and maybe get to see inside the house. Speaking of rooms…"

"Just up the hall on the right."

When he returned, Mrs. DeWitt was clearing the table, and he thanked her for the breakfast and hospitality.

For the third day in a row, Bill started his work day heading out Godfrey's Store Road. The road wasn't nearly so slick today as it was yesterday. It wasn't muddy, just wet. Tires, wagon wheels, and hooves left marks that stayed until something else came through. As cold as it was and early, just past eight-thirty, he felt like Mack Poole would still be holed up in his cabin.

About the same time Bill hit Godfrey's Store Road, Mack, riding his old mule, turned onto the lane to Mt. Nebo Church and Annie's cabin. Poole met Travis Jackson in his wagon coming out and they nodded to each other but passed by without speaking. Travis kept checking for Poole behind him, but he never showed.

When Bill got to the road to the Mattox cabin, he slowed and stopped. From the wheel ruts and mule tracks it looked like two wagons had come out this morning. One turned toward town, and one up the road toward Godfrey's Store. He decided to stop at Godfrey's store. Joe always had something to tell. He was standing in his usual place behind the little counter when Bill walked in.

Bill called his name and Joe looked up, "Deputy, glad to see you. I've got questions for you."

"What questions?"

"First tell me about the Brunsons," Joe said.

Bill gave Joe a complete story of everything he wanted known about what they found, including he and the sheriff believed it was a suicide. He saw no use in calling Mr. Brunson a murderer.

Godfrey allowed as how he had figured that out himself. He said the way his wife carried on, she would have nightmares the rest of her life. Godfrey asked him about the hobo camp up near the paved road.

Though he knew the answer, Bill asked, "How did you hear about the hobos?"

"Poole walked in here late yesterday looking for something

to eat. He told me you said you were going to see about the hobo camp. That didn't make no sense to me. When you came by here yesterday morning, I figured you were heading to the Brunson's."

"I was, but I didn't care about Mack knowing about them, so I made up the story about the hobos. What else did Mack say?"

"He said he told you it was Annie Mattox, and that's about all, except that he kept saying he didn't have any food at his place. He wanted me to give him credit. Of course, I didn't, but I did give him some meal, a little lard, and a piece of fatback. He thanked me, sorta, and started up the road toward his place."

"Did you say anything to him about the Brunsons?"

"No, I didn't. I was ready to go home and be done with him. But, I stayed here until I was sure he was gone."

"If Mack comes here, how about give the sheriff a call. I see a car track in the road that looks like it was made this morning. You got any idea who it was?"

"It was Neal in his county truck. He had two fellows with him. I thought they might be going to Brunson's to check on the cows."

"I suspect you're right. See you later."

The path down to Mack's cabin still showed the scars of Bill's exit yesterday. Bill steered the car down the path and stopped where he had the day before. Everything looked pretty much the same. There was still a hint of smoke coming from the chimney, but other than the smoke there were no signs of anything or anyone around. Bill rolled down his window and leaned on the horn for a long blast. The sound stirred up some crows down behind the cabin, but that was all. The old mule didn't come from his shed to investigate. The dog raised his head and laid it down. Another blast of the horn yielded nothing more.

Bill shut off the car and got out. He took a couple steps toward the cabin and called out, "Mack, Mack Poole, this is Deputy Brown. Mack, are you in the cabin?" No reply.

Bill walked closer to the house. As he got close, he noticed the gap gate to the pen for the mule was down and there were tracks coming out going toward the road. He called out again, "Mack, this is Deputy Brown, I need to talk to you. Are you in there?" Again nothing.

He stepped on the porch, pulled his night stick and rapped loudly on the door frame. When he had no response, he pushed the door open with his foot and went in. Mack was not there. It didn't look like he had been gone long, and he was planning to come back.

Bill walked out to the gap gate and found boot prints in the wet dirt back and forth between the house and where the mule had stood. From the footprints and hoof marks, Bill decided Mack had gotten on the mule. He followed the tracks to behind where his car was parked. From there they led down the path toward the road. In the car, Bill drove to the place where the path started up to the road and got out. He could easily follow the tracks up to the road, but there they got lost in the jumble of other marks. He couldn't tell if they went down toward Godfrey's or up toward Brunson's farm. He reasoned if Poole had turned toward Godfrey's he would have run into him this morning, or at least, Godfrey would have seen him. If he had gone up the road, Neal or whoever came from the Jackson place in a wagon might have seen him.

Bill headed up the road and reached the Brunson's farm before overtaking the wagon. By the time he got to there, he was sure Neal's truck had gone up the road first and the wagon had come after.

The truck was up by the barn and he could see one cow tied to the fence. He pulled in and walked toward the barn. A man came out and greeted him by name. Bill recognized him as Oren Hall, a farmer who had a small dairy just out of town, "Hello, Oren. Y'all looking after these cows?"

"Yeah, we fed 'em good and milked 'em. Neal's been away from the farm too long, he weren't much use as a milker. Me and my boy are going to drive 'em down to my place. You need any milk or fresh eggs?"

"No, I don't do much cooking. Did you see anybody on the road coming up this morning?"

"Nary a soul coming. But a few minutes ago, Travis Jackson came by in a wagon."

"I wonder where he'd be going. There ain't much up this way."

"I think his daddy, Moses, has a sister who lives a little way up, Their place ain't far off the road. You looking for somebody?"

"Mack Poole." Bill answered, figuring it was time to get the word out. "He's been helping us with the girl's murder. He identified her and we have some more questions for him."

"Annie Mattox?" Oren asked.

"Yes. If you see him when you're driving the cows, how about stop at Joe's and get him to call the sheriff. Is Neal inside?"

"I'll do it for sure, Bill. Neal's inside. We got him doing something he's good at." Oren laughed at his own joke.

Inside, Bill found Neal shoveling manure out of the little barn and greeted him with, "Good job there, Neal."

Neal turned and said, "Hello, Bill," and he walked over. Bill and Neal had the same conversation inside the barn as Bill and Oren had outside. Neal was going to drive to town ahead of Oren and his son, and could look for Poole all the way to town.

Bill left the Brunson's and followed the wagon track for about half a mile until it turned off on a little lane to the right. In a hundred yards or so he came to a nicely kept cabin with a wagon and mule tied out front. He got out and started for the cabin when a young man came from the cabin. "Are you Travis Jackson?" he called.

"Yes sir. Is something wrong?"

"No, I want to ask you a question or two. Did you come from your place this morning?"

"Yes, sir."

"Do you know Mack Poole?"

"Yes, sir, I know him. I saw him this morning riding on his mule down my road."

"What time was this?"

"I don't know, exactly but it were a little more than an hour ago, I guess."

"Did you talk to him?"

"No, sir, he don't talk much to colored folk, we kinda dipped heads as we passed."

"He was headed down toward the church?"

"I 'spect he were going to Miss Mattox's cabin. He's there a lot. Is she the one what got killed up at Indian Rock?"

"Yes, it was Annie Mattox."

"It's a shame, she was nice. Nice to everybody, even Mr. Poole."

"Thank you, Travis. I might have some more questions about Miss Mattox later."

"Yes, sir. Deputy, there be another man who come to see Miss Mattox, too. But, I ain't seen him in a while. I don't know his name, but I think my daddy do."

"Thanks, Travis. I'll ask your daddy about him." Bill was in a hurry now, but the road was still too wet to hurry much. Past Brunson's he caught up with Oren and his son driving the cows, and he had to slow down and stop and wait for them to make a way for him to get around them.

At the turn to Mt. Nebo Church, he stopped to look at the road and tracks. It appeared the other wagon that had gone out earlier had come back and it was pulled by two mules. With all the tracks of mules and wagons going and coming he could not pick out the tracks that might have belonged to Mack's mule.

He drove on past the church to the turn to Annie's, and he got out and walked to the path leading to the cabin. There was a fresh set of hoof prints which went in and another set that came out. He couldn't tell which way the set that came out turned, but it made no sense Mack would head toward the Jackson's.

Back in the car, Bill drove down the path like he had done on Monday afternoon. He got out and followed the tracks across the bare ground to the fallen down porch. From their visit on Monday there were a good many foot prints in the dry dirt around the door. He went into the cabin and found it empty and like they had left it on Monday.

On foot, he followed the mule and boot tracks around the cabin and down a foot path into the woods. After about a hundred yards, the path petered out and it was harder to find the mule's tracks on the pine needles, leaves, and undergrowth, and he saw no more boot prints. In another fifty yards the track he was following disappeared completely in a swampy area. He scouted back and forth, but found nothing more to track.

Back at the cabin, he found the mule tracks leading out from the woods to the road. He back tracked along them, but lost all connection when they came out of the swamp. He didn't know where or why Mack had gone into the swamp and come out, but it didn't look like he was there now.

In the car, Bill radioed the sheriff and told him what all had happened. Bill could tell he wasn't pleased they didn't have Mack, but he agreed he couldn't have gone far, and would likely show up at his place by night fall.

The sheriff ended their radio conversation with, "You make one more run up and down the road. If you don't turn him, we'll go to his cabin before dark."

Bill drove up beyond the Brunson's place to where he had turned off to talk with Travis Jackson and down to the turn to Mack's place. There were no new tracks anywhere around the cabin. He drove down Annie's road and into her place, and there were no new tracks there either. He pulled onto the road and decided not to stop at Joe's again and headed to town.

6

Heading into town, Bill made up his mind to stop and talk to the conjure woman. I'll ask about knowing Annie Mattox and when she last saw her, and nothing about spirits or plat-eyes or haunts. Yeah, and Mack Poole, I will ask if she knows him. He hesitated slightly and made the turn into the lane leading to the big white house on the hill. The lane made a left turn at a big oak tree and went straight to the house.

The house was two-stories, narrow across the front and deep. There was a porch with columns, not round columns, but square, tapered and in pairs. The porch on the second floor he thought might be off a front bedroom. He could see at least six gables and a lot of windows. If the house came in a rail car, it had to have come from somewhere else. I've never seen a house like this one anywhere around Greene County.

He stopped on the left side of the house and could see eight big windows, four down and four up. On both floors, three of the windows made a bay under one of the gables. The light he had seen on Tuesday morning had come from the upstairs bay. Today, there was a light in the downstairs bay. The other window downstairs, at the front, was completely dark. He walked up the broad steps to the porch. The front door was in a little open alcove to the right of the front room. The window there was covered by heavy drapes inside. Bill started to knock, but saw a little brass plaque with a black button. He pushed it and heard a four-note chime from inside.

In a moment, the door was opened by someone wearing overalls and a plaid flannel shirt. Even in a man's clothing, there was no mistaking this was a girl, a very pretty girl. She had dark red hair, green eyes, and no freckles. Bill stood silently looking. He tried to remember what it was he was doing.

A voice from behind the vision before him called out, "Momma, he's here."

Bill looked and saw the nine or ten-year-old girl who had spoken go into what must be the room with the bay windows.

Gathering himself, Bill got out, "Ma'am, I'm Bill, Deputy Bill Brown and I would like to talk with Mrs. DuBose. Is she here?"

"Yes, she is, Deputy Bill. Won't you come in? I'm Bet...Elizabeth DuBose."

Bill removed his hat and walked into a large hall. Stairs to the second floor were on the right. On the left were double pocket doors held closed by a brass lock. In front of him was an open door to the dining room and to the left was the short hall to the bay window room.

Elizabeth spoke, "Come this way into the parlor. Momma will be with you in a few minutes." She led him into the room with the bay windows and gestured for him to have a seat on the sofa. The sofa was on the shared wall with the front room and it blocked a closed door. Elizabeth looked at the younger girl and said, "This is my little sister, Connie."

"Pleased to meet you, Connie, and you too, Elizabeth. Connie, how did you know I was coming to see you? Did you see me driving up?"

Connie looked at Bill and said, "No, we knew you would, me and Momma." Turning to Elizabeth, "Betty May, why did he call you Elizabeth?"

"Don't you remember 'Elizabeth' is my real name?"

Connie turned to Bill and said, "Cornelia is my real name, but Momma and Betty May call me Connie. What's your name?"

"My real name is William Brown, but most folks call me Bill. You can, too. May I call you Connie?"

Bill took his seat on the sofa and Connie answered, "That will be fine, Bill." She sat on the sofa next to Bill.

Elizabeth took a chair by the door to the dining room. Bill wanted to look around the room more, but he found it hard to take his eyes off Elizabeth. He was trying find a question to let him learn how old she was, when she asked, "Can you tell us why you are here?"

Connie answered before Bill could speak, "I already told you. Me and Momma told you. It's about the ones who passed. First Annie and after, the two right together. I'm sad about Annie, but the other two were old. It was close to their time, especially one of them."

Fully surprised, Bill asked, "Who told you about all of that?"

Elizabeth answered, "Nobody told them anything. Connie and Momma know about things like this all the time. They call it a gift. I'm glad I don't have it."

Connie, sitting to Bill's right, looked up at him and said, "You hurt your arm bad didn't you and it's hurting right now? How did you hurt it?"

Bill's right arm did hurt right now, his elbow. It always hurt when it was cold and damp. He answered, "I was in an airplane crash in the war and I broke my arm. I had to stay in hospitals for a long time. Now it hurts when the weather is bad."

"I'm sorry," Connie said, "Is this where it hurts?" Connie put her hand on the exact spot on his elbow where the pain always started. Her hand was warm. More than warm, it was almost hot and warmth moved from it up and down his arm, and the pain eased and was gone.

"How'd you do that?" Bill asked.

"Don't ask," said Elizabeth who understood what had happened. "Just be glad."

A small woman walked into the room. Bill stood.

"Momma," Elizabeth said, "this is Deputy Brown. He wants to ask some questions."

"I know, Betty May," and she walked over to Bill and extended her hand. "I'm Mary Greene DuBose." Bill accepted her hand, and it was soft and warm, but not warm like Connie's. "Sit down, please, I am." She took a seat in a big chair in the corner of the room.

Bill didn't know what he expected of Mary Greene DuBose, but what he got was not it. She was small, not any taller than five-two. Wiry, might be the word and she looked strong. She was gray all over. Her hair was not visible but hidden in a gray wrap tied in front. She had on a long sleeved, gray dress that covered down to her ankles. The only skin visible was her face and hands and they looked so pale they almost matched her dress. She had little spectacles, with no rims, perched way out on her nose. The only colors about her were her pure green eyes, like Elizabeth's, and a large gold cross hanging by a gold chain around her neck. She touched it often as they talked. She could be forty or she could be sixty. She was, in fact, only thirty-eight.

Mrs. DuBose began, "I know you want to talk to me about the ones who passed. We seldom know the names of those who pass, but we sense the change. If the passing is violent or mean, we sense that, too.

"Did you see anything?" Bill asked.

"We had gone to my sister's this weekend and were there until late Monday. When we came back, Connie knew there had been a passing close by. She cried all night because she felt like a soul we knew. Tuesday evening, we heard it was Annie Mattox."

Bill continued, "You knew Annie Mattox?"

"Yes. She was sweet and friendly. Annie and Betty May went to school together some. But, we don't know about the other two. Their passings happened together and were violent. We didn't sense much more except they were old."

Bill decided to tell a little about the Brunsons to see their reaction, "The two who passed on Monday were Mr. and Mrs. Brunson. He had a little farm up above Joe Godfrey's store."

"Oh yes, we know them; poor Mrs. Brunson has been ill. Connie sensed a gun. Were they shot?" asked Elizabeth.

"Yes," Bill answered. "Mrs. Brunson had been sick, paralyzed, and Mr. Brunson couldn't take care of her. We think..."

"He shot her and he shot himself," Connie finished Bill's sentence.

"Yes, Connie, that's what we think."

Together, Connie and her mother bowed their heads and prayed.

When she raised her eyes, Mrs. DuBose asked, "What's the connection between Annie and Mr. and Mrs. Brunson?"

Surprised again, Bill answered, "Annie had helped to take care of Mrs. Brunson."

"Deputy Brown, we want to help. We didn't see anything. But sometimes if I go to where there has been a passing, I get a sense of things. Will you take me to where Annie died?"

"Me, too!" said Connie.

"Yes, you, too," answered her mother.

"Yes, ma'am. I'll be glad to take you. It is close by, across from Indian Rock. We can go right now."

"We were about to have dinner. Please join us, then we can all go," said Mrs. DuBose.

Bill said, "Thank you, I would like to."…and to spend some more time with Elizabeth.

They all stood and Mrs. DuBose gave instructions, "We will eat in the dining room. Connie, please put some ice in the glasses for the tea, and Betty May, you can help me in the kitchen. Deputy, if you would like to wash up, the bathroom is at the top of the backstairs, through the kitchen and up."

"Thank you," and he started for the kitchen. As he passed the door, he looked into the dining room and saw the table already set for four. He realized no one had been in the dining room since he arrived so it had to have been set before he came.

Bill was very glad for a few minutes alone. All of this was much different from anything he could have imagined. Elizabeth, oh, I do hope she is at least seventeen. If she went to school with Annie she could be eighteen or nineteen. I want to see more of this house.

At the top of the stairs he turned right into a long hall going to the front. There was a room on his left, a bedroom, he guessed, and the bathroom beyond on the right. He went in. It was a big room with a toilet and a hand sink on either side of a large tub on one wall and a long dressing table with a mirror on the other. When he finished washing, he walked out into the hall. He stood for a moment looking to the front of the house. There must be a bedroom over each of the rooms downstairs, one over the parlor, one over the front room that's all closed, one over the dining room, and there must be one at the end of the hall where he saw a door. Five bedrooms upstairs, this place is huge.

Downstairs, he found all seated in the dining room. The four places were in the middle of the table, two on each side. The empty place was beside Elizabeth, opposite Connie and Mrs. DuBose. Tea had been poured into glasses at each place, and the food was in serving pieces in the center of the table. He sat down and said, "This looks very good. My dinner is usually a sandwich."

"We hope you enjoy this," Mary said, "Would you return thanks?" As she spoke she extended a hand to each of her daughters and they extended their other hands to Bill.

He managed a "Yes, ma'am," as he took Elizabeth's hand and reached across for Connie's. He knew a table grace, but decided not to use it. He felt like he had covered everything in a reasonably short time and ended with, "Bless us to thy service. Amen."

All echoed his amen, and Connie released his hand. He held on to Elizabeth's a fraction of a second longer and gave it the slightest of a squeeze. For an instant, he felt like she squeezed back.

The meal was wonderful, a kind of chicken perlo with slices of spicy red-skinned sausage that made the rice pink. It looked strange, but was very good. There were butter peas. Bill had noticed the big green glass canning jars in the kitchen, and corn bread. Everyone ate almost silently, but as they were finishing up, Mrs. DuBose asked Bill if he knew his Bible.

"Not too well. My momma took me to Sunday School and all. When I was in the hospital, I started it and read through *Second Kings*."

"Did you ever read any of St Paul's epistles?"

Bill guessed, "Just verses in Sunday School" was a good answer.

"Do you know who St. Paul was?"

"Sort of, I mean, I know he wrote some books of the New Testament and we call him an Apostle, like Peter and John. He wasn't one of the twelve, was he?"

"No, he came after Jesus died and rose. Amen. He taught about Grace and the Holy Ghost or the Holy Spirit. Do you know about that?"

"Oh, yes, ma'am. The Father, Son, and Holy Ghost, the Trinity."

"In *First Corinthians*, Chapter 12, Paul says the Holy Spirit gives us gifts. He says different ones get different gifts. Some can teach, some can heal, some can prophesy, some can speak in tongues, and some can interpret tongues. We call them gifts of the Spirit. Have you heard of this?"

"I've heard of the things you're talking about, but I didn't know the Holy Ghost gave them."

"The Holy Ghost did give them and there are more than

what I told you. What Connie and I have are gifts of the Holy Ghost. My gift is I can sometimes be in touch with the spirits of those who have passed. Connie has the gift of healing and speaking in tongues. This is not black magic and it is certainly not from Satan. It is a gift of God by the Holy Spirit and we treasure and honor our gifts."

"I think I understand a little."…and Elizabeth is a gift of the Spirit all by herself.

"We will clear the table and straighten up and be ready to go in a few minutes."

"Please take your time. I'm going out to the car and radio the sheriff to let him know I will be in later than planned." He stood and pulled Elizabeth's chair back as she stood up.

She looked right at him, smiled and said, "Why thank you, sir."

As he walked out, Mrs. DuBose said, "Betty May, Deputy Brown seems to be a very nice young man. Don't you think?"

"Yes, ma'am," she replied.

"He's nice looking, too," Mrs. DuBose added and finished silently with, "He could be helpful here."

7

Bill stood beside the car and flexed his right arm. It simply wasn't sore now. What happened? Did that little girl really do something? The DuBose family came out, and he walked around to the passenger side and opened the front door for Mrs. DuBose.

Mrs. DuBose said, "Elizabeth, you get in the front."

"Good," Bill thought as he opened the back door. Mrs. DuBose paused and Connie jumped in and she followed. Elizabeth stood to the side and Bill stepped around to the open front door and looked at her and said, "Ma'am."

Driving, Bill asked, "Elizabeth, when were you in school with Annie?"

"Most of elementary school. I remember fifth grade most, she was in sixth. They moved her to fifth because she missed so much. She was smart; they didn't need to punish her because her daddy wouldn't let her come regular. After her mother died she didn't come any more."

Exactly what I wanted to know. Elizabeth is at least nineteen.

Mrs. DuBose broke his thoughts with, "Deputy, please tell us what you think happened. Betty May is old enough and Connie understands, sometimes more than I."

"Annie Mattox was stabbed. Dr. Parker thinks somewhere else and brought to the spot I'm going to show you, and she died there."

Connie broke in, "Annie did die somewhere close by."

"Let him finish, Connie," said her mother.

"There's not much more. She was wearing a dress she was making, but it wasn't finished. It was like she was trying it on when she was attacked."

"The dress was blue and it didn't have a hem yet. And she had lost her shoes."

"Yes, Connie, you're right." Bill said. How the hell does she know?

Standing by the road where Annie's body was found, Bill pointed, "She was there, on her back, with her legs in that direction and her arms in this direction."

"May we get closer?" asked Mrs. DuBose.

"Yes, but there are a lot of briars, be careful and follow me."

Bill led them through the path beaten down by all who had come and gone on Monday. He stopped to pick a place to stand so Connie and Mrs. DuBose could get closer.

Connie screamed as if she were in pain.

In the same instant, a shadow passed over, and Bill felt like he had been hit by a blast of cold air. He felt the chill in every bone in his body. The pain returned to his right arm, and he reached for his elbow. Turning, he looked up to see what had caused the shadow. He saw nothing. There was only a bright sun in a clear sky.

Elizabeth grabbed him and covered her face in his chest.

Connie's wail slowly diminished into sobs.

Mrs. DuBose put her arms around her daughter, "I felt him

too, Cornelia. He's looking for her. He will not bother us, but be wary, he may return."

Connie sobbed on and clung to her mother.

Mrs. DuBose asked, "Deputy, what time is it?"

Confounded by this question, Bill answered, "Twenty minutes after two. Why?"

"The one who murdered Annie Mattox just passed. His spirit came here seeking her spirit. Connie and I felt his spirit here. His presence was very strong. You may have noticed."

Not sure he understood, Bill asked, "You say Annie's murderer is dead?"

"Yes," Mrs. DuBose replied, "he died just now, at twenty minutes after two."

For a few minutes, the four of them stood silently in the little patch where Annie Mattox died. Mrs. DuBose finally spoke, "The murderer's spirit will not find Annie's spirit here. Her spirit is at peace. It will not be a hag or a haint in this place."

Connie said, "Amen."

"Deputy, who do you think murdered Annie?" asked Mrs. DuBose.

Bill was trying to make sense of what had just happened and what Mrs. DuBose told him about Annie's murderer. Even with what she had said, there was nothing in anything he had learned about police work that would suggest he answer her question, but the next words from his mouth were, "Mack Poole."

Connie sobbed, "No."

"Where do you think he is?" asked Mrs. DuBose.

"I don't know. I have looked for him all morning," Bill answered.

"Take us to Annie's cabin. We may be able to sense something."

"No, it might be too dangerous."

Before anyone said anything else, all four turned toward the road at the sound of a wagon. Four ears appeared over the little rise, then heads and eyes. Bill reluctantly released Elizabeth and took several steps toward the road to see Moses Jackson on the seat of his wagon rise over the brow of the little hill in the road.

"Deputy Brown," he called out. "I seen your car. I need to tell you something." Not waiting for a reply, he continued, "My boy, Travis, come home about an hour ago, and he say you be looking for Mack Poole. He say he told you he saw him coming down our road this morning."

By now, Moses had the wagon stopped and Bill was beside him, "Yes, he told me, but I didn't find Poole."

"Yes suh. I had come out our road before Travis went out and I ain't seen Mr. Poole. I took my Liza and Travis' Clara and baby down a little ways to Liza's sister's, and I came home pretty soon after. When I got past Miss Annie's place, I looked behind me and Poole's old mule was following me. He came right on in at my place and tried to find something to eat. It were powerful hungry. I run him into the pen and gave him some hay."

"Go on," Bill said.

Moses continued, "I drove up to Miss Annie's and looked around for Mr. Poole and hollered and played a call for him, but I didn't hear him or see him. I didn't go in the cabin or nothing. If he'd come in there on the mule, he ain't gone out on it cause it's still in my pen. After I did some chores and ate my dinner, I come out here looking for you and to go get Liza and Clara."

"Moses, what's back of the cabin? I followed the mule tracks around behind the cabin and down a little foot path, I came to a swamp and I lost the track. When I came out I saw the mule tracks heading out to the road. I back tracked the mule to a different place in the swamp."

"It ain't no big swamp at all. Fact, in summers it dries up and there's dry ground between the cabin and the creek."

"Moses, where are you headed now?"

"As soon as I get Clara and Liza and take them home; I was going to look for Mr. Poole. I ain't want him to think I took his mule."

"Don't worry about the mule. I need you to help me look in the swamp for him."

"Yes, suh. If you say so, I will. Mr. Poole be a torment to Miss Annie."

Mrs. DuBose led the others up to the wagon and Moses took off his hat and said, "Good evening, Miz DuBose, Miss Betty May, Miss Connie; hope you all are well."

"Thank you, Mr. Jackson, we are well."

Bill said, "Head on to the Mattox cabin, Moses. I'm going to take Mrs. DuBose home."

"Yes, suh I'm going to go down the next path to Liza's sister's house and get my family. I won't be long," and Moses clicked to his team and started down the road.

Riding to the house, Bill asked, "If Mack Poole did this, you believe he is dead because his soul came looking for Annie's just now?"

Mrs. DuBose replied, "Whoever killed Annie is dead now. I am sure. But, deputy it was the murderer's spirit, what some call ghosts, who came here. His soul is waiting to join his body at

Judgment Day. God willing, body and soul will burn in hell for eternity."

Connie added, "Amen. The one who did this was somebody who knew her, but not …"

Mrs. DuBose pulled Connie close, "Not right now, Connie. We will talk inside."

Standing beside the car at the DuBose home, Bill said, "You have given me a lot to think about. I'm not sure I understand it all."

Elizabeth took his hand and said, "Bill, I don't understand all of the time either, but have faith. Momma and Connie can help."

Bill rubbed his right arm and said, "I'll try. I will come back to tell you what we find out. Oh, thank you for dinner. It was delicious."

Mrs. DuBose looked at him, at Elizabeth, and back to Bill and said, "You're welcome and we would like to know what you find. But, I think you would come to see some of us if you didn't find anything."

Connie stepped close to Bill and held his right elbow. "Did it start to hurt again when the spirit came?" she asked.

Bill nodded, "Yes."

Connie bowed her head and said words Bill didn't understand, all the while moving her hands up and down his arm.

The heat from her hands warmed him more than the spirit had chilled him. Bill closed his eyes and felt the cold and pain leave his body. He opened his eyes and looked down at Connie who was looking up at him. He took both her hands in his and said, "Amen, Connie, Amen."

8

Bill called the sheriff on the radio and told him about Moses Jackson finding Poole's mule. The sheriff said he would get a couple of others and come on out to help in a search.

Bill met Moses and his family as they were coming out of the path down to Liza's sister's. "Moses," he called as the car and wagon rolled along the narrow road side by side, "I'm going on to the cabin and look around there."

Moses reached under the seat of the wagon and pulled out a feed sack and took an old bugle from it and showed it to Bill, "I'll blow three long notes when we come."

Bill drove on to Annie's cabin and took a flashlight, a hatchet, and the camera from the trunk. He put the camera on the backseat. When Moses and Travis reached the cabin, Bill asked Moses to blow something loud to see if they could get a reply. Moses stood in the wagon, wet his lips and lifted the bugle. He played the loudest "Reveille" Bill had ever heard.

Even after Moses moved the horn from his lips, the sound seemed to continue for minutes. "That's as good as I can do, deputy."

Looking at Moses, "Up on the road, you said Poole tormented Annie. What did you mean?"

"Well, suh, he'd come to see her some. We'd see him in his wagon or riding his old mule of an evening. Sometimes he'd go to the cabin, but sometimes he'd tie up out by the road, and I don't think he'd go to the cabin unless he sneaked. Travis' wife talked to Miss Annie some and she say Miss Annie told Mr. Poole not to come around. But it appears he did, no matter."

Bill looked around to see the sheriff's car with at least one other in it and following him was the game warden with another in his truck. Good. We can do a decent search in the light we have left.

When he got out of his car, Bill saw the sheriff had changed from the black suit he had on this morning to a uniform. He took a couple of steps toward Bill and returned to his car, and took his revolver from under the seat and put it in his jacket pocket.

Bill would take Travis, and Buddy Wilson, who they used as an extra deputy, with him. They would start in where the mule started in. The game warden, the fellow who came with him, J. P., Moses, and the sheriff would try and backtrack from where the mule came out. All except Moses, Travis, and J. P. had pistols.

One shot would be the signal they found Poole, two would mean they needed help. They would stay together while they searched, and start out before dark at five-thirty. It had been cool all day and now since the sun was getting low, the temperature had dropped.

Bill went to where the mule tracks disappeared into the swamp and he did like he had done working out how Annie's body was dragged to the spot where they found her. He looked ahead and tried to find an opening a mule could go through and would walk along until he needed to make a turn. He and Buddy would call out for Mack from time to time, but their calls yielded no response. After about twenty minutes of wading through ankle deep water they reached the higher ground Moses had mentioned. There the trees were old oaks and hickories that had lost their leaves so they had better light.

Travis found a couple of marks that looked like they were made by a mule. The three followed them a way before they petered out. They had been searching about an hour and would have to start working their way out of the woods before it got dark. As they scouted around the spot where they lost the track, Buddy said he heard the creek. They all walked over and looked.

Bill could see a big oak tree downstream. "We'll go as far as the big oak, and then get out of the woods before it gets dark. That big tree will be a good starting point if we come back," he said.

They spread out and started. Buddy stayed closest to the creek bank. He cried out and was silent for a for a few seconds. He called, "Bill, come help me. I've fallen in a hole."

Bill and Travis hurried and found Buddy. He had gotten too close to the bank and stepped into a washout created by the creek undercutting the bank.

"Are you hurt?" Bill asked.

Buddy answered, "I think only my pride, but my foot is caught in roots or something and I can't pull it loose."

Bill used the flashlight, and looked over the edge. He could see what happened. Buddy's right foot, toe first, had wedged open a space between two roots. When his foot passed through, the roots snapped back, trapping his ankle. "Buddy, I think we can pull you out. When we start pulling, you work your foot loose."

Bill and Travis knelt and each reached under an arm and started pulling. Buddy moved his foot as much as he could but it didn't come out. After two attempts, Bill and Travis sat back.

Bill said, "We need more help and it is nearly dark. I'm going to signal the others to come." He stood and fired two shots in the air. In the distance, they heard two long notes from Moses' bugle.

"Daddy heard us. They be coming," Travis said. "Deputy Brown, if you hold my legs, I can go down over the edge with your hatchet and maybe chop one of those roots in two, and Mr. Buddy can pull his foot out. Mr. Buddy might have to hold the light."

"Buddy, do you want to try or wait for the rest of them to get here?"

"Let's try, my foot is getting numb."

With the hatchet in his right hand, Travis snaked his chest over the edge of the bank and pushed aside roots as he worked his way down. Bill sat behind him with both hands on his ankles.

Travis said, "Far enough, I think this will work, 'cept I can't swing too far. It's going to take a little while." Travis started chipping away at one of the roots. After ten minutes, Travis said, "I'm about through, but the last piece is hard to get to."

Bill said, "Hush a minute. I think I hear them." In the distance, were two more bugle notes. "Sounds like they are down to where we started. I'm going to fire two more shots." Bill fired his revolver into the air while still holding on to Travis' ankle.

Rather than echoing, the full darkness simply absorbed the sound and complete silence returned. A few seconds later, two bugle notes broke the quiet.

Bill said, "They are closer, and coming this way."

A couple of more thumps from the hole and Travis said, "I'm

through. Mr. Buddy, I can move this piece of root away from your foot. Can you pull loose?"

"I think, but I can't hold the light because I need my hands to push," Buddy said.

Travis answered, "I don't need the light, I've got a hold of the root."

Buddy pulled his arm with the flashlight out and dropped it. Buddy said he was ready, Travis pulled the cut root away. Buddy pushed up with his hands and freed his foot.

"My foot's loose," he said with relief in his voice.

Bill tugged on Travis' ankles, and Travis worked his way up. Bill and Travis both crawled around behind Buddy and from their knees pulled him out. All three of them lay on the cold wet ground, breathed deeply and let the pain in their strained muscles ease.

There were two bugle notes much closer now, and Travis responded with a loud, "Daddy!"

Bill rolled over toward the flashlight, and as he reached for it, his eyes followed the beam up to a spot on the large oak tree just beyond where they lay. Most of the beam hit the trunk, but where it missed the tree it lit up a branch on the other side of the tree. A rope was dangling from it.

Bill waved the beam of the flashlight back and forth on the rope and said, "See, in the light. Did you see the rope before?"

Both said no.

Buddy said, "That rope looks kinda new, not like it's been out here in the weather."

Bill agreed.

"Help me up, Travis. And thank you for cutting me loose."

Bill and Travis rolled up to standing and both helped Buddy to stand. "Can you walk, Buddy?" Bill asked.

"Yeah, my foot's coming to life now," Buddy replied. "Bring the light and let's see where the rope goes."

Bill kept the light on the rope as the three walked around the bush. The light showed the rope hanging from a limb about seven feet off the ground. He followed the rope, now tight, with the beam of the light, up and over to another large branch a couple of feet higher in the tree. From there it dropped straight down behind the bush. As they moved around the bush, Bill brought the light beam down the rope to the face of Mack Poole.

"Goddamn!" yelled Buddy.

Travis cried out as if in pain and recited, "The Lord is my shepherd..."

"Jesus!" Bill swore.

Mack seemed to be looking down at first one, then another as he twisted at the end of the rope. Bill brought the light down his body, and they could see his arms hanging straight at his sides. His pants had fallen from his waist. They were dangling from the toes of his right foot.

"Bill!" Buddy asked, "Who in the hell could have done this? We ain't seen no tracks but the mules'."

"I don't know. There weren't any other prints around Annie's cabin either. Travis, is there anybody else who stays down here?"

"...I will dwell in the house of the Lord forever. No suh," Travis answered. "It's just me and Daddy and our families. Don't nobody even come to hunt down here no more."

"A still?" Bill asked. "Anybody been down here making 'shine?"

"No, sir, Deputy Brown," Travis answered. "Me and Daddy watch for that. We don't want nobody making likker around us."

Bill shined the light under the body, "Buddy, see where everything is torn up under him. Could that be from his mule standing there?"

Buddy moved a little closer and stepped back. "Yeah, I think. It does look like hoof marks. You think somebody put the rope on him when he was on his mule and ran the mule off?"

"Maybe. That could explain the mule coming out alone and following Moses," Bill answered.

"That makes sense," said Buddy.

Bill said, "Buddy, he could have done it to himself."

With fear in his voice, Travis asked, "You think Mr. Poole done gone and lynched hisself, Deputy Brown?"

"Yes, I think it's possible," Bill answered. "If somebody hanged him, they might have kept the mule."

The two notes from Moses' bugle were very close now and they could see a point of light. Bill moved everyone away from Poole, and both groups started calling back and forth. In a few minutes, all seven were standing around the corpse of Mack Poole.

"I can see how Poole could have hanged himself, but why?" asked Warden Copelan.

Sheriff DeWitt answered, "Bill had caught Poole in lies about Annie's death. He knew we were on to him. We know he was scared. He might have figured this was better than jail."

"Still, it don't make much sense," said the warden.

Buddy said, "It don't make sense to me either, but if somebody else hanged him, I think they would have tied him up, leastways his hands."

Bill said, "Tied his hands and the end of the rope to the branch instead of just wrapping it. And the noose is nothing but a slip knot."

Moses and Travis stayed out of the white men's conversation. J. P. offered an occasional grunt of agreement. At the end, there was nothing to make any of them think there was anyone with him in the swamp. They concluded Poole hanged himself.

Bill said, "The way I see it is Poole rode to the tree with the rope, made a loop with a slip knot and put it around his neck. He tossed the end over the higher limb, still on his mule, he moved over to the lower limb, pulled the rope tight and wrapped it around the limb several times. He kicked his mule who ran and left him swinging."

Versions of the possibilities were voiced with slight variations. Warden Copelan thought if Poole had been hanged by someone else, they would have tied the rope instead of wrapping it around the lower limb.

Buddy said, "A murderer would have picked a higher limb."

As they talked through all of this, Bill would direct the beam of his flashlight to what was being discussed. At a point, the beam of light hit Mack's feet, and his pants soundlessly fell off his right foot. Mack's body twisted like he was turning to look at them. No one spoke.

After a moment Sheriff DeWitt said, "We need to get his body down before morning. I ain't going to carry it back in my car, and I don't want it in the county patrol car either. Moses, you, Travis, and Warden Copelan will go with me. I'll get on the radio with office and get Fred out here to take the body. Bill, is your camera in your car, and can you take anything at night?"

"Yes, sir it's in the back seat and there is a flash gun in the box. I haven't used it but it's worth a try. Send the whole box."

"I have a small canvas tarp in my truck." Copelan added. "We can wrap him in it to carry him out."

"Moses, can you get me out of here?" Sheriff DeWitt asked.

"Yes, sir. I know this old tree from hunting on this creek. When I was growing up this tree was on the edge of a field." Pointing, he said, "We can go out this way and won't have to walk in so much water or woods."

"Good, let's get going. Bill, why don't you build a fire. You have matches?"

"Good idea, sheriff," said Buddy, "I've got matches."

Turned out the fellow who came with Warden Copelan was his brother-in-law and a banker who was visiting from Atlanta. He had ruined a new pair of shoes, and had never seen a dead man except at a funeral home. Unfortunately for the warden, this evening became the adventure of a lifetime for J. P., and his role in it became more and more significant as time passed. But right then J. P. was glad to help gather wood for a fire. They built it on the side of the tree away from Poole.

The fire helped. The heat, the light, and even the busy work of bringing in branches made the time pass quicker. In about thirty minutes they heard the others heading in from the same direction they had left. In a minute, they could see the flashlights and what looked like a couple of oil lanterns.

They came to the fire and Travis handed Bill the camera case. Bill sat it by one of the lanterns and opened it. He loaded the camera. The group walked with him around to Poole's side of the tree.

It was too dark to focus the camera on the glass so he set the distance on the focus knob. Standing about fifteen feet away he figured he could get the ground, Poole, and the limb he was hanging from in the picture. He lined up the shot and pressed the shutter release. There was a satisfying pop and a flash of white light.

There was a collective gasp from the small assembly. To this point, they had only seen Poole in bits and pieces as the beam from Bill's light played over him. In the burst from the bulb, the whole brightly lit and horrible scene was instantly before them. The image of Mack's bulging, staring eyes, his swollen tongue filling and pouring out of his mouth, and bare legs swollen and dark with pooled blood was forever burned into their memory.

With Poole's image still in his mind, Bill swore loudly as he tried to remove the still hot flash bulb from the gun with his bare hand. With the lesson learned, he had Travis hold the flashlight so he could see to wind the film. He took a picture from behind and several more from different angles. Bill took a couple of the ground underneath Poole, hoping they would show hoof prints. In the last picture, he got Warden Copelan to hold his night stick under Poole's feet to show how close to the ground he was.

"All right," Bill said. "Let's get him down and go home. But be careful, I would like to come back tomorrow and look at the tracks and see if I can figure out if there was anyone else here. Warden, you and Buddy lay out the tarp under him. Me and Travis will unwrap the rope to let him down."

Bill could pull Poole up a little and get some slack on the rope which they unwrapped with no problem, Travis tried to catch the freed rope, but it slipped through his hands, and Poole's stiff body dropped, hitting feet first. It teetered an instant and fell like a log with a little bounce and a wheeze of air. Except for his feet, Poole missed the tarp.

Muttering, Warden Copelan dropped to his knees and grabbed Poole's shoulders and worked his head onto the tarp and pulled his body onto it. The rope was still around Poole's neck. Copelan coiled the loose end and tossed it on the tarp. The coil landed on Poole's hand and it almost looked like he was holding it. Before he wrapped the tarp around the body, J. P. picked up Poole's pants with a stick and dropped them onto the tarp. The warden rolled the tarp around Poole and tied it with a length of rope. He wiped his hands in the dirt and with a hand full of leaves and finally on his own pants. He looked up and said, "As stiff as he is, I'd say he's been dead for a while. If he was a deer, I'd say he died this morning."

"This morning?" Bill asked remembering what Mrs. DuBose had said about when the murderer died. "Do you think it could have been later?"

"Hell, Bill. I don't know," the warden answered. "A man hanging in the cold air, I don't know what difference it would make. Doc'll know."

"Yeah, I guess," Bill answered. He directed, "J. P., you and Buddy get a lantern. Buddy, lead the way, J. P., you bring up the rear. The rest of us will carry the body. Two on each side." And they walked out of the cold woods.

Moses had brought his wagon and they were happy to put their dismal load in it. They all walked behind as Moses drove to the Mattox cabin. Soon they saw the red lights of the Thompson Funeral Home hearse on the road behind the cabin. Bill looked at his watch, it was nearly ten. By ten-thirty the white men were ready to head to town.

Just before Moses and Travis started home, Bill saw the sheriff talking to Moses, and reach into his pocket and pull out his wallet. He put out his hand to Moses with a bill or two. Moses held up his hands like he didn't want anything, but the sheriff never brought his hand back until Moses took the money. As the hearse pulled out to the road, Bill, who was behind it, saw the lantern on Moses' wagon moving down the lane toward his cabin.

9

Bill did not mind being the last in the line of the four vehicles moving down Godfrey's Store Road. In fact, he let the red tail lights get smaller and smaller in front of him. Even poking along as he was, he would only gain a few extra minutes before he'd be waiting at the funeral home. The heater was on high and the fan blowing on his damp feet felt good. As the DuBose house came into view, he realized he was hungry. The chicken perlo was good, but Elizabeth DuBose was better. *A girl hasn't made me feel like that since I took Mary Nell Jenkins home the night before I left for active duty. But Mary Nell is no Elizabeth May DuBose.*

Pete was cleaning out the hearse when he drove into the lot. He would have to wash it again tomorrow. He stopped and asked, "Dr. Parker here yet?"

"Yeah, he was waiting when Fred got here."

"Pete, y'all have had a busy week in three days."

"Hell, Bill, sometimes I'll go two or three weeks without washing this thing. Then I only wash it because I haven't in a while. But, the Brunson's bodies, what a mess! I damn near bathed in Lysol after getting them out. Fred had to embalm the bodies and heads separately. He put both in the same casket, locked it, and screwed it closed. He said he wouldn't open it even for their children. But the Brunsons still weren't as bad as dead children. God, I hate to handle dead babies. You better go in there. Geer's sent over a mess of sandwiches this afternoon."

"Good, I'm hungry."

The sheriff, Buddy, Warden Copelan, and J. P. ate around a little table in the hall. A few drinks and some paper cups were on the bench along with a bucket holding a small block of ice and a pick. The sheriff said, "Get you something to eat. What took you so long?"

"I took my time and tried to dry my feet. I'm going to wash my hands," Bill said. When he returned he grabbed a hamburger and ate most of it before chipping off some ice for a Coca-Cola. "Whoever did this, thank you."

"Diane called Geer's and had them bring this down to the office. When I called and told her we had a body, she brought them up here. She's a smart girl." Looking at the game warden, "Thanks for your help today, Frank. I owe you a favor. And you, J. P., civilians don't often get caught up in this kind of mess." Turning to Buddy, "You, too, but you'll get paid, but not what is was worth tonight. Now get on and get your foot put up so it don't swell too much. Frank, can you drop Buddy off?"

Getting up, Copelan said, "No problem, Ben. I suspect you'll help me next time I call. Good job tonight, Bill. I think you've wrapped up the murder with the suicide. I sure as hell wouldn't go looking for more. Come on J. P., Buddy let's go."

As they walked out, the sheriff turned to Bill and said, "Unless, doc finds something, I think we are done. Do you have any other ideas?"

Bill explained, "Soon after I saw him, I thought he had done it to himself. As low as he was, a plain slip knot tied around his neck, and the way the rope was wrapped on the tree doesn't make me think there was anyone else there. There were only a few tracks under his body. The mule walking out to the road fits, too. If the pictures turn out, they might show something else. I'll take the roll of film to Mr. Ben first thing tomorrow and I'll go back and take pictures in the daylight."

Before the sheriff could reply, they heard Dr. Parker coming up the steps. "Doc, come sit down and get something to drink. I think there's a sandwich left."

"I'll have a drink," Dr. Parker said, "but I don't have an appetite right now."

"That's no surprise. What did you find?"

"There's no doubt the hanging killed him. It was a strangulation, not a broken neck. From what you described, he didn't fall far enough to break his neck. Short-drop hanging is a tough way to die. It probably took at least twenty minutes, maybe an hour, and I suspect his mind knew what was happening until it was over. It looks like he might have had second thoughts and fought the rope."

"Did you see anything to make you think someone hanged him?" Bill asked.

"Not really. There were some scrapes and rope burns on his neck. As long as it took him to die with a slip knot and a small rope, it's no surprise there were marks. He did have a cut and bump on his head that could have knocked him out, but it had been cleaned up some, so I think it happened yesterday."

"Would you have any problem saying he hanged himself?" asked Bill.

"I could sure say I found nothing to rule it out."

Sheriff DeWitt asked, "Are you a lawyer, too?"

"No, but spend a few years in the Army and you learn how to keep your own ass covered. But, I am going to sign the death certificate and say the cause of death was strangulation, likely self-inflicted. It's after eleven o'clock and way past the time I'm usually in bed. I'm going home now, and I suggest you do, too."

As Dr. Parker stood, Bill asked, "Dr. Parker, when did he die?"

"*Rigor* had set in pretty good so I'd say he died before noon. It could have been as early as ten o'clock."

"You don't think it could have been later in the day?" Bill continued.

"No, he was too stiff and too cold. Noon is as late as I would say he died."

After a pause, Bill said, "Noon or before works out for when Poole's mule showed up at Moses' place." Silently he completed the thought – but it sure doesn't work for what Mrs. DuBose said. I didn't think I believed in ghosts.

At his apartment, Bill lit his heater and took out his bottle and glass. Tonight, I'm going to finish my whiskey before I do anything else, except take off my shoes and damn wet socks. Before bending to his laces, he took a good pull of his drink. He twisted off his shoes off and put one on each side of the heater. The wet socks didn't come off easily and were tossed in the general direction of his laundry bag. They bothered him, one on the floor and one hanging from the edge of his table. So, he had another sip, stood and piled the socks into the bag and found this morning's towel from the bathroom rack in his chair, looked at amber liquid behind the crystal glass, swirled it around and finished it.

He rubbed his feet hard with the towel. First one and the other until it was time for another sip. Bill looked at his feet and worked his toes a few times. By God, I think I can feel my toes. When he reached for his glass with his right hand, he realized two things, the glass was empty, and his arm didn't hurt. I haven't hurt since Connie touched it the second time this afternoon. It always hurt in this kind of weather. He rubbed his elbow, there was no pain. What the hell did Connie do?

The room was no longer cool, but it wasn't warm yet. At the sink, he rinsed his glass and dried it inside and out with the cleanest dish towel there. He poured another two and decided on a third finger of whiskey in the nearly sparkling glass and added the drops of water. He sat about two sips longer, and decided the room was warm. He put his revolver, holster, and belt in the closet. I need to clean it and reload in the morning, not now. He took off his pants and shirt and more or less hung them over a chair. In the morning, not now.

Wearing his boxers and undershirt in a warm room with a good drink of whiskey, Bill's mind wandered, I'm not going to think about work, I'm going to think about Elizabeth. But he couldn't keep his mind on her. It was Mary Nell Jenkins on the last night before he reported to Bush Field in Augusta. He arrived at her house at six. Her mom and dad were getting ready to go to a Grange meeting in Siloam. Her dad told her they would be back at ten and she should do the same.

Mary Nell answered with an insincere, "Yes, sir."

Shortly after arriving at the friend's house, Mary Nell said,

"Bill, I don't feel so good. Please take me home." Back home, she said, "Sit on the sofa and wait for me. I'll be back in a minute." She returned in her bathrobe. "I feel better," she said, and sat close to Bill. "I want you to feel better too," she said as she kissed him.

In a few minutes, Bill found out how much better Mary Nell was, and that she was wearing only her bathrobe. She meant to give all for the war effort and would have, but her daddy's early return from the Grange meeting put an end to her plans and nearly Bill's military career.

When he returned to Greensboro, he looked up Mary Nell and found out very soon after he left, she married a boy from Putnam County who had been exempt from the draft because he ran a dairy farm. They already had three children. The memory of the night nurse in the seersucker uniform started to form, but he pushed the thought out of his mind. It always led to other things. The whiskey and warm room had done their jobs.

10

Bill knew it was late before he opened his eyes, because of how badly he had to pee. He didn't hear the alarm. Standing, he looked at the clock, twenty minutes to eight. First things first, he stood at the toilet. With that resolved, his mind turned to the other tasks for the day. It is Thursday morning, quarter to eight by now. I've plenty of time to shower, dress, and get to work by eight-thirty, but no time for breakfast or anything around here. Breakfast is no problem. I am going to Mr. Ben's in Greene Pointe. The drug store there has a counter and it will be okay to eat somewhere else for a change.

In due time, the water was hot and he showered. Out, he had to retrieve the towel from where he had dried his feet. He used it in favor of digging in the laundry bag for a cleaner dirty one. If he were going into the woods he was going to be dressed for it today, combat boots and long woolen socks. By the time he was dressed, it was quarter after eight. He took his revolver and holster from the closet and wiped both with the oily tack rag he kept there. He reloaded, checked himself in the mirror, and locked up. He knew Diane or the sheriff would have a pot of coffee going and he hoped it was Diane.

When he walked into the office he was a little surprised to see Buddy there. "How's the foot, Buddy?"

"Better, I put an ice bag on it last night for a little while and it didn't swell much. Sheriff DeWitt wants me to go with you today."

"Good, I wasn't looking forward to being out there by myself, even in broad daylight. We'll go to Greene Pointe and drop the film and come in from the other end of Godfrey's Store Road. Is there any coffee left?"

Diane answered, "I made a fresh pot. Give it a minute."

"Thanks for getting those sandwiches last night. I was cold and hungry when we got back to the funeral home."

"You're welcome. The sheriff says it looks like Mack Poole killed Annie and hanged himself. So, this wraps itself up into a tidy little package."

"I can't figure it any other way. I don't have any idea of who would want to kill Poole. Maybe we'll see something out there today."

"I hope not," Buddy inserted.

"Yeah, me, too."

When the coffee was ready, Bill poured himself a cup and Buddy a second or third. While he worked on the cup, he unloaded and did a better job of cleaning his revolver and reloaded it. As he finished the coffee, he asked Buddy, "You ready?"

It was nine-thirty when they pulled up to Joda Ben's store and went in. There were no customers and Joda motioned Bill to the small counter near where his portrait camera was set up.

As Joda was spreading the Brunson pictures from the envelope on the counter, he said, "You were right, Bill, these are about as bad as anything I've ever seen. But you're doing a good job with your exposure and focus." Pointing, he said, "these marks look like powder burns to me. If you need to, we can enlarge this part to show them better."

Buddy came closer to the counter and started looking at the prints, "Damn, I can't believe this. I'm glad I wasn't out there."

"It was pretty bad. I don't want to do anything like that again. Or, anything like last night."

Joda asked, "Last night?"

Bill pulled the roll of film from his pocket and related the events of the previous night, explaining he had taken the pictures in the dark with the flash gun.

"I ought to have these ready about three."

"I'll be here before five," Bill replied. The timing pleased him as it would give him a chance to go by the DuBose house later and come pick up the pictures. "I'll have another roll or two for you. Give me three more rolls of 120 and two packages of flash bulbs. Buddy and I are going to where we found Poole and look around in the daylight."

Stopping at the drug store, Bill said to Buddy, "I overslept this morning and I'm hungry. Do you want anything?"

"Not to eat, but the coffee's kicking in and I think I'll make use of the indoor facilities."

They didn't fix breakfast at all and only made a few sandwiches at the soda fountain later in the day. Bill convinced the lady at the counter to make him the fried baloney sandwich on the menu. It started with a thick round cut from the cloth covered stick in the refrigerator. On the flattop, the slice started to sizzle and get a little burned. The center popped up like a ball.

She cut a cross in the pop-up and flipped it over and pressed it down, buttered one side of two slices of white bread, and put them buttered side down on the grill. When she turned the bread over, the buttered side showed a warm toasty brown. "You want lettuce and tomato?" she asked. When Bill nodded no, she quickly assembled the sandwich, adding mayonnaise and some yellow mustard. Her work was cut on the diagonal and a dill slice was attached to each half with a toothpick.

Bill asked for a glass of chocolate milk. She fixed the milk with syrup pumped from the soda fountain. He finished the sandwich and milk quickly except for the last swallow of milk. It was mostly syrup. He seriously considered a slice of apple pie from under a glass dome on the counter, but he saw Buddy coming from his extended stay. He settled with the lady at the counter. As they walked toward the door, Bill looked at Buddy and said, "I hope you had a match left."

Buddy asked a few questions about the Brunsons on the ride to Godfrey's Store Road. After they turned, it was only half a mile to the Brunson farm, and when they went past there were several cars and a couple of wagons under the trees.

"Family, I guess," said Bill. "Fred said he got in touch with Mr. Brunson's son."

Bill slowed as they passed the turn to Poole's cabin and again at Godfrey's store. When they turned onto Mt. Nebo Church Road, they could see signs of the traffic from the last two days. There had been enough coming and going the track to the cabin from the road was pretty well beaten down. Bill didn't hesitate to drive to the cabin.

Bill said, "Let's check out the cabin before we go to the

woods. I'm going to take some pictures. Buddy, get a couple of those 'Keep Out' cards and put them up."

Buddy rummaged in the trunk and found the cards. At the cabin, he tacked one up on one of the cedar posts holding up the porch roof and one on the front door. He joined Bill inside. Looking around, he said, "She sure kept this place clean. I bet she wouldn't let Poole chew in here."

"What are you talking about, Buddy?" Bill asked.

"Nothing really. I found a cud of chewed tobacco out by the post. The wife don't let me chew inside, don't figure Annie let Poole chew inside."

"I guess, but I don't think I ever saw Poole with tobacco," Bill said as he took a couple of pictures of the outside of the cabin. Inside he took several with the flash. "I don't see anything that's changed since the first time I was here," he said. "We are going to take this sewing machine, hem marker, and quilts with us. I don't know what to do with them, but the machine and quilts are too good to leave here."

"What's a hem marker?" asked Buddy.

Bill pointed it out and explained how it worked.

Buddy tried the bulb and was rewarded with a full puff of white. "Yeah, don't leave this here," he said.

"I think I can drive to where Moses brought his wagon last night. I don't remember any bad places and we ought to be able to follow his tracks."

In the daylight, they could see they had come out in an open area, and they could drive close to where they found Poole. As they bumped along, Buddy said, "I think I can see the big oak. This sure looks different in the daylight."

"Yes, that is the tree. Buddy, I want to see if there is anything around here to make us think Mack didn't do this to himself. I don't know what we are looking for. And I don't really want to find anything."

They worked their way to the big oak. There was plenty of evidence of their being there the night before. But there was nothing either of them saw to make them think any others had been there with Mack. Bill tried to take pictures from the same places he had taken them the night before. Buddy found the place where had fallen and asked Bill to take a picture of it.

"I didn't find anything to change my mind. Let's pick up the stuff at the cabin and get back to town." Bill dropped Buddy off at his house and went on to the office. He gave the sheriff the Brunson pictures and run down of his morning.

"I ain't used to this much paperwork," Sheriff DeWitt said. "Bill, you need to write up your part on going to the Brunsons on Tuesday, and finding Poole last night. Don't be so danged long winded like you do sometimes, but don't leave anything out. Unless we have another murder or two today, I'm going to try and get the judge here next week so we can be done with all of this."

"I'll get started on the Brunsons right now. Damn, I hate looking at those pictures. Did Fred get any shot out of the bodies?"

"Yeah, he found some," answered the sheriff as he held up a Thompson's Funeral Home envelope that rattled as he handled it. "These look like #6 shot to me. I guess we might get GBI to say so, if we had to."

"I have the empties with the shotgun. There was an open box of Winchester shells on the kitchen table with three left in it. They were #6's, just like the casings. I brought them, too. I think if we opened one of them and compared the shot we'd have all we need."

"That ought to do."

"I'll do it and put it in my report. I'll get finished before I go to dinner. Mr. Ben says he'll have the pictures from last night this afternoon. I'll head to Greene Pointe later and give him the roll I took this morning and pick those up. I'll have them to use on what I write on Poole."

Sheriff DeWitt looked over to Diane and said, "I'm going home and to the funeral home. Fred says the Brunson children are coming this afternoon and he wants some help if they think they want to view the bodies. The funeral is supposed to be in the morning. Since Bill is going to be here, why don't you go on to dinner, too?"

She said she would, and in a few minutes, Bill was alone in the office. He took a Greene County Sheriff's Department envelope from Diane's desk and one of the shells from the box he took from the Brunson house. With his pocket knife, he pried open the crimped top of the shell and pulled out the top wad and poured the shot into the envelope. He took one shot and taped it onto a sheet of paper with Scotch tape. Beside the shot, he wrote what he had done.

He opened the envelope from the funeral home with the shot recovered from the Brunson's bodies and removed one and taped it to the paper and wrote where it had come from. It was clear the shot were the same. He signed and dated the paper and put it, along with the two envelopes, on the sheriff's desk. He went to work writing his report. He had about finished when Diane returned.

He gave the report to Diane who read through it. She made bad faces two or three times and asked him about words, and what he meant in places. When they agreed on everything, Diane said she would get it typed. Bill left, saying he wasn't planning to return until the morning. He headed for Geer's and a late dinner.

11

At a quarter to three, Bill drove to the DuBose home and was ready to ring the bell when Elizabeth opened the door. She wasn't in overalls this time. It was a dress and her hair, that dark red hair, was brushed out to the top of her shoulders. Bill stood staring for a time longer than polite and finally stammered a "hello" and "you look nice."

Elizabeth said, "Come in, they've been waiting for you."

Why didn't she say "we've" been waiting for you?

Elizabeth led him to the bay window room where her mother was seated in her chair near the window, and Connie was on the ottoman. Connie had on a dress, too. And though the daughters seemed to be dressed for company, Mrs. DuBose appeared as she had the day before.

Connie said, "Hello, Bill, we are glad you came to see us today."

Mrs. DuBose pointed to the sofa where he had sat yesterday, "Please have a seat."

He sat down, not all the way at the end by the arm, but not in the middle either. When Elizabeth joined him on the sofa, she didn't sit at her end. Her hands were on the sofa cushion beside her. Bill knew if he put his hand down, their hands would touch. For now, he folded his hands in his lap.

Quickly Connie asked, "There was another passing yesterday, wasn't it?" Her mother reached over and touched her on the shoulder and nodded "no" to her.

"Tell us what you've found out, please," Mrs. DuBose said.

"Yes, Connie, there was," Bill answered, "Mack Poole is dead. We found him early last night. We are pretty sure he hanged himself because we were on to him about killing Annie."

Connie started to speak, but her mother's touch stopped her.

Mrs. DuBose asked, "If you found him last night, do you have any idea about when he died?"

"Dr. Parker said it was before noon, maybe as early as ten o'clock."

"Deputy, if he died before noon, he is not the one who killed Annie. Whoever killed her died right before their spirit visited the scene of Annie's death. The time was two-twenty, wasn't it?"

"Yes, ma'am," Bill replied.

Mrs. DuBose continued, "If the doctor is right about when he died, Mack Poole's spirit wouldn't have waited to come looking for Annie's spirit. Connie never did think Mack killed Annie. Yesterday when you said his name, Connie said "no." Do you remember?"

Bill looked around the room, "I'm afraid, I don't understand all of this," and he let his hands fall.

Elizabeth put her hand on his and said to him, "There's always a lot we don't understand about what Momma and Connie know. Sometimes you have to have faith they know."

"Momma, I told you yesterday morning there had been a

passing close by and it had been a hard passing," Connie said. "The spirit kept fighting to get out of the body and the body kept trying to bring it back. Momma, I think he did do it to himself. We need to pray for his soul to have peace. We need to pray a lot for him. We have to pray for Mack Poole."

"We will."

"I'm going to say a prayer now, Momma," Connie said as she slid to her knees and knelt over the ottoman with her hands folded in front of her. Mrs. DuBose bowed her head and moved her hand from Connie's shoulder to her head. Elizabeth bowed her head and took Bill's hand, and Bill bowed his head.

Connie spoke clearly, but Bill did not understand any of the words until she ended a phrase with, "our brother Mack Poole." More he didn't understand followed, until, "our sister Annie Mattox." Connie ended her prayer with a loud shout and an amen. She held her face in the cushion of the ottoman.

Elizabeth raised her head and looked at Bill. Taking his hand in both of hers she said, "Sometimes, Connie speaks words I don't understand when she prays. Sometimes Momma doesn't know them either."

Mrs. DuBose spoke softly above Connie's now still body. "Speaking in tongues is another one of the gifts of the Holy Spirit. Some have the gift to speak and some have the gift to interpret. I understand Connie most of the time."

"I've heard of speaking in tongues," Bill said.

Mrs. DuBose continued, "Connie prayed Mr. Poole's soul would rest in peace because the one who killed Annie is now dead, and the killer's spirit will wander and have no peace. She prayed God would forgive our brother Mack for taking his own life. He did it because he loved Annie Mattox, and she was dead. And, he didn't help her when she was attacked."

No one said anything for several minutes. Connie stood and wiped her eyes with her hands and looked over at Bill. She walked over and held out her hands to him. Bill never let go of Elizabeth with his right hand, but took Connie's hands with his left. Her hands were warm, but not like yesterday. "Bill," she said, "You look troubled, don't be. I can tell you love the Lord so you have nothing to fear."

"Connie," and he pulled her and she came closer, "I am troubled, but I am not afraid. You give me comfort. But my job is to find who killed Annie. And if Mack Poole didn't do it. I don't know where to start looking again." He looked at Mrs. DuBose, "You do understand I can't take what you've told me to a court."

"We understand," she replied, and added, "Remember, whoever killed Annie Mattox is dead now. He died at two-twenty yesterday."

Perplexed, Bill asked, "But who is it?"

"I don't know now. Would you like to ask Annie?" Mrs. DuBose replied.

Not understanding the question, Bill said, "Ask Annie?"

Elizabeth turned toward him and released his hand, "Bill, Momma sometimes can get in touch with spirits, and they will give her messages or signs." Pointing to the room behind the sofa, "She uses the front room for sessions where she tries to make contact."

Bill looked from Elizabeth to Mrs. DuBose and back.

"Momma is asking if you would like to have a session and try and get in touch with the spirit of Annie Mattox? If you learned anything from Annie's spirit, maybe you could find out enough on your own to show Mack Poole didn't kill her, and who did."

Connie, now standing beside the end of the sofa with her arm on his shoulder said, "It would give Mr. Poole's soul real peace. Please try."

Not believing what he was saying, Bill asked, "What would I do?"

Mrs. DuBose replied, "We need some things of Annie's, personal things she cared about. Where is Annie now? Has she been buried?"

"Her body is still at the funeral home, but we are planning to bury her tomorrow afternoon at three-thirty. As for personal things, we have the spool of thread from her sewing machine, a quilt off her bed and scraps of cloth from the dress she was making. I guess I might get her sewing machine or the dress she was in or her shoes."

"Get her shoes," Connie said. "She loved those shoes."

"And the thread and quilt are good, too, but the most important thing you should bring is some dirt from her grave. If you can get the dirt, that's all we need. Except, we need more people. I would like to have five, but Connie and Betty, uh, Elizabeth can't be there. Who can you bring?"

In his mind, Bill started with the sheriff, but dismissed him and quickly ran out of other male possibilities. The first and only woman who came to mind was Diane. "I can bring Diane."

"Who is she?" Elizabeth asked pointedly.

"She's the lady who works in the sheriff's office and does our paperwork."

Elizabeth said "oh" and her mother agreed Diane would be okay if she would come.

Bill knew she would come. She would do nearly anything to get inside this house and say she knew Mary Greene DuBose. That's three. Who else? His mind was turning, he remembered the exchange with Moses Jackson and the DuBose family at the road side. He asked, "Would it be good if it was somebody who knew Annie?"

"Yes, someone who knew her would be best," replied Mrs. DuBose.

"Would Moses Jackson be okay?"

"Yes, he would be excellent. He knew Annie, and he's been to a session before. His wife should come, too. Do you think Diane would mind?"

"No, I think she would be fine with them. When would we do this?"

"Sunday afternoon would be best. Come at two-thirty. You talk with Diane, and you come to supper Saturday at six. Bring Annie's shoes and the other things. We don't need the sewing machine. It's too big."

Surprised Bill said, "Afternoon? I thought it would be at night."

Mrs. DuBose continued, "Spirits don't care about night or day, but they don't like noise. It is quieter at night and that's why we, the living, notice them more at night. If we give them a suitable place during the day, and if they want to, they will come."

"Sunday afternoon will be fine." Bill looked at his watch and saw it was nearly four o'clock. "I have to get to Greene Pointe right away. Thank you, but I do have to hurry."

"Bill, we dress for supper on Saturdays." Mrs. DuBose paused a moment and added, "I'll drive down to Moses' cabin tomorrow and make arrangements with him. I need to tell him some things. Oh, and Deputy Bill Brown, you must pay me for this session. It will be two dollars."

Elizabeth said, "I'll see you out," and walked with him to the front door. "Don't worry about the session. It will be good. You'll see."

"I won't worry, but I am looking forward to seeing you Saturday. I hope we will have some time to talk. By the way, what does 'we dress for supper' mean, a suit?'"

"A suit would be perfect, but a jacket and tie would be fine. And I'm looking forward to seeing you, too, and I'll make time for us. But on Sunday, you might not see me nor Connie. Oh yes, you dress for a session, too, and Diane will need wear a hat, or some other head cover."

As Bill walked down the steps, he looked at his car and read *Greene County Sherriff's Department.* What the hell have I done? Just what the hell have I done? Stupid, stupid, stupid!

12

As Bill opened the door, Joda Ben looked up and said, "I was about to give up on you this afternoon. Your prints turned out okay, given the subject."

"Here's another roll for you. I shot it today. The same place in daylight and no body hanging from the tree. Mr. Ben, I don't know what we have in the budget for photography, but I'll bet we've gone through a year's worth this week."

The first print, the one of Mack hanging and staring with bulging eyes and a black tongue, was as bad as his memory of the real thing. It was going to be like the image of his co-pilot impaled by the tree limb that came through the cockpit wall when they crashed. It would be with him always. Wonder if Mrs. Du-Bose could contact the spirit of Jimmy Brabham?

As he came to the last print with Warden Copelan holding Bill's nightstick under the body, Bill asked Ben, "Do you have a ruler handy?"

"Sure," and Joda opened a drawer and handed him a one-foot ruler, "What do you want to measure?"

Bill answered, "Some things on the picture and compare them to the nightstick. I was going to see if I could determine how far Poole fell. Dr. Parker said his neck wasn't broken because he didn't fall very far."

Measuring on the picture, Bill explained, "In the picture, my sixteen-inch-long nightstick is three-quarters of an inch long. From his ankle to the ground it measures nearly an inch and a half. See, it's two nightsticks or thirty-two inches."

Now, with a bit of excitement in his voice, "And in the picture, Poole's neck is just over seven inches off the ground." Bill made a quick calculation on a scrap of paper and said, "So his neck is up a little more than five and a half nightsticks high or," a pause for more calculations, "seven feet four inches in the air. I'll put somebody about Poole's size on his old mule and measure how far their neck is off the ground. With that, I'll know how far he fell."

"Pretty good, Bill. But it doesn't matter. He's dead no matter how far he fell."

"I know, but it might make a difference if we thought someone else was there."

For the first day this week, Bill was going to get home before full dark. If he hurried he would make Caldwell's before five and pick up a week's laundry. From there he'd go to the Hot Spot and pick up some ribs and Brunswick Stew. When the white deputy came on Thursdays, Bobby always told him he was getting the ribs cooked this morning, not the ones left over from the weekend before. True or not, it didn't matter. The ribs were always good.

Even though only a one-room garage apartment, it had become home and he was glad to be home. First thing, he took off his uniform and put on blue jeans and an old gray Tech sweatshirt.

This evening was the first and only time he had been in civvies since last Sunday. Bill enjoyed the routine of cleaning and tidying up the place a little, putting up his clothes, and changing his bed. He had the radio on and the guy was playing some Bob Wills and talking about the Georgia–Florida game on Saturday in Jacksonville. He said nothing about the Tech-Navy game in Atlanta.

Bill decided he would spend Saturday afternoon listening to the games and cleaning up his truck for Saturday night. If he could get across the county line tomorrow or Saturday morning, he would get a couple of bottles of beer for the afternoon. Supper with Elizabeth made Saturday look like a pretty good day.

The night guy was on the radio now, and he never did play much country. It was mostly Sinatra, Como, and bands. Hot Spot ribs and stew was a fairly regular Thursday supper. But before he ate, a drink, but not too much tonight. He took out his glass and bottle. It wasn't going to take will power to keep him to one drink tonight. One good one was left in the bottle.

A plan adjustment for Saturday was in order, he would head toward Athens and stop at the liquor store outside the city limits and pick up a bottle and maybe some beer. It didn't seem to matter if he stopped at the beer joint across the county line, but he knew driving almost to Athens in the patrol car to a liquor store probably wasn't a good idea.

He turned the oven on to its lowest setting and raked the cole slaw from the now soggy paper plate of ribs onto one of his two dinner plates and put the ribs in the oven. The radio night guy put in his two cents worth on the game on Saturday and played "Time After Time" by Margaret Whiting. I like her. I'll listen to this and finish my drink and my supper will be ready.

Still in a good mood and with a little energy, Bill cleaned up his supper mess and washed his few dishes. He listened to the radio a while longer and picked up one of the old *Life* magazines his landlords left for him in the garage below. There was an article about GI's wounded in the Pacific returning home. Being *Life*, there were lots of pictures, including one of a nurse in what looked like the seersucker uniform his nurse had worn. Tonight, the memories of her and their encounter led to the usual conclusion.

Up at six on what looked to be a clear but cooler day, Bill made it to Geer's by seven and talked Mack Poole, the ball game, and weather. He enjoyed the conversation and being the center of information about Poole. Without his input, it seemed most had determined Poole had killed Annie Mattox, and hanged himself in shame or because he was scared. From Geer's he drove to the chain gang camp past Godfrey's Store Road and left his patrol car to be washed.

Diane turned to the opening door a little surprised, "I didn't see you drive up."

"I dropped my car at the camp to get washed. After this week, up and down those muddy roads, it was a mess. Lindbergh dropped me off. Is the boss here?"

"Not yet, but he'll be here soon, Diane answered. "He wants to call the judge and set up a coroner's jury to wrap all of this up before GBI gets too involved."

"Diane, I want to talk to you about something. Do you have plans for Sunday afternoon?"

"Nothing particular, what's up?"

They heard the sheriff's car pull in and Bill said, "I'll tell you about all of this later, but keep Sunday open."

Diane replied with a puzzled, "Okay."

"Morning, Bill, morning, Diane, do we have any new bodies today?"

Diane answered, "No, sir, it's a regular morning."

"A lull may be troubling after this week. Diane, go ahead and call Judge Morrow's office and let's see if we can get a hearing scheduled for Tuesday. I know he won't care about doing it on Monday. Bill, you have anything for me?"

"I have the pictures I took when we found Poole. I can't see anything in them to make me change my mind about what happened. I think I've worked out how he did it to himself."

"Let's see them." Ben DeWitt worked through the prints, asking a few questions as he looked. "No, there's nothing here to make it look like anyone else was there. Tell me what you think happened."

Bill pulled out the picture of Poole hanging in the air with the warden holding his nightstick and explained his calculations.

"All this makes sense to me. Especially with what Dr. Parker said about no broken neck," the sheriff replied.

"Sheriff," interrupted Diane.

"Mm?"

"Mary says Judge Morrow has to hold a hearing there in Crawfordville on Tuesday, a suicide. But if we can get him all the information on our four deaths on Monday morning, he will be here first thing Wednesday. What should I tell her?"

The sheriff asked, "Bill, can you get everything together by this evening?"

"Yes, we have pictures, Dr. Parker's reports, and my reports. If nothing happens today, I don't see a problem. Of course, we don't have anything from GBI on Annie Mattox."

"Hell, GBI don't matter. Diane, tell Mary we'll have everything to him early on Monday."

"Yes, sir," replied Diane, and she relayed the message to Mary.

Sheriff DeWitt asked, "Bill, can I help you with anything?"

"No, sir. I don't think so. When I get everything put together, you can go over it all with me. Did you see what I did with the shot Fred took from the Brunsons?"

"Yes, I did. Put them in with the pictures." The sheriff continued, "Diane, did you say Mary said they had a suicide in Taliaferro County?"

"Yes, sir."

Ben DeWitt leaned back in his chair, "Three suicides and two homicides in less than a week and within thirty miles of here, I think that's as many as I have had during my whole time here. And Chief Deputy Bill Brown solved all of ours. Hot dang! I'm going to the court house to pick up our pay envelopes before they get the bill from Joda Ben for pictures."

As the sheriff pulled the door closed, Diane spun her chair toward Bill and said, mocking the sheriff, "Chief Deputy Bill Brown, what the devil is going on Sunday afternoon?"

"What do you know about Mary Greene DuBose?"

"Well, she's supposed to have money, a lot of money, because her husband did something with railroad cars in the twenties. She's has two daughters, one's about eighteen and the other is younger. And a whole bunch of people, colored and white, say she can call up the dead and talk to them. Oh yes, and she has what looks to be a mighty fine house. She doesn't mix with folks in town or go to church, but I don't think I've ever heard anyone say she was mean or not friendly. What does she have to do with Sunday?"

It took Bill about twenty minutes to give Diane the short version of his encounters with the DuBose family and the proposed outcome set for Sunday afternoon. He left out a good bit about Elizabeth, but did tell her about how Connie made his arm stop hurting. Diane only asked a few questions as he talked and a couple of more when he finished. He asked her, "What do you think?"

Diane's reply was quick. "I wouldn't have thought you'd have anything to do with anything like what she does. But, as the sheriff says, hot dang." She paused, "Hell yes, I'll come. I'd come just to see the house, but to get in on a 'session', is that what you call it? Oh, yes, sir, Diane will be there. Reckon what you wear to a session?"

"I am supposed to have supper with them tomorrow and Mrs. DuBose told me to dress for supper. Elizabeth said I was supposed to wear a suit or a jacket and tie, and I should dress the same for the session."

"Elizabeth told you? Okay, I'll need to work what to wear. I sure didn't know you had to dress for ghosts. The afternoon time thing doesn't make much sense to me. Bill, everything seems to add up for it to be Mack Poole. Do you think she can actually tell you anything about Annie Mattox's murderer?"

Bill answered, "Remember, I told you about the younger daughter, Connie, knowing about the two other deaths and the blue dress and the shoes. I mean, there are some things there I don't understand. But, no. I don't think there's anything more to find out. I kind of got backed into this."

Diane pushed, "Yeah, I guess, but you know, somebody might have told her. You said there was a colored man there who told you about DuBose. He would have known about the dress. He could have told them about it."

"Maybe, but he wouldn't have known about the shoes or anything about the dress not being hemmed. And, it was the way she said it."

Changing her line of questions, Diane asked, "What about the older daughter? You haven't said anything about her. I understand she is very attractive."

A pause might have been prudent, but Bill spoke honestly and quickly. "Her name is Elizabeth and she is nice looking, beautiful, in fact. She doesn't seem to have any of the gifts Mrs. DuBose and Connie have."

"Now I understand your interest in all of this. Elizabeth makes way more sense than a ghost. Well, bless your heart. I'll still go. You can always count on old Diane for some help in the romance department."

"I think I can do okay on my own, but you're welcome to help. Now, if I don't get things put together for Judge Morrow, there won't be enough of me left to romance anybody."

Bill set to work on getting all the information on Annie Mattox together. When he was done, he felt like everything was there to prove the victim was Annie Mattox and she had been killed by a single stab wound by an unknown assailant sometime on Saturday evening, November 2, 1946. Since Mack Poole was dead, he wasn't going to sign anything, and no one knew where Tommy Coles was. He added his signed statement saying each had identified Annie Mattox in his presence.

The Brunsons were next. The pictures pretty much told the whole story. Dr. Parker's statement stating both were shot at very close range hardly needed any explanation beyond the photographs. He added his statement quoting Mr. Brunson to say, "We'll be all right, it will all be over soon." And, as the sheriff instructed, he included the paper with the #6 pellets taped to it.

As he was packing all the Brunson photographs into a big envelope, the sheriff walked in with their pay envelopes. "Diane, you can go to eat now and make it to the bank before they close for dinner. We'll stay here and go over the files Bill is going to take to Judge Morrow."

"Thanks," Diane said as she took the small brown envelope from the sheriff's outstretched hand. "I'll be back before one."

"When she gets back, I'll take you out to the camp to pick up your car. We can eat out there. I saw Monroe at the court house and he said Troy cooked some backbone and rice."

"Good plan," Bill replied. "We'll still have plenty of time to go with Fred to bury Annie. Here's what I finished on the Brunsons."

"Okay," said the sheriff, "but I'm going to let you represent the county at the funeral, burial. Poor child. Show me what you have for Judge Morrow."

When Bill returned from dinner, he loaded his washed car with the envelopes for Judge Morrow and put in Annie's shoes, the scrap of cloth Diane said was to be a pocket, the spool of thread, the quilt, and the hem marker. He hadn't mentioned the hem marker to Mrs. DuBose, but he felt like it was a bit different and personal, and if any of this made any sense at all, the hem marker fit. The sheriff hadn't come back and likely would not, it being a Friday. Bill guessed he had gotten a tip on the location of a still.

Diane asked some more about Sunday. Bill had planned to pick her up in his truck and ride her out, but she insisted she would drive herself and she would be there at two-fifteen.

It was getting close to three-thirty when he drove to the far end of the cemetery where the poor were buried. Fred hadn't arrived yet but he saw the pile of red clay from the freshly dug grave and drove to it. The gravediggers knew they didn't have to open a big grave for the simple casket the county paid for. "That hole was an awfully small place for a life to go," Bill said to himself.

Bill heard the hearse; Fred was driving, and the Methodist pastor was in the front seat with him. It was the Methodist's turn. Pete was in the back with the body. It looked like it was going to be the four of them, but at least she had a real preacher. Bill walked over as Pete opened the door and rolled the plain, unfinished coffin out. It was no problem for the four of them to carry it to the grave and rest it on the ropes staked over the opening.

Bill looked up to see another car stop on the path to this part of the cemetery. It was a Packard. Three women, all dressed in black, came from the front seat. Elizabeth DuBose had driven and her mother and Connie walked around to the driver's side and stood there. One of the four who came from the back seat was Moses Jackson. The others must be his wife and Travis and his wife. The Jacksons assembled on the passenger side of the car behind the long hood. The sun was low and behind the car so the car and the people became a silhouette on the low ridge.

The pastor put on his stole over his open shirt and walked to the head of the small grave and began to read from the *Gospel of*

John. He didn't read much, then he prayed and Bill thought it was a good prayer for Annie.

Fred showed them how to handle the ropes. Bill and the preacher only had to hold theirs while Pete and Fred let theirs play out, lowering the coffin into the grave.

As the coffin went down, the preacher recited the Methodist committal. He and Bill pulled their end of the ropes up and out. The minister picked up a handful of dirt from the pile and tossed it onto the coffin below.

Fred signaled to the diggers who started over with their shovels to begin filling the grave. As Fred, Pete, and the minister started to the hearse, Bill took a manila envelope from his pocket and put in a handful of grave dirt from the pile.

At the first note, they all stopped and looked to the ridge. Against the low sun, they saw the shape of a man standing alone in front of the Packard and holding a horn to his lips. Moses Jackson played "Taps" for Annie Mattox.

13

Since the Greensboro Tigers were in town this week, Bill's evening was planned. All he had to do was be at the game, walk around and be seen. He usually enjoyed the duty. He could talk to some old friends and the kids. Most of the time he didn't feel much different now than when he was on the field playing for the Tigers. He went by the booster club's concession stand when it opened and bought a hot dog and a drink. He didn't really want it after what he and the sheriff had eaten at the camp.

The Tigers were playing Waynesville, and they were pretty good. Greensboro was struggling. The game started good for the Tigers when Junior Moore picked up a fumble on the second play and ran it 42 yards for a touchdown. Unfortunately, it was the home team's only score; the final was 26 – 7. Bill stayed until they turned out the lights. He was home by ten-thirty.

He woke up at eight. There would be no shower, no shave, or no breakfast at Geer's this morning. The shower and shave would wait until the afternoon. He cleaned up a little, combed his hair, and put on his jeans and a sport shirt and walked out and down his stairs, grabbing his cloth jacket. It was going to be a perfect fall day, crisp this morning and mellow warm in the afternoon.

His truck was parked inside the garage under his apartment. In it, he sat for a moment and let the cool of the seats work its way through his jeans and shirt to his skin and the warmth of his body back to the seats. He breathed in and smiled. His truck always smelled like a truck. It may have been because he didn't drive it as much anymore and he never became accustomed to the smell, but it smelled like a truck and that made him happy.

He stepped on the clutch and put the key in and turned it. When he pressed the starter button not a sound came from under the hood for a long second. Then there was a grind and a pause, two grinds and a shorter pause, the engine started turning over. He pulled out the choke and there was a sputter and a pop and the engine was running. He knew the drill, the battery had to wake up after a week of not doing anything. He turned the radio on and knew it would take about as long for the tubes in it to warm up as it would for the engine.

With the choke in, he eased the truck out of the garage to the sound of the kid who worked weekend mornings give a report on last night's game. From the way he told it, Waynesville was lucky to get out of town with a three-touchdown win. He didn't need gas but would stop at Jim's and top off and get a cup of coffee.

When he was closer to Athens he punched the third button on his radio which was set to the big station there. At ten, they had started coverage of the game. Right now, it was some local guys still in Athens, but at eleven they would go live to the Gator Bowl in Jacksonville. Georgia was 6-0 and Florida was 0-5, so none on the radio thought Coach Butts' boys were going to have a problem with the Gators.

When he was closer to the liquor store where he usually stopped, he decided to drive on to Athens. He was a little hungry and he knew he could find a place to get a late breakfast or a sandwich. He might find a new tie.

Since Thursday, Bill had been thinking about what he would wear to supper and to the session. He had a gray suit he bought in San Francisco when he returned from overseas. It was supposed to be a nice suit and the coat fit fine, but civilian life and breakfasts at Geer's had made the pants impossible to button. He had a pair of black gabardine slacks that would work with the suit coat, and he had his high school graduation coat, a blue and gray plaid sports jacket he had hardly worn. It fit if he didn't try to button it. It would go with the black slacks, too. He still had the tie he bought for the suit. He planned to wear the suit coat and tie on Sunday. If he could find a tie to go with the plaid jacket, he would be okay for supper tonight.

The Gallant Belk store wasn't near as impressive as I. Magnin's in San Francisco where he bought his suit, but given The Big Store in Greensboro, it was impressive, even though it didn't have groceries in the back. Inside the front door was a polished brass plaque with the word 'Elevator' and arrow pointing to the rear.

As he stood at the front of the store, he saw nothing like men's clothing so he headed for the elevator. At the elevator were four others waiting. A sign by the elevator door read "Gentlemen's Clothing 2."

The brass pointer above the doors showed the elevator was coming from the third to the second floor, and the five there watched it intently. After a long pause at 2, the pointer started down toward the G. All shifted their weight from foot to foot and moved very slightly toward the door as the pointer neared G.

There was a bump as the elevator arrived. The bump was followed by a metallic sound, the mahogany door slid into the wall revealing a small chamber of more polished mahogany, sparkling brass, and mirrors. To the right stood an older gentleman with gray hair and a thin gray mustache. He was dressed in a dark red blazer with G B stitched on the pocket, gray slacks, and white gloves. He stepped out and offered his hand to an older lady who stood waiting for his assistance. She was followed out by a porter carrying several packages.

When they cleared the area, the operator stepped inside and faced the group, now grown to six, and said, "Going up." He welcomed them in with his white gloved hand.

When all were in and facing forward, he worked the bar to close the outer wooden door. He reached across and pulled the polished brass lattice-work gate closed. When it locked in place, he squeezed the handle on the lever coming up from the floor and moved it forward. The chamber lurched slightly and all eyes looked to the brass pointer above the door as it started moving from G to 2.

In a continuous move, the white glove pulled the floor lever and the chamber stopped with the brass pointer directly on the 2, and floor aligned perfectly with the wooden outer doors of the second floor. The brass lattice gate was pushed aside, and the wooden door slid into the walls revealing a new scene. To the riders he announced, "Gentlemen's Clothing here and Better Ladies Wear ahead," and to those standing in front, "Going up."

After two ladies exited, Bill walked out into the Gallant Belk Company Gentlemen's Clothing Department.

Directly in front of him was a display of sweater vests. There were solid colors and argyles including a white one with a red and black pattern, UGA colors. It was displayed on a bust mannequin over a crisp white dress shirt, a matching red tie, and under a black Georgia blazer. He looked closer and did the arithmetic. The whole outfit cost almost fifteen dollars. He liked the tie, but it was two dollars and UGA red. On the side wall, a sign read "Clearance Sale" and he decided to go there.

He paused at a rack of double breasted blazers, with sharp looking brass buttons.

"Forty-eight long." Bill turned to the sound.

"I'd say you were a perfect forty-eight long." The speaker was a slender and well-dressed man of about fifty with snow white hair. He was taking a blazer from the rack, and motioned to Bill to take off his jacket and extend his arm. "My name is Jack, Jack Breeden and we have a special on these jackets today," he said as he slipped the jacket on Bill. "Button the inside button, and we'll see how it falls." Jack was standing behind Bill now and ran his hands across the shoulders of the jacket. "Yep, forty-eight is right for you, and I see the sleeves are the right length. Old Jack doesn't often miss on size."

Bill looked down at the jacket. It was black with silver buttons, most on the rack were navy. Speaking to Jack, "I'm really not in the market for a coat today, just a tie."

"I'll bet you were looking for a new tie for a big date tonight. But let me tell you about the special we have today. These jackets are $5.98. If you buy it today, you can get a pair of slacks, a shirt, and a tie for only four dollars more. A pair of gray slacks, a new white shirt, and a Bulldog tie would look good."

"I'm a Georgia boy and pull for the dogs except at the end of the year, and like I said, I'm looking for a tie."

"I have a great looking gold Tech tie. It would look good with this black blazer."

"I'm a deputy sheriff in Greene County, and I don't need to advertise Tech or Georgia."

"Deputy Sheriff? Well deputy, we give peace officers ten percent off. With the discount, you can buy everything for $8.98 and since you don't live here, I can get the pants cuffed and pressed while you get you a bite of lunch. What is your name, young man? I'll bet you are a veteran, too."

"I'm Bill Brown and I was in the Army Air Corps."

"I can't give you the veteran's discount and the peace officer's discount, but I can throw in another tie. Let's look at the slacks. Thirty-six waist?"

"Yes," Bill replied. It took him only a second to realize when he replied "Yes" to his waist size, he had said "Yes" to everything and he was going to spend about one-third of the money in his pay envelope at one time. This is all right, he rationalized. I have a little cash tucked away at home and almost a hundred dollars at the bank.

The pants fit in the waist and Jack measured them to length and suggested one inch cuffs with a half inch of break. Bill agreed.

"Go around to Tony's and get a bowl of vegetable soup and some corn bread. It's good and it won't take long. Come on back here. I'll have your pants done, and I'll pick out some ties. If you have the soup, tell Tony to put it on Jack's tab, but you leave a tip."

Bill took a booth close to the counter at Tony's and a waitress came over. "What'll you have to drink, dear?" she asked as she handed him a menu.

"Tea," he answered. "Jack Breeden said he would buy me a bowl of soup and corn bread."

"Bought a new suit, did you?"

"No, a blazer and slacks, they were on special."

"You did good. Jack doesn't spring for a meal unless it's a suit. Vegetable soup and corn bread coming right up, hon."

As she walked away, Bill decided it would look better if the money to pay for his new clothes was in his wallet rather than the small pay envelope. He took it from his pocket. The net this week, and most weeks, was $32.20. He put the six fives and two ones into his wallet and the two dimes in to his front pocket. The two dimes would make a good tip for his waitress. Just as she brought his tea, a man got up from the counter and stuffed the newspaper he had been reading under his arm. As he came by Bill's booth, Bill asked, "Excuse me, but do you know of a package store close by?"

"Turn right out the door, right at the corner and it's about halfway down the block past the florist shop. You can't miss it."

"Thanks."

The soup was good, but the corn bread was wonderful, thin and crispy on top and a little bit sweet. It crumpled perfectly into the soup, and his waitress earned her big tip when she brought a second helping without his asking. He took his time with the soup and had a second glass of tea.

He guessed he still needed to give them time on his pants so he headed for the liquor store. He recognized the man behind the counter as the one who had given him directions in Tony's. As he walked over to the counter, Bill said, "I guess you did know where this place was."

The man looked up puzzled until he recognized Bill from the restaurant. "Yeah, I make the walk at least six times a week. What can I get for you?"

"Two fifths of Johnnie Walker Red."

As Bill walked out he looked in the window of the florist shop next door. Damn, I do need to take something tonight. I really have been out of it for a long time. Flowers will be good. I can give them to Elizabeth, but they will be for all of them.

He walked out with a nice bouquet of red, white, and pink rose buds. The lady said they would open and last a week but he had to get them in water as soon as he could. Between the liquor and the flowers, he was loaded down, and he decided to go to his truck and drop off the liquor and flowers before going to pick up his clothes.

Jack was standing by the blazers when he walked on to the second floor from the elevator. He waved, disappeared, and re-appeared holding a wooden hanger with a large paper envelope on it. He hung the clothes by the cash register and showed Bill the cuffs of the pants and the new shirt, unfolded and ironed so it would be ready for tonight. Bill really liked the two ties he had picked out. One was red, not Georgia red, but a lighter color with white diamonds in diagonal rows, and the other was a regimental with a repeating pattern of a narrow black stripe, a gold stripe, a red stripe and a broader green stripe. The green is the color of Elizabeth's eyes. Bill paid, and Jack showed him the card he had made with his name. It had all his sizes and what he bought today. Jack said if Bill needed anything, all he had to do was call or write and he would get it together and send it to him. Jack handed him his business card.

As he walked along Clayton Street to his truck he was pleased with himself, and knew he was going to look sharp tonight.

14

When he reached his truck, he realized it was a quarter to one. He didn't think the Georgia game started until one, but the Tech-Navy kickoff was at noon. He knew he could find it on WSB out of Atlanta and listen all the way to Greensboro if he wanted. He listened to Tech awhile, and it didn't seem like they were going to have any problem with Navy. Shortly after one o'clock, he tuned in the Georgia game and they were handling poor Florida.

He had forgotten to get beer, and the games weren't very interesting, so he nixed the truck washing in favor of a haircut and barber shop shave. He swung by his place and put the flowers in water and hung his new clothes in his small closet.

Scotty was sitting in his chair in the barber shop reading the paper. The Georgia game was on the radio. "Hey, Bill," he said, "you had a busy week according to all of the talk this morning."

"I'd just as soon not have another week like that. You have time to give me a trim and a shave?"

Scotty stood and looked around the empty shop, and said, "I think I can work you in. Have a seat." Scotty's service was quick or slow depending on his mood, the number of men waiting, and what the current customer had to offer for conversation.

Bill estimated he was in for a slow haircut and a fast shave; he couldn't talk while he was getting a shave. He was right. During the cut, Scotty gave his short report on the week's activities as compiled from the morning's haircuts. Bill corrected some of the misinformation Scotty had picked up.

Scotty was tickled for words from the horse's mouth, especially when Bill added a detail or two that had not yet been reported. He was set up for the week. Bill told him about Judge Morrow coming for the hearing on Wednesday. The hearing notice would be posted on the court house door by noon Monday, but for Scotty to know on Saturday afternoon was another plum to share today and at First Baptist's Men's Sunday School tomorrow.

Of course, Bill never mentioned the DuBose family's involvement in the investigation, or his involvement with the DuBose family. Although he knew neither would remain a secret long in Greensboro.

Bill leaned forward in the big chair as Scotty shaved the back of his neck finishing up his haircut. That always felt good and he liked the sound the straight razor made sliding across his skin. "I'll comb it when I finish your shave," Scotty said as he pulled the head rest out and tilted the chair to almost horizontal. He added an extra towel over the cape and turned on the hot water. He wet the bristle brush and worked up a good lather in the small bowl he held and worked the lather onto Bill's face and neck.

Now for the best part.

Scotty went to the steamer and pulled out a small towel and touched it to his cheek to test the temperature. He folded it longways and lay it on Bill's upturned neck. The next two towels were tested, and wrapped around Bill's entire face leaving only his nose uncovered. Bill relaxed under the warm towels and listened to the rhythmic swoop-swoop as Scotty worked the straight razor against the big leather strop hanging from the chair.

In a few minutes, the towels were beginning to lose their heat, and Scotty removed them. He worked up a new batch of hot lather he brushed onto Bill face. With short strokes of the freshly honed razor, Scotty started at Bill's left sideburn and worked down his cheek. Every stroke or two, he would wipe the lather from the razor on the towel on Bill's chest. After the cheeks, he did Bill's neck, his chin, and finally above his lip. Scotty cleaned him up with more hot towels, dried his face, put on a bit of Bay Rum, and put the chair up and combed Bill's hair. With a bit of a flourish he removed the cape and Bill stood in front of the chair while Scotty took a corn whisk broom and went over Bill's shoulders and the front and back of his shirt.

"You must have a hot date tonight to get a shave on a Saturday afternoon?"

"Your shave will last me two or three days. Scotty, you know I might be planning to go to church tomorrow." Bill found a quarter from his pocket and laid it beside the cash register and rubbed his cheek. "Yeah, two or three days, see you later."

Hot date. Big date. The phrases tumbled through his mind on the short ride home and upstairs to his apartment.

Is it a date? Her mother invited me. Invited me to tell me about the session. But I do want to see Elizabeth, I want to see her a lot. Every time I think about her holding on to me out by the road, I get a hard on. I might not get to talk to her alone.

Why the hell am I going out there anyway? To solve a crime us-ing hoodoo I've already solved with hard work and a little luck? Wait until the sheriff finds out. And, Diane's going. We both might get fired. What if somebody sees me all dressed up go-ing out Godfrey's Store Road? They'd guess I was going to the DuBose's because there isn't anybody else out there for me to go see on a Saturday night. He paused the conversation with him-self and, in a moment of reflection, the memories of Elizabeth squeezing his hand following the blessing, her taking his hand when Connie prayed, and her being in his arms by the road all came flooding back. He damn well knew he was going and why.

He did make a plan. He would dress and leave at five and drive toward Greene Pointe on the Atlanta highway and come the long back way to Godfrey's Store Road. If anyone saw him, they'd think he had a date with a Greene Pointe or Madison girl. He figured he would go the same way on Sunday. After Ath-ens and back and two planned trips nearly to Greene Pointe, he thought he'd better get gas. He made a quick run to O'Neal's and filled up. He was going through this week's pay like it was water. At least, I had a free lunch and I'm getting a free meal tonight. Then he remembered the $2.00 he was going to have to pay Mrs. DuBose.

Back at home, he moved the things of Annie's he was taking for tomorrow from the patrol car to his truck. The next trip he brought the flowers down. If someone saw him all dressed up and carrying a big bunch of flowers, they would know something was up. This way if he were seen, he'd only be dressed up.

He found the black shoes from his Army dress uniform and gave them a good brushing. He showered and dressed slowly.

When he put his new shirt on he realized it had French cuffs. He panicked for a second and remembered his dad's cuff links stashed in his shaving kit. It took him several tries to get the links through four button holes and he had to redo the first one because he put the cuff link through backwards. He chose the striped tie, he really liked all the color against the white shirt. He slipped on the jacket and buttoned it. Jack really had the size right on the first try. The only mirror was the one in the bathroom and he could only see his head and shoulders, but he liked what he saw. He took the jacket off and put it on the hanger. He wouldn't wear it while he drove. He didn't think anyone noticed him as he drove through town and out toward Greene Pointe.

15

It was nearly dark when he pulled up to the DuBose house. Out of the truck, he put on his jacket, buttoned it, and adjusted the sleeves. He took the flowers, locked the door of the truck, and started up the steps. As he reached for the button to ring the bell, the door opened. Connie was standing there. She had on a navy-blue jumper over a white blouse with a small gold cross on a fine gold chain around her neck. Her hair was neatly brushed.

"Connie, you really look nice."

"Thank you, Bill," she said as she crossed her feet and made a small curtsy. "You look very handsome." She took his hand and led him into the parlor. As they entered, Elizabeth walked in from the kitchen.

"I didn't hear the bell," she said to Connie.

"It didn't ring," she replied.

Bill stood holding the flowers in one hand and Connie's hand in his other. Elizabeth was stunning. Her dress was burgundy with the skirt falling from her small waist, but the top was fitted with short sleeves and a neckline showing a hint of cleavage. Close around her neck were three strands of pearls. And her auburn hair, he now knew it was auburn, was up on her head.

"Bill, good evening," she said.

The sound of his name brought him back. "Hello, Elizabeth, you look lovely," and he held the flowers out to her.

As she took them from him, she turned to the corner of the room. "Look what Bill's brought us," she said.

For the first time Bill's eyes, left Elizabeth and looked where she was speaking.

A young lady rose from the big chair by the window and started toward Bill. "I suspect he brought them to you, Betty May. You might put them in some water. Good evening, Bill. I love your tie."

He recognized the voice, but the woman who had spoken bore no resemblance to the Mrs. DuBose he had met earlier this week, but she is who it had to be. This was a young woman, who hardly looked older than Elizabeth. She had the same auburn hair as Elizabeth, except hers was down and to her shoulders. After another step toward him with an extended hand, he realized her long black dress was really pants. She had on a deep green satin blouse which was open more at the neck than Elizabeth's dress, but her large gold cross provided a level of modesty. The short black vest she wore had gold metallic threads which made her green eyes sparkle.

"Thank you, and the flowers are for all. Looking first at Mrs. DuBose, Connie, and finally at Elizabeth, Bill said, "I don't think I have ever been in the company of three such lovely ladies as I am this evening." He couldn't take his eyes off Elizabeth.

"Bet...Elizabeth and I were going to have a glass of wine before our meal. Would you care for one, or perhaps something else? My husband kept a well-stocked bar."

Connie dropped his hand and ran across the room. Admonished by her mother to not run, Connie slowed and lifted what had appeared to be a drawer on a sideboard on the kitchen wall. She unlocked something and the second drawer front dropped down making a shelf in front of what was, indeed, a well-stocked bar. Elizabeth went into the kitchen with the flowers.

"Whiskey perhaps," offered Mrs. DuBose.

Accepting Connie's waved invitation, he walked over to the cabinet. Looking over the array of bottles, he saw one which caught his eye, *The Glenfiddich*. He noticed a crystal bucket with a sliver handle filled with chunks of ice and a small footed pitcher filled with water. He lifted the dark green bottle and asked, "May I?"

"Certainly," replied Mrs. DuBose, "Connie, please get Deputy Brown a glass."

Connie opened the lower doors of the cabinet and looked again at the bottle Bill had picked and for a glass. Elizabeth returned from the kitchen and filled two stems with white wine. She filled a third from a bottle of ginger ale also in the bucket. Connie gave him exactly the right glass for his whiskey and he poured a good inch, and added water from the pitcher.

"Bill fixes his whiskey like Daddy did," said Connie as she accepted her stem of ginger ale from Elizabeth.

"Yes, like Daddy," said Elizabeth as she now handed her mother her glass.

Mrs. DuBose held her glass up and spoke, "To our good health and to a successful session tomorrow."

Bill said, "Hear, hear," and they all touched glasses.

"Now, let's all sit down and enjoy our drinks before we eat.

And no more talk of the unpleasantness of this week," Mrs. Du-Bose said as she sat in her chair.

Connie climbed on the ottoman. Bill took his middle left seat on the sofa, and maybe a little more middle. Elizabeth joined him there and maybe a little closer.

Mrs. DuBose continued, "Deputy Brown, I understand you grew up in Greene County, but I don't believe I know your parents."

"Yes, ma'am, I did, and please call me Bill. We had a small dairy farm near White Plains, in fact some of our land was in Hancock County. My daddy died in 1943 while I was overseas. Mother sold the place and herd, and moved to Sandy Springs with my sister and her husband."

"Connie said you were in an airplane crash and hurt your arm," Mrs. DuBose continued.

"Yes, ma'am. I am a bomber pilot and we were trying a new plane. We caught some anti-aircraft fire. I tried to make it to our base, but had to crash land on an island. My co-pilot was killed when we crashed, and I was hurt pretty bad. My gunner survived the crash. He pulled me out and saved my life. My arm was broken at the elbow. I spent most of the next year in hospitals. My arm used to hurt, especially when the weather was damp and cold, but since Connie touched it, it hasn't hurt. Thank you, Connie."

"You are welcome. How did you learn to fly an airplane?"

"Connie, before the war I was in school at Georgia Tech. After Pearl Harbor, the Army went to colleges and started pilot schools. I was already in the reserves, ROTC, so I signed up for pilot training and learned to fly airplanes while I finished school. When I graduated, I went into the Army Air Corps and they taught me how to fly big airplanes, bombers."

"A Tech-man?" Elizabeth asked, not so much as question, but more as an accusation.

"I don't advertise it around here, too many Bulldogs. I went to Tech to play baseball and be an engineer. The war changed everything, and I ended up a pilot and engineer."

"My daddy knew engineers but I don't think any of them knew how to fly an airplane," Connie said.

"I'm not that kind of engineer, Connie. I'm a mechanical engineer. I could come closer to building a locomotive than driving one. I wouldn't mind another bit of whiskey. It is quite good."

"Please," and Mrs. DuBose pointed to the bar.

As Bill fixed his second drink, he continued, "Since I was in the Reserves, I have only been taken off active duty, not discharged. But I don't think I will be recalled. When I came back from overseas, I went to my sister's home to see Momma. I visited for a few days and bought my truck. I came here to visit my dad's grave and see some old friends."

When he returned to the sofa, he closed the gap with Elizabeth. "I got here late on a Saturday and never thought how there was no place in Greensboro to get a room for a night. Jim O'Neal sent me to Mrs. Littlejohn's. If I hadn't been in uniform, and she saw I was a major and a pilot, she would have sent me on my way. She would only rent me a room for a week. And of course, she wanted it paid in advance.

"Sunday, I visited my dad's grave and drove to our home place and met the new owners and looked around a little. Monday, I looked up a couple of guys from high school and found out about a couple more who didn't make it."

Bill shifted in his seat on the sofa and rested his right arm on the back over Elizabeth's shoulders. "I was eating dinner at Geer's on Tuesday, and planning to leave for my sister's a little later when Sheriff DeWitt came in. He recognized me and sat down. He asked about me and the war. I told him after my crash, the Army decided I wasn't able to fly any more. They offered me the choice of going to the Military Police officer's training in Honolulu or quartermaster's officers training at Fort Leavenworth, Kansas. I picked Honolulu. When my MP training was over, I had to take the Military Police physical. When I passed it, the Army decided I could fly airplanes again. They assigned me to Alamogordo, New Mexico to learn to fly B-29's."

"Those are really big airplanes, aren't they?" Elizabeth asked.

"Yes, and sometimes tricky to fly. But, when we dropped the A-bombs, the Army Air Corps decided they didn't need reserve Major Brown any longer."

Bill paused for a sip of his whiskey and ended his story, "Anyway, Sheriff DeWitt said he needed a deputy and said it was my job if I wanted it and could stay as long as I wanted. When he made the offer, it sounded good and right now, I'm really glad I took it," he let his hand touch Elizabeth's shoulder.

Mrs. DuBose rose and said, "Now, I think we are all glad you are here. Connie come help me with the rolls. Bill, please sit. We are about fifteen minutes from eating. If you need to wash up, there's a bathroom under the stairs in the front hall. Elizabeth, come in a few minutes, I'll need your help, too."

Elizabeth turned to Bill and put her hand on his knee and said, "Well there were some real surprises in your story. You're a Georgia Tech man. My daddy didn't like Georgia Tech men." But after a short pause, she added, "He would have liked you.

I need to go help Momma." As she leaned forward to rise, she gave him the slightest kiss on the cheek.

He watched the dark red dress float out of the parlor into the kitchen and looked at the last of the whiskey in his glass. He finished it. In a moment, they all came into the parlor and Mrs. DuBose announced their supper was ready. She led all into the dining room. The table was set as before, two on each side facing. In the center of the table were some of the flowers he brought arranged in a bowl which matched the table setting.

Mrs. DuBose and Connie went to the left and stood behind their chairs and Elizabeth went to the right. Bill was far enough behind to understand, and went without hesitation to Mrs. DuBose and pulled out her chair and seated her. She thanked him. He did the same for Connie and at his side of the table, he seated Elizabeth. Her thank you included a look and a touch of her hand on his.

When he was seated, he saw Connie's hand extended to him and to her mother. He took Connie's hand and reached for Elizabeth's. With all joined together, Mrs. DuBose announced she would return thanks. It took a moment for Bill to realize she had begun her prayer of thanks because it was in the same conversational manner she usually used. Only Connie's bowed head convinced him the blessing had started.

Between his mother's conviction he and his sister would grow up to be 'gentile and refined' and the Army's that an officer was also a gentleman, Bill felt reasonably comfortable seated behind the array of plates and tableware. As he unfolded his napkin and placed it in his lap, he studied the salad plate on his dinner plate. He recognized small chunks of apple and chopped pecans and he was fairly sure the main ingredient was beets, likely pickled beets. The mystery was the spots of soft very white material topping the dish. Farmer cheese, he reasoned. That was no hill for a dairyman. With his salad fork he took a bite and confirmed all the ingredients except the cheese, and it was cheese. It had a pleasant taste, but tart. "This is very good," he said, "please tell me about the cheese."

"Thank you," answered Elizabeth, "it's goat cheese."

"Me and Betty May made it," added Connie.

"Betty May and I made it," corrected Mrs. DuBose.

"Betty May and Connie, I like it very much."

Supper was a pork roast cooked with onions and carrots until it was so tender it barely kept its identity as a roast. It was served with potatoes and a rich brown gravy, green beans, and the hot rolls. Dessert was peach cobbler made from home canned peaches. When Bill said it was very good, Elizabeth smiled to let him know she had made it.

"Elizabeth, Connie, please clear the table and put up the food. The dishes may wait until morning. Bill and I are going into the front room to talk about tomorrow.

Mrs. DuBose rose and walked to the closed pocket door in the hall.

16

Mrs. DuBose worked the lock on the pocket doors and pushed them into the wall, revealing heavy black drapes. She pulled them open, but it was still pitch black in the room. "We seldom use the electric lights in here," Mrs. DuBose said. "People concentrate better in candle light, and spirits prefer the higher level of attention. Darkness or light makes no difference to the spirits."

By now she had found the switch on the wall and pushed it on. A dim bulb overhead and sconces on either side of the front windows and the permanently closed door to the parlor came on. Bill's eyes adjusted and he began to make out the details of the room. It was paneled with the same dark wood as the trim in the rest of the house. The drapes were plain, black, and heavy. In the center of the room was a round table surrounded by six identical side chairs and one matching arm chair. The arm chair faced the door. Around the room against the wall were eight more of the side chairs. The room was large enough the fifteen chairs could be put in a circle around the table and he expected the table could be made large enough for all the chairs. The most striking feature in the room was a large painting of Jesus suspended from the ceiling by gold chains. It was in front of the draped window and directly behind and above the arm chair.

"Bill, we will only be five tomorrow. Would you move two of these chairs to the wall and help me arrange the others. Put that one against the wall there and this one over here." When the chairs were moved to her satisfaction, she continued, "I will be there." indicating the arm chair. "You will be at my right, your friend, Diane, Mrs. Jackson, and finally Mr. Jackson will be seated to my left. During the session, our hands will be joined. We shan't be here longer than an hour. If we have no contact in an hour, we will not succeed in reaching the spirit of Annie Mattox."

In the four corners of the room were candle stands. Mrs. DuBose went to each, setting its position and looking at all the candles. Bill turned to the right and saw another large painting. This one on the wall. It was in three parts, two smaller ones on either side of one with a round top. In the round part at the top was the image of God or Jesus looking down through the clouds at a man fallen on the ground who was looking up. All the others in the picture were turned away from the heavenly being. One soldier was holding his shield over his head.

Mrs. DuBose had gathered several new candles from a chest in the corner and was replacing some of the candles in the stands. She lit each new one and let it burn a minute or two before snuffing it out between her thumb and forefinger she wet in her mouth. Noticing Bill looking at the painting she explained, "The painting is the *Conversion of Saint Paul* by Benjamin West, a copy of course. Jefferson found it in one of the rail cars. He understood how important Saint Paul is to me." Having made the circuit of the candles, Mrs. DuBose asked, "Do you have the things we asked you to bring?"

"Yes, they are in my truck, should I bring them in?"

"Yes, there is a switch for the porch light by the door. Be sure to turn it off when you come in."

The porch light made little difference. With a full moon in a clear sky, there was almost enough light to read. Bill was thankful for the moonlight because the dome light in his truck did not work. He unlocked the passenger door and reached in to gather the things he had brought. The quilt and one shoe were there on the seat as he had left them, but the other shoe and the scrap of dress were on the floor board. The hem marker with its heavy base was leaning against the seat instead of standing straight up as he had left it. He didn't see the spool of thread at all. He ran his hand over the floor board and finally found the thread where it had rolled under the seat. Strange. I must have knocked these off the seat when I closed the door. He put the thread in his pocket, wrapped the shoes, cloth, and envelope of grave dirt in the quilt and held them under his arm. He picked up the hem marker and started up the steps when he heard the front door open. It was Mrs. DuBose.

"It seemed you were taking a long time. Is something the matter?"

"Not really, a couple of things must have fallen off the seat when I closed the door. It took a minute to find everything."

"Is anything missing?"

"Oh no, the door was locked."

"Good, but it wouldn't have mattered about the door."

"Ma'am?"

"Never mind, bring everything in." Mrs. DuBose turned off the porch light as soon as he entered the hall. She told Bill to put everything on one of the side chairs. From there she arranged them on the round table. First the quilt was refolded and placed on the table directly in front of the arm chair. It took up nearly half the table. The shoes were placed in the center with the hem marker on one side and the scrap of dress and the thread on the other. The envelope of dirt was left in her chair. She adjusted the chairs one last time and looked at Bill. "We need to leave this room right now. Go to the parlor." Bill walked ahead and into the hall and to the parlor. He heard the click of the light switch and the bump of the pocket doors closing.

Standing in the parlor he looked into the kitchen where Elizabeth and Connie were taking off their aprons and wiping their hands. Connie came running into the parlor from the kitchen as her mother entered from the hall. "Momma, Momma," she called out.

"I know, Connie, and it is all right. Bill had left the things for the session outside. Everything has been taken care of now."

Elizabeth entered the parlor, "Bill, Connie felt Annie's spirit here while we were eating, but she didn't say anything."

"In my truck?"

"Bill, everything is fine now. If Annie were here tonight, that's not a problem. Her spirit may have been searching. This all bodes well for our success tomorrow. Now, Connie, it is time for you and me to go upstairs for the evening. I have a big day tomorrow and it is close to your bedtime. Tell Bill good night. You know you won't see him tomorrow."

Connie stepped in front of Bill, "Thank you for coming tonight, we enjoyed having you visit. Oh, and thank you for the flowers, they were lovely."

"Thank you for having me. I enjoyed supper very much. I really liked the goat cheese," and he held out his hand to her.

Connie closed the gap between them in an instant and wrapped her arms around his waist. With her head to one side she pulled as close as possible to him, "Oh, Bill, I like you so much. I'm so glad you have come to our house, please, please come back."

Bill put his arms around Connie and held her close. "Connie, I like you too, a lot." He pulled away a little and dropped to a knee so they were face to face. Looking into her eyes he said, "I want to talk to you and learn from you. And I do want to come to see you and your family." He kissed her on the cheek. Connie turned and ran to the hall and up the front stairs.

When she reached the top, she called, "Good night, Bill.

"I'll add my goodnight and thanks, too. This has been a very pleasant evening and you are certainly welcome here. Elizabeth, don't be too late coming up."

Elizabeth made no promise to her mother when she said, "Good night," and kissed her on the cheek.

Bill added his goodnight and thanked Mrs. DuBose again for the meal. She followed Connie upstairs.

Finally, we are alone together.

Elizabeth may have been several steps ahead of Bill in her plans for the rest of the evening. "Please sit down, I'm not planning on going up any time soon."

Bill took off his jacket and hung it on a chair and sat in his usual position on the sofa. The lights in the kitchen and hall were off. Elizabeth walked to her mother's chair and turned on the reading lamp beside it, she turned off the overhead light in the parlor. "Sit down at the end. I want to put my feet up." Bill moved to the end of the sofa and Elizabeth sat right beside him, pulled her knees up and kicked off her shoes and lay her head against his shoulder. "Now, that's better."

"Yes, it is." Bill dropped his arm around her shoulders and pulled her closer.

"Connie misses her daddy, doesn't she?" he asked.

"Bill, we all miss him. In many ways, he was all we had, and we were really all he had. His death changed our lives. Momma wouldn't let Connie go to school this year. Daddy wouldn't have liked that."

"What do you mean?"

"You should know. I mean everybody in Greene County thought he was a thief and had stolen things from the railroad. But he didn't, he made money for the railroads and he tried get things back to people. No one knew what he was doing, and they were mad and jealous. Some think he stole a rail car full of money and has it hidden somewhere. He didn't and we don't have much money."

"I've heard about the railroad cars all my life, but I never understood," Bill said.

"Nobody understands," Elizabeth continued. "And there is Momma and her gift. Nobody understands her gift, not even me! Some in town call her a voodoo woman or worse, but some of the ones who do the talking and name calling show up for sessions and pay."

Elizabeth propped herself up and looked at Bill. "And Connie, is Connie worse or better than Momma? I don't know. Momma doesn't know. Most of the time neither of us know what do with her. Sometimes she can pick up something that belongs to somebody and tell all about them. Two years ago, we were in the May Company in St Louis and there was a woman going through her pocket book looking for something and making a fuss. Connie walked over to her and told her to look behind the sugar jar in her pantry. The woman looked at Connie like she was crazy, she paused, smiled, and told Connie she was right. Connie told her goodbye and walked away. The woman never said what she lost, so I asked Connie. She said the woman had some dollars rolled up with a rubber band and she had hidden them behind the sugar jar."

They didn't speak for several minutes. Elizabeth let her head fall lower on Bill's chest and he pulled her closer. Elizabeth sat up again and braced her left hand on Bill's shoulder and looked directly at him. "You said you would like to know our family. If that's true, I hope you are up to it."

"I think I can handle the DuBose ladies."

"I hope you can, Bill Brown, because I like you. I like you very much." She put her head on his chest and sighed.

"I'm coming tomorrow, but your mother says I won't see you. When can I come again? Or maybe we can go out. What do you think about our going out, maybe to the picture show?"

"I would love to go out, but it's so hard with us. Momma and Connie are so different, we are so different and I don't want to be sometimes." She turned in his arms, and looked up at him from his lap. Even in the dim light, Bill saw the glint of a tear on her face. "Bill, on Wednesday, we are going to New York for Thanksgiving. We won't be back until the first week in December."

"Why so long?"

"We used to travel all over on the railroad. We've been to New Orleans, Memphis, St. Louis, Chicago, and one time all the way to California. The big trips are over now. But we've gone to New York every year as long as I can remember, even when Connie was a tiny baby."

"Why would you go to New York every year?" Bill pressed.

"Daddy would go with us, but he wouldn't stay the whole time. He had business to do with his bankers. And I'm supposed to meet with them this time, me and Momma. Momma would hold sessions. We'd stay at The Drake Hotel and had two bedrooms and a sitting room. They would set up a room for Momma's sessions."

"Who would come to her sessions in New York?"

"People from up there; I don't know who they were, or how they found out about Momma. Daddy would set up the sessions and the people she saw paid a lot of money. Daddy would collect the money before they ever came to the sessions. Momma never touches the money. I've have Daddy's book, but I haven't figured it all out. Oh, you're supposed to pay me tonight for tomorrow or leave it in an envelope on the table tomorrow. And ..."

"Listen a minute, Elizabeth. That is an awful lot to be on you."

Finishing her thought, "I don't know how to make you work with all of this."

"Let me tell you a short, but true story." Bill began, "A few months ago I asked out a girl who lived at Mrs. Littlejohn's. We went to a supper and dance and had a nice time. I asked her out again and this time we went to Athens, ate supper and went to a picture show. It was different for both of us and we both had a good time. Driving back to Greensboro, she sat close to me and started telling me all about the things we were going to do, our wedding, our house, and our children. When we got to Mrs. Littlejohn's, I said goodnight and never asked her out again."

"Why?" Elizabeth asked.

"What she talked about didn't scare me, and I might have wanted some of the same things. She was pretty and smart. I guess she would have been a good wife, but she didn't let me be a part of what she was planning for us. Elizabeth, what I'm saying is that you and I need to figure things out for ourselves, together, not separately. And we can. Now it is late and I don't want to get on the wrong side of your Momma, or Connie. I think I need to go."

"I guess, but I don't want you to," Elizabeth said.

Bill stood and took the two dollars from his wallet and gave them to Elizabeth, and stepped toward his jacket hanging on the chair.

As she got up from the sofa, Elizabeth said, "My little sister had a goodnight kiss before she went to bed."

"Your little sister had a little sister goodnight kiss. Big sisters get big sister kisses." Bill didn't know what experience Elizabeth had in kissing and he didn't care. What mattered was she was fully committed to this kiss.

When they had to stop, they held on to each other tightly. Finally, Bill said, "If I don't leave now, I never will." And he turned and walked through the hall to the front door, all the while holding on to Elizabeth's hand. At the door, Elizabeth turned the porch light on, they kissed again and Bill walked out to his truck.

The full moon was still high in the sky and he hardly noticed when Elizabeth turned off the porch light. Starting down the drive he looked to the seat to his right. I wonder if I'm riding home alone?

17

Bill walked from his bathroom to the door and pushed it open into Sunday morning. Looks to be a copy of yesterday. Except today, I'm going to meet a ghost. He looked down at his truck, or did I bring one home last night? His thoughts stayed on last night and there were no more ghosts to think about, only Elizabeth and her family. Mrs. DuBose drank wine. She looked like somebody's old maid on Wednesday, twenty years younger and a movie star on Saturday night. I've never seen a real woman dressed like she was, not even in Honolulu. She holds 'sessions' in New York City, apparently for a good deal of money! And Elizabeth might have to manage everything.

What did I tell them about me? Most everyone knew I'd had been a pilot in the war and had crashed, but few know I've been trained to fly B-29's. How could all this work now? I've known all along being a deputy sheriff in Greene County, Georgia was a respite, a pause from flying, from being shot at, from dropping bombs and killing people, from having to think about things, hard things, from doing all the things I've been taught and trained to do, from being who I am supposed to be. I know I will never live in Greensboro very long. Whatever else I said last night ended this vacation from my life.

The worst thing about Sunday mornings now was coffee. He had instant, but it wasn't the same. He looked at the bottle of milk in the refrigerator, plenty for coffee and enough for cereal. If he had enough cereal for the milk. Breakfasts on Sunday were right there with the coffee. He shook the box of corn flakes and from the weight and sound he knew there would be enough, but at this point the description flakes didn't apply. For a second, he had an image of the breakfast the teacher would make for him on a Sunday morning, but breakfast was quickly replaced with an image of waking up next to Elizabeth, and food didn't matter anymore.

The rattling of the glass top on the gutted percolator called him from his thoughts. He turned off the eye and fixed his coffee. For whatever reason, it wasn't so bad this morning. Nothing could be bad this morning. After his coffee, he decided to ride to the office and call Diane before nine o'clock and make sure everything was okay for today.

Diane said she would go to church this morning because going seemed like a good idea if she was going see a ghost later. She, too, had plans to take an indirect route to the DuBose house. Bill told her about the session room, seating arrangement, and joining hands. The seating and the hand holding didn't matter to her, but she was interested in hearing more about the painting of St. Paul.

She said, "Everybody's has a picture of Jesus, but St. Paul, you've have to know a little Bible to have a picture of him." She was real glad the whole thing wasn't going to last much more than an hour. She said she hadn't been looking forward to driving from there in the dark. And she reminded Bill, he owed her one big time for doing this. Bill agreed.

"Diane, I did tell you, you are supposed to wear a hat, didn't I?"

"Oh, no you did not, Bill Brown. But I always wear a hat to church so a hat is not a problem today. I guess if St. Paul is in the room, then women must cover their heads. He said so. Bill, that's two you owe me."

Bill agreed.

On his way home, Bill went by Moon's Gulf station. It was the only place in town open on Sunday mornings. There was probably a law against it being open, but nobody minded, least of all Shorty Moon. They had one copy of the *Constitution* left and Bill bought it. At home, he sat down with the paper. There was a good story about the Army-Notre Dame game.

In the business section was a picture of a big new airplane that had its first flight. It was the Lockheed Constitution and the Navy had it. They didn't have much of the technical information which really interested him. When I was at Tech, Dr. Williams, or somebody, would get information for us. All the professors knew people who worked at Lockheed or Boeing. Some of them worked at those places and taught at Tech.

Bored and anxious to leave, he took a shower. He thought about the restaurant the other side of Greene Pointe toward Madison with an outside window where you ordered sandwiches. He could leave a little early and go there and eat in his truck. As he worked that out, it occurred to him Edna's, the restaurant, would be a good place to bring Elizabeth. Maybe he could take her on Tuesday before they left for New York. He tried the crossword puzzle but he was not really interested and it seemed like every other word reminded him of Elizabeth. Finally, he decided it was time to get dressed.

In no hurry, he slowly drove to Edna's Restaurant and Drive-In. When he turned into the parking lot, he saw a window covered by metal awning. On both sides of the window were hand painted menus with prices for sandwiches and a fried chicken basket. At the bottom was the line, "Come Inside for a Full Meal." Good to know. With plenty of time, Bill read through the menu.

He ordered at the window from a friendly lady and opted for the tailgate as his table. He didn't take off his tie, but he did unbutton the second button on his shirt and pushed the tie inside and tucked one of the napkins in at his neck. After getting everything prepared he sat on one side of his tailgate and ate as he watched the comings and goings. For a little town like Greene Pointe early on a Sunday afternoon, this place is doing well.

He went to the restroom on the outside of the building to wash his hands. It was pretty rank, but at least there was soap and water. The towel machine was supposed to let you pull-down clean cloth towels from a roll and take up the used part. The pull-down part worked. But the used part of the roll piled up on the floor. He was glad the lady had given him extra napkins. He tucked three or four into the seat. He looked at his watch. Even if I poke along I'll get there about two. No matter, I will have a better chance to see Elizabeth.

18

When he stopped in front of the DuBose house it was ten minutes until two o'clock and Connie was sitting on the top step in her overalls. She ran to meet him with a hug.

"I didn't think I was going to get to see you today."

"Momma says things like that sometimes, especially when she's not sure about people. She likes you better now. Betty May has gone to get the Jacksons. Where is your friend? She needs to come. We need to have at least five."

"She will be here in a few minutes. She is driving her car."

"Momma told me you brought Annie's shoes last night. Those shoes are why Annie's spirit came here. Will you let me hold them when the session is over?"

"If your mother says so."

"Me and Betty May will have to stay upstairs during the session so we won't disturb anyone. Bill, you like Elizabeth a lot, don't you?"

"Yes, I do, Connie. And I like you and your mother a lot, too."

"But not like you like Elizabeth."

Bill was a bit surprised by this conversation, but he figured he needn't be anything but honest with Connie. "You are right, Connie."

Taking his hand and leading him toward the front door, Connie continued, "Elizabeth likes you like you like her. Maybe I do, too."

In the front hall, his flowers from last night were in a tall vase on a table by the pocket doors. The hall seemed more open and brighter. He heard a sound on the stairs and looked up.

"Bill, Connie said you would be early. But it's no matter. Where is Diane?" Mrs. DuBose asked.

Bill repeated, "She should be here any minute. She is driving her car."

Mrs. DuBose was now standing before him in the hall, and it was the third completely different version of her he had seen. This afternoon she was not glamorous and youthful like she had been last night. She wore a skirt and a matching jacket, and he could tell she had on make-up, not a lot but it was there. Last night her hair had been free and loose, today it was neat and tidy under a small beret.

Connie said, "I see somebody coming."

And they all turned to the window. Bill said, "It's Diane's car, she is right on time. Connie, come out with me and meet her."

Bill opened the door for Diane. "You look very nice, Diane," he said.

"Thank you."

"Diane, this is my friend Cornelia DuBose. We call her Connie."

"Pleased to meet you, Connie." Not waiting for Bill to complete the formal introduction, "My name is Diane, Diane Weston. You have a lovely home."

"Thank you, Diane. Let's go in," Connie said.

As they started up the steps, they heard the Packard coming up the drive. Connie looked up and said, "Betty May will drive to the back. We should go in now."

Connie introduced Diane to her mother. Diane complemented her on the house, and Mrs. DuBose asked about Diane's work. Both looked to the parlor door as Elizabeth led Mr. and Mrs. Jackson into the hall.

Mr. Jackson had on a dark gray suit with a fine pinstripe. Mrs. Jackson was a small, but heavy woman. Her dress was black with some white piping and a large red cloth flower on her left breast. Her hat had matching flowers. Mrs. DuBose introduced Moses and Eliza to everyone, but she never called either by their first name.

Neither Bill nor Diane took their eyes off Elizabeth. She wore a simple green dress and green matching shoes. Her hair was brushed back into a short pony tail tied with a green satin ribbon. Diane poked Bill in the ribs, hard, and gave him a second poke when Elizabeth came and stood close beside him on the other side. Mrs. DuBose and Bill made it through the introductions. By the time they were done, Elizabeth was holding Bill's arm.

As Mrs. DuBose walked to the closed pocket doors she said, "If you will all wait here a moment, I will prepare the chamber and return for you." She looked to Elizabeth, opened the doors slightly, entered, and closed them behind her.

Reacting to her mother's look, Elizabeth said, "Nice to have met you, Miss Weston. Connie and I are going upstairs now. We will see you after."

The four of them stood in front of the closed pocket doors. We look like the ones at Gallant-Belk waiting for the elevator, except we don't have a brass pointer to watch.

Fortunately, the wait was not long and Mrs. DuBose opened the door. "Please come in, I'll show you where to sit." As she pointed to chairs, they took their places.

Bill seated Diane and stood waiting for Mrs. DuBose who was still at the door. "Please take your seat, Mr. Brown," she said as she closed the door. The candle stands in each corner held seven candles and they were all burning brightly. There was enough light to see the faces of those at the table. A light from somewhere was shining on the picture of Jesus.

It appeared to Bill the table was as they left it last night, except in front of each place was a small pile of dirt. In front of Mrs. DuBose's chair was an open Bible.

Mrs. DuBose took her seat and extended her hands, "Please, let us all join in a circle." She continued, "Let us pray. Father God and Creator, Giver of your Son, the Holy Spirit, our life, our soul, our spirit, and our life eternal, be with us and bless us and help us as we search for the spirit of one of your own."

Mr. and Mrs. Jackson added, "Amen."

Mrs. DuBose continued, "We search for no gain, but for truth and comfort for the spirit of our sister, Annie Mattox. We know her soul is with you waiting for the final judgment, her body has gone to the dust before us, but her spirit needs comfort and we are here for her. Amen."

"Brothers and sisters, I am going to call on the spirit of Annie Mattox to join us now, and I feel she is near. If you knew her in life, call up a memory of her, a good one. If you didn't know her call up the memory of a treasured loved one who has passed and cling to it as I speak."

When she started to speak again, Bill remembered his Dad hitting grounders and pop ups in the corner of the pasture. His Dad had spent days scraping it smooth so they would have a place to practice.

"Sister Annie Mattox, we are your friends and neighbors. Some of us you knew in life, and some you have come to know from the other side. You know we all care about you. In front of us are some of your earthly treasures. Things which brought you comfort and joy in life. Through us they can bring your spirit peace. Come be with us and let us know who hurt you. We know he has passed over, too. Come and be with us. We will be silent and wait for your sign."

As they sat holding hands and waiting, candles started going out, one by one until only the middle candle on each stand burned. It was so dark now no one could see across the table.

Mrs. DuBose repeated her call to Annie Mattox.

There was a sign, the sound of a wind outside on an afternoon when no storm was possible. The four burning candles flickered and went out. The room was into total darkness. They all heard a sound of something falling on the table and felt the bump. Then there was silence.

After a moment, Mrs. DuBose began again, "Bless your soul and peace to your spirit, Annie Mattox. We are your friends and will be with you as you need us. Thank you. Amen."

Mrs. DuBose said, "Brothers and sisters, our sister Annie Mattox visited us and left us a sign. Please sit still and don't touch anything while I light the candles."

They all dropped hands, except Diane held onto Bill's hand and put her other hand on his, and would not let go. After a moment, Mrs. DuBose rose. Slowly the room grew brighter as she lit the candles. When Mrs. DuBose lit the last of the candles, both Diane and Mrs. Jackson called out as they looked at the table.

The hem marker had fallen over and the heavy base was on its side. The chalk contents of the vessel had spilled out and covered the toes of Annie's shoes with a coating of white dust.

There was a collective gasp as all looked at the toe of Annie's right shoe. In the white chalk dust was a mark that looked like it may have been made by a small finger scratching away the dust to reveal the black leather below. Neither recognized the mark but it looked like some sort of writing.

"What is that?" cried out Mrs. Jackson.

Bill stood and looked at the mark. "It looks like Pi," he said.

"What?" Diane asked.

"Pi," Bill said. "The Greek letter, the one you use for circles. Pi r squared, from math."

"I never was much in math, but I remember talking about Pi," Diane answered.

Looking across the table, Bill asked, "Mr. Jackson, Mrs. Jackson do you recognize the mark? Does it look like anything you know?"

"I know a little music writing, but it don't look like anything I ever seen in a music book. No sir, I don't know what it is," replied Moses Jackson.

Mrs. Jackson shook her head.

Bill started to stand, "May I stand, I want to make a copy of the mark?"

"Yes, we are done. I will open the door. Please be careful and not disturb the table."

They all looked at Mrs. DuBose as she was speaking. Her formerly perfect hair was all out of place almost as if someone had run their fingers through it, and her make-up was streaked from perspiration and perhaps tears. She looked tired and much older. Diane who still had not let go of Bill's hand squeezed it even tighter.

"Diane, let me get your chair," Bill said as he gently freed his hand from Diane's. He stood behind her and moved the chair back as she stood.

"I'm going to the hall," she said. Mr. and Mrs. Jackson rose and went with her.

Bill stepped towards Mrs. DuBose, "May I help you?"

"No thank you, Bill. I need to sit a minute. Go on and draw the mark. It will be important."

Bill drew the mark several times as he moved around the table. He held his pencil close to the mark and gauged its height and width by moving his thumb up and down the pencil. He made marks on his paper to match his measurements.

"Mrs. DuBose, is this a mark or sign you know?"

"No, Bill. I agree it looks like Pi, but otherwise, I don't know it."

"Connie asked to see the shoes. When I move these things to my truck, will it be okay to show them to her?"

Sounding much more like herself, "Connie gets such strong connections from things she touches. Sometimes they hurt her, but I don't think I can, or even have the right, to keep her from doing and feeling. She may tell you something that will help."

Neither of them moved or said anything for a long moment. "Bill, you may be a part of our lives for a time to come. Not now, but soon, I want you to tell me your feelings and thoughts about this session today."

"Mrs. DuBose, I think…"

"Really, not now Bill. I want you to have time to think, and I want Annie's story to unfold for you. Now, help me up and let's see to the others." They walked out together, and Mrs. DuBose closed the doors behind them.

Connie was standing at the top of the stairs when her mother came out. Mrs. DuBose looked up and nodded. Connie turned and called down the hall, and ran down the stairs to her mother. She held on tightly to her and was uncommonly quiet. Elizabeth walked down the stairs and gave her mother a kiss on the cheek.

Diane stepped over to Bill and asked, "Are you going home now?"

In a whisper Bill replied, "I hope not, I hope to stay."

Still whispering Diane said, "I can see why. She is beautiful. But, I want to talk to you, and soon."

In more of a normal voice, Bill said, "Remember, I have to go see Judge Morrow first thing tomorrow. I had planned on being in Crawfordville at nine."

"Okay, we will wait, but this may be important to you and to Mrs. DuBose," Diane replied quietly.

"Brothers and sisters," Mrs. DuBose began, "thank you for coming today and helping. I believe we were successful in making a way for Annie's spirit to find peace. We will see. Elizabeth, are you ready to take Mr. and Mrs. Jackson home?"

"Yes, ma'am." Elizabeth started through the parlor with the Jackson's close behind her.

Diane started for the front door with Mrs. DuBose holding her elbow and barely keeping up. "Miss Weston, it was a pleasure to meet you. I hope to see you again soon. Bill, thank you for inviting her."

"Thank you, too, Mrs. DuBose. Bill, I'll see you tomorrow," Diane said as she hurried to her car.

The three-remaining stood at the door and watched the Packard come around the house with the Jacksons and Diane's car fall in behind. At the road, the Packard turned right toward Mt. Nebo Church Road, and Diane turned left toward town.

"Momma, I know she came, I felt it. What happened?" Connie asked.

Mrs. DuBose moved to the door of the session room, "Connie, I want you to see. She wrote something we don't understand."

"Momma, I can't read much. But I will try."

"It's not words, honey. It's, it's…well you tell us if you know. Look there on her shoes."

Connie stood at the table staring at the shoes and the mark. "Momma, I don't know what the mark is." She looked at Bill and said, "but it will tell you who hurt Annie. Can I hold her shoes?"

Bill answered, "Yes, but be careful, if I could get home with the mark still on the shoe, I could take a picture."

Connie reached out and took the left shoe. Immediately her shoulders fell and she pulled the shoe to her chest and dropped her head. She sniffled and turned her body back and forth holding the shoe close to her. "We're sorry, Annie, so sorry. You won't hurt anymore."

Her mother said, "Put the shoe down, baby. Annie knows you love her."

Connie carefully put the shoe on the table and looked at Bill. "The person who stuck Annie with a knife, is that person." She pointed at the mark on the right shoe. "But someone ran with her, and it hurt her. The running hurt her a lot."

"Do you mean, she tried to run away and he chased her?" asked Bill.

"No, she was picked up in his arms, and he ran with her, and she was in a wagon. It bounced on the road and the bouncing hurt her."

"Connie, that all seems very strange to me. Does it seem strange to you?"

"Yes, Bill, it does. Annie didn't know why he ran with her and put her in a wagon. Maybe he was sorry she was hurt and was trying to take her to a doctor."

Bill said, "I'll have to think about all of this. When we find out who did this, it might all make sense." *I know who killed her and none of this makes a damn bit of sense.*

"Bill, Connie and I have done enough for today. It's time for you to put Annie's things in your truck. Connie come sit with me in the parlor."

Bill quickly and carefully picked up the quilt and hem marker without disturbing the shoes and went to his truck. I thought for sure she was going to say it was time for me to go. I'll take my time and Elizabeth will be back.

He spent as much time as possible arranging the quilt and hem marker in his truck, and then walked inside. He heard Connie talking in the parlor so he took his time collecting the cloth scrap, thread, and envelope he had used for the dirt from her grave. Outside he shook out the envelope and put the thread and cloth in it and tucked it under the quilt. He looked up and saw the Packard turning in the drive. He waited by his truck, Elizabeth stopped, and walked to him and hugged him and added a quick kiss.

"Are you leaving?" Elizabeth asked.

"I hope not. I'm putting Annie's things away for tomorrow. I still must get her shoes. There is a mark on one of them. I want you to see."

"The Jackson's talked about the mark, something about a Greek pie?"

With a little laugh Bill said, "Almost, but I want you to tell me what you see."

"Where are Momma and Connie?"

"In the parlor."

"Good, I'll put the car up and meet you in the hall."

Bill busied himself until he heard the back-door close, then he walked up the steps and into the hall. He heard Elizabeth talking to her mother, and she appeared in the parlor door. They walked quickly toward each other and greeted with a proper kiss. "I missed you," Elizabeth breathed.

"And I missed you, too," Bill answered and they kissed again.

"Momma said to fix us some…ooo," Connie stopped in mid-sentence as she entered the hall and saw her sister and Bill embrace. She dropped her head and stopped.

Elizabeth turned from Bill, "Connie," and she walked to her little sister and put her arm on her shoulder, "what did Momma say?"

Connie looked at her sister.

"It's okay," Elizabeth said, "I told you Bill was going to be my boyfriend."

"Supper, Momma says to fix us some supper. You know how tired she is after a session. She wants to eat and go to bed."

"Tell her I will be right there. Bill wants to show me Annie's shoes and the writing. I'll come and fix us something. See what she wants. Don't tell Momma you saw us kissing."

A pause, "Okay" and Connie walked into the parlor with her head still down. "Momma, Betty May said she'll…" and the sound of her voice was lost.

As Bill and Elizabeth walked into the session room, he said, "Take a look at the shoes."

Elizabeth said, "Not a Greek pie, but the Greek letter Pi, that's what Moses was trying to tell me. Yes, it looks like the Greek letter Pi." She walked around the table to see the mark from all angles. "No, I don't see anything else. Now, I'm going to make some sandwiches for supper. That's all Momma will want. She will go to bed and sleep all night. I'll fix you a sandwich, too."

"Good, but will it be all right with your mother?" Bill asked.

"She'll say if it isn't, but don't worry. She's going to bed and will be asleep in a little while."

Carefully picking up the shoes and walking toward the door, Bill said, "I am not going to try and get anything past any of the DuBose women, one I love and the other two would figure it out."

Elizabeth looked at him and smiled. As he went out, she turned to the parlor, "Momma, what do you want to eat?"

19

Carrying the shoe to his truck, Bill saw the chalk dust fall off. I don't know why I think this is important. I was there and I couldn't even swear to what happened. Pi? What the hell does it mean? It means something to Mrs. DuBose and right now because of Elizabeth, it means something to me, but it doesn't make sense, and it sure as hell doesn't mean anything to the law.

Mrs. DuBose was in her chair when he walked into the parlor and Connie was sitting on the ottoman. Connie didn't look up at him, and he thought she might have turned away.

"I have everything packed up. I have to take some of it to Judge Morrow in Crawfordville tomorrow. He has to have a hearing here on Wednesday to rule on the manner of Annie's death." Turning to Connie, "Connie, thank you for looking at Annie's shoes. I hope it didn't hurt you. You are very important to me."

"Not like E-liz-a-beth," Connie whined, drawing out her sister's name.

"Cornelia, mind your tongue, young lady," scolded Mrs. DuBose.

"Yes, ma'am."

Bill looked straight at Connie, "No, not like Elizabeth is important to me. But you are very important to me, and more than anything I want to be your friend. In less than one week, all the DuBose ladies have become important to me. Can we be friends?" Bill stepped closer to the ottoman and held open his arms.

Connie looked at him for the first time since she caught him kissing Elizabeth. "Oh, Bill, I want to be your friend, too." She ran into his arms. "I love you and I love Betty May, too. This is hard, I don't understand, I usually understand."

Mrs. DuBose answered, "Yes, Connie, it is hard. Real love is hard to understand. We miss Daddy because we loved him so much and he loved us. We love Bill because he is our brother in Christ. And we love Bill because he is our friend, and he has helped our neighbors. Elizabeth and Bill may have another kind of love important to God."

"Like you loved Daddy," Connie asked.

"Perhaps," her mother replied.

Bill looked at Mrs. DuBose and said, "You told me about Paul explaining about the gifts of the spirit. I don't know where it is in the Bible, but didn't Paul write about love, too."

"Yes, he did, Bill. I'm proud of you for remembering. I will use it for our blessing tonight."

Elizabeth stood in the door and said, "I've made some sandwiches, and we have some potato salad and some pickles. It's not much, do we need anything else?"

"That will be a gracious plenty for me, dear. Bill, can you get enough?"

"I will be fine," Bill answered.

Elizabeth continued, "I set places in the kitchen. I didn't think we needed the dining room tonight."

A small dining table with painted yellow legs and white porcelain top had been pulled away from its place close against the wall and it was set for four with plain light blue plates. Matching painted chairs were at each place. Bill imagined this was the setting for many DuBose family meals when Jefferson Davis DuBose was alive. All seated, Bill reached for Elizabeth's and Connie's hands without a prompt.

"We talked about love a few minutes ago and Bill reminded us of something St. Paul wrote about love nearly two thousand years ago. I am going to tell you what he wrote. Connie, in our Bible, Paul uses the word charity in this part, and how you have heard it before. But he means love, and he means all kinds of love. I'm going to change the word charity to love as I tell you in my words a part of what he said."

Mrs. DuBose continued without a pause, "Paul said he could teach wonderful lessons in words we could all understand, or he could talk like an angel using words like Connie uses. And he said, if he didn't have love, what he said was noise like someone banging on a brass cymbal. Paul said he was smart and could understand great mysteries and tell what was to happen in the future, but if he didn't have love, he was nothing. And he knew no matter what good things he did, if he didn't do them with love, they didn't help him."

Mary Greene DuBose now bowed her head and continued, "Father help us to learn love. We know a little of what love is, but we need to learn what love is not. Love is not wanting what others have. We are happy for them. Love is not being proud of ourselves, but we are happy to be humble. Love is not being angry at others because anger makes us and them sad. Love does not let us think what others are doing, saying, or thinking is evil. Love does not like sin. Sin makes us unhappy. When everything around us seems to be falling apart, love helps us to know now, a little of what is to come. When Jesus' perfect love comes, we will know it all. It is like when I was little, I spoke, understood and thought like a child because I was a child. Now I am grown up, I have put away my childish ways and understand like a grownup understands. But even now it is hard. Seeing Jesus and His love is like looking at him in a cloudy old mirror, but when He comes again, we will see Him just like we see each other now, face to face. While we wait, we must have faith and hope and love, but love is the most important. Amen."

"Momma when I say those words people don't understand, am I talking like angels?"

"Connie, I think those words are talking like an angel."

"And I understand mysteries, don't I?"

"Yes, sometimes you do."

"Momma, did I misbehave when I wanted Bill to love me and not Betty May?"

"Yes, Connie, wanting what others have and not being happy for them is envy."

"I need to love everyone."

"Yes, Connie. You have been blessed with many and strong gifts of the Spirit. But if you use them without love, then they are noise, like someone beating on the brass cymbal Paul talked about."

"I don't want to be a noisy cymbal. Bill, I'm sorry I got mad about you kissing Elizabeth. I think I was speaking as a child. Betty May, I'm sorry I got mad at you, too."

Bill looked at Connie, "Sweet Connie, I accept your apology. Tonight, you have put away childish things and shown us true love. But, Connie, don't stop being a child and try to grow up too quickly. You are supposed to have fun when you are nine."

"I'm ten."

"When you are ten, too. Let's eat, I'm hungry," said Bill.

The conversation for the rest of the meal was pleasant. Bill was pleased to know both Mrs. DuBose and Elizabeth knew the outcome of the Tech game and of the Army – Notre Dame game. Understandably, they were Georgia fans, but since he had gone to Tech, they didn't hold his loyalty against him. Connie seemed willing to take Tech as hers until she remembered how little her daddy thought of Tech. All three seemed to adopt Bill's Army team as their own. Bill mentioned how good the bread was and Mrs. DuBose quickly pointed out Elizabeth was the family baker. Connie remembered there was peach cobbler left from Saturday night, and all but Mrs. DuBose decided on a serving. It was just dark as they finished the meal, a little after six o'clock.

"Thank you, Elizabeth, for fixing supper. Bill, I need to rest and am going up to bed. Connie, your bed time is eight o'clock. We have a busy week to get ready for our trip."

"Good night, Mrs. DuBose. I have a busy week, too. I have to go to Crawfordville first thing in the morning. I won't keep Elizabeth or Connie up late, I promise."

Mrs. DuBose stood and said, "Good night, Bill. I'm glad you are in our life. Elizabeth, beware of unguarded moments."

Mary Greene stepped to Bill and kissed him on the cheek

and walked to the back stairs and up. Connie and Elizabeth stood staring at Bill until their mother had disappeared.

Connie looked at Elizabeth and said, "Betty May, does Momma love Bill?"

"Yes, she does, but it was not a boyfriend kind of kiss."

"Love is confusing."

"It is sometimes, Connie. Now help me clear the table. We will wash the dishes in the morning."

"Okay, can we listen to the radio?" Connie asked.

"Sure, Bill see if you can find Jack Benny. That will be fun."

They listened to the last half of Jack Benny, mostly talked during Phil Harris and Alice Faye, but laughed at Edgar Bergen and Charlie McCarthy. It was still a half hour before her imposed bedtime, but Connie was sleepy. She agreed to go upstairs if she had a goodnight kiss from Bill, and if Elizabeth would go up with her.

Bill found some music on the radio and took off his tie. When Elizabeth returned, she had changed into the same plaid shirt she was wearing when he first saw her. But instead of overalls, she wore jeans, and the shirt was not tucked in.

"I hope you don't mind my changing, I had been in that dress long enough and I needed to get comfortable," she said.

"You still look lovely, in fact, you're beautiful. Come and sit here," and Bill patted the sofa beside him.

Elizabeth took two quick steps and jumped onto the sofa landing beside him on her knees. "Kiss me," she said and she wrapped her arms around his neck and pulled him to her.

By the time their kiss ended, they had worked into a much better posture with Elizabeth lying across Bill's lap and facing him. Her shirt had moved up, revealing a band of bare skin above her jeans.

Neither had opened their eyes following the first kiss and in this new and more comfortable position, they were both ready to continue. Bill shifted his hand and it found her tummy, flat and smooth with a firmness underneath. He moved his hand slowly across and back.

Elizabeth gave an encouraging "yes, good, yes," and she nuzzled her face against his neck. Elizabeth's reaction to his touch aroused Bill completely. Bill moved his hand under her shirt around to her back to pull her closer.

Elizabeth shifted. "Rub my back," she said as she turned more toward him.

"How is this?" Bill said as he spread his hand and cupped it so only the tips of his fingers were touching her, and moved it up and down her back from her waist to her neck in a zigzag pattern. He felt nothing but her warm skin. Elizabeth sighed a pleased "mmm." Bill spread his hand flat and rubbed gently all the way down to her waist.

"Oh, that feels so good. I told you I wanted to be more comfortable," she said. "This might be one of those unguarded moments Momma warned me about."

"Do you need to beware?" Bill asked.

Looking up she said, "No, not at all." And she unbuttoned two buttons of her shirt and pushed it open. "Do you?"

"I might," Bill replied as he leaned to her and pressed his lips on her forehead. When he pulled back, Elizabeth was still looking directly at him with the slightest smile. Meeting her eyes with his and holding them there, Bill moved his hand from her back, unbuttoned the last button on her shirt and opened it completely. "I see," he said.

"No, you don't, you're not looking," she said with a bit of a pout.

He repeated the forehead kiss. This time when he raised his head, his eyes found her breast at the same time as his hand. As he filled his hand. He moved his thumb slowly across her nipple, and she responded with another "oh" and a "yes" that had a little surprise in it.

She brought her hand up and covered his and pushed it firmly to her. "Hold me tight."

Bill started to pull her closer, "Wait," she said, and raised up. With Bill's help, she took off her shirt. It fell to the parlor floor as she lay back in his lap.

Bill lowered his head down and worked his tongue against her nipple deep in his mouth. Elizabeth gasped in pleasure. She took his right hand, shoved it between her legs, and squeezed it tightly. As she did, she brought her knees up and turned toward him murmuring, "Oh yes."

The music on the radio stopped and the announcer ended the program and signed off for the night. With only soft static from the radio, the quiet of the Georgia country filled the house. There was a creaking noise, possibly the floor under a foot somewhere in the house, or not, then another creak.

With some fear in his voice, Bill raised his head, "What was that?"

Neither spoke for a few seconds as they listened. They heard nothing more.

Bill knew their moment was lost. Their time on the sofa had

too quickly taken him to a place he neither expected, nor was quite ready for. And, Elizabeth, she had surprised him in ways he never imagined. "Who is this wonderful creature?" he thought. "No matter now, this is only the beginning."

Elizabeth broke the silence, "You know, Bill, we do have ghosts in this house."

Bill laughed at her comment and his reaction to the sound, and said, "Elizabeth DuBose, I do love you. But now, as much as I hate it, think I had better go."

"Yes," she said as slipped into her shirt.

20

He knew it wouldn't take long, and he knew too Mary Nell Jenkins' open bathrobe and the nurse's uniform were likely to become distant memories. He was right on the first point. When he crawled into bed it was only nine-thirty. As he lay there, he hoped his thoughts would become dreams. Unfortunately, the only dreams he remembered when the alarm sounded at five-thirty were of a chalk covered shoe with a crude Pi scratched on it. He showered and dressed quickly and went down to his truck to move Annie's things back to his patrol car.

The quilt, hem marker, and shoes would go to the office, but the thread and scrap of cloth needed to go into the envelope he had prepared for Judge Morrow on Annie Mattox. The envelope contained his photographs, Dr. Parker's report, and Annie's dress. The scrap and thread connected her cabin to her body as another form of identification. In his apartment, he took out the drawing he had made following the session. As he looked at it he thought it would have been a good idea to have signed it, and gotten Diane to initial it. He realized again this would never be evidence in any court. But, he did draw a copy and add measurements to the originals. He put the originals in the kit with his father's cuff links and the copy in his wallet.

He thought about what Connie said when she held Annie's shoes. Annie running away from the killer makes sense, but the killer running while carrying Annie doesn't. But, talking to the spirits of dead people doesn't make sense at all. I need to put all of this out of my mind.

Bill had breakfast at Geer's, and got to Crawfordville before nine. The fellow sweeping the brick sidewalk told him Judge Morrow's office was on the second floor, but the judge was not there yet. Bill headed up the stairs with his box of envelopes. The door to the judge's office was open, but there was no one at the secretary's desk. A hand-written note was taped to the door frame. It said, "Out on an errand. Have a seat. Be back shortly." He settled into the chair with cushions opposite the desk.

In a moment, he heard someone walking down the hall. Before he reached the door, a man called out, "Mary."

A tall man in a shirt and tie, carrying his jacket, pulled the sign from the door and walked into the office. He looked at Bill and asked, "Were you here when she left?"

Bill stood, "No sir, no one was here when I came in. Are you Judge Morrow?"

"Yes, and I guess you are the deputy from Greene County," and he extended his hand to Bill.

Shaking the Judge's hand, "Yes, sir, I'm Bill Brown."

"Come on in to my office and we'll talk about all the troubles in Greene County. How is Ben?"

"Ben is well. He is up for reelection next year and thinks he might have some opposition this time. And, well, I have brought you a box full of troubles." Bill picked up his box of envelopes and followed the Judge into the office.

"Just leave the door open so I can see when Mary gets back. Hell, Ben won't have any trouble, he knows too much about everybody in the county. Bill, you are new aren't you. When did you come to work?"

"I started last March. I had some MP school and Sheriff De-Witt needed somebody right away."

"Military Police, that's good. Where were you stationed?"

"I never did any police work in the Army. I was a pilot and after I crashed they sent me to the MP officer's school because they didn't think I could fly anymore. When they decided I could fly, I got back to being a pilot."

"A pilot, what did you fly and where?"

"B-17s and 24s in the Pacific."

"You say you went back to being a pilot before you did any police work in the Army?"

"I guess when the Army found out I passed my MP physical they decided I could fly and shipped me to New Mexico to learn to fly B-29s. The war ended and the Army Air Corps decided they didn't need so many reserve officers so I was given my separation orders."

"How did you get to Greene County?"

It dawned on Bill the judge wanted to know as much, if not more, about him than his potential girl friend's mother did. "I'm from Greene County. My family had a dairy farm down near White Plains."

Bill followed with his story from separation from the Army to being hired by Sheriff DeWitt.

"Have you kept up with the talk about starting an Air Force?"

"Yes, it is interesting. I know some of our Air Corps brass

didn't think the regular Army brass gave us our due. Bombers made a difference in the Pacific and Europe. Even with the A-bomb, big bombers are going to be important. Jet engines are only on fighters now, but we can use jets on big airplanes. I think having brass who understands the air war will make a big difference."

"Would you go back?"

"I've thought about it. I know I won't do this much longer. I have some other interests now that make a return to the service a little less attractive."

"Yes, she will, Major Brown, yes she will. Let's talk about what brought you here. Have you ever been to a coroner's inquest?"

"No, sir."

"It's pretty simple. All we want to do is determine the manner of death as a public record. I'll preside and there will be seven men who make up the jury. Most of them have done it before and know what's going on. You or Sheriff DeWitt will present the evidence you have, and what you think happened. We will ask questions, and the jury votes. Mostly, it's pretty cut and dried,

"Yes, sir."

"Okay, show me what you have."

"I want to start with the girl who we believe was murdered. There's a connection among all three that makes sense when we get to the man who hanged himself."

Bill went through his evidence and the identification of Annie Mattox by Mack Poole and Tommy Coles. He explained Poole couldn't testify because he was the one who hanged himself, and they couldn't find Coles because didn't have a regular home. The judge let him finish, looked at the photographs and statements, and asked if she had been raped.

Bill said, "Dr. Parker's examination showed no evidence of rape, and Annie had on her underwear." He described the location of the body.

Next, he went to the Brunsons. First, he told the judge one of the on-lookers where they found Annie's body said she had been working for the Brunsons. He told of his conversation with Mr. Brunson and how he said it would all be over soon.

Judge Morrow didn't spend any time on the photographs, but he did ask who had taken them and gave a satisfied nod when Bill explained he taken them all. Again, he had no questions for Bill.

Bill ended with, "Judge Morrow, we believe Mack Poole committed suicide, and he did so because he killed Annie Mattox. He knew we were close to catching him and he was afraid."

"Suicide seems a poor choice. Why didn't he run?" asked the judge.

"Mr. Poole was not real smart. I don't think he had ever been out of the county. He wouldn't have known how to run away. He may have figured hanging was his only way out. I doubt he had money to buy a shotgun shell even if he still had a gun."

"Why did he think you were close to catching him, and were you?"

"I had caught him in lies about when he last saw Annie and how well he knew her. He was at the crime scene and told me it had been most of a year since he talked to her last. Later, I found out he had given her a ride in his wagon on the Friday before she died on Saturday. When I confronted him about the lie, he said he was scared."

"Anything else?" asked the judge.

"I took him to her cabin with me. When I found her sewing machine, he told me she sewed. He admitted she had given him a shirt she had made for her father. Also, Annie had a dress maker's hem marker in her cabin. I didn't know what it was and he told me what it was and how it worked. The only way he would have known about the hem marker was to have seen her using it."

"Is it one of those things that blows out puffs of chalk dust to make marks on a dress?"

"Yes, sir. When I took him to identify the body he was very upset. Both the Sheriff and I felt like he would have run if we had not been right beside him."

"Did you ever question him? I mean an intense questioning."

"We were going to question him right after he identified the body, but we got the call about the Brunsons. We felt like he wouldn't run, and we'd pick him up the next day. I took him home on my way to the Brunsons."

Judge Morrow continued his questions, "Why would he have stabbed her in the first place?"

"We think he wanted to marry her. He told Coles he was going to get married. Later, we found out Annie had plans to move to Athens. Poole couldn't have survived in Athens. They may have fought about her leaving. Supposedly, Poole had a real mean streak and could fly hot."

"About the hanging. What makes you sure it was suicide and not murder?"

"The biggest things were his hands weren't tied, there was no sign of a struggle or evidence of other people at the site of the hanging. The rope was wrapped around a limb rather than being tied to it. Tying a knot wouldn't have been easy from the back of his mule."

"Makes sense," Judge Morrow said.

"There's a little more," Bill added. "According to the doctor, he died of choking, not of a broken neck. He didn't fall far enough to break his neck. I did some calculations and it looks like if he came off his mule like we think, he only dropped a foot or so. Dr. Parker said it would have taken at least twenty minutes for him to choke to death."

"Anything else?"

"Nothing, but we don't have any other suspects for the murder. Not many people live around there. There is a colored family down at the end of her road, but they are good people and there's no reason to suspect any of them, no motive. In fact, they were probably the best friends Annie had. And we don't know of anyone who had anything against Poole. He was a loner and pretty worthless. Mean streak or not, he hadn't made enemies we knew of. Suicide sort of fits."

"The place where you found the Mattox girl's body, is it close to the DuBose house?"

Surprised at the question, Bill answered, "Yes, sir, it is."

"Have you met Mrs. DuBose?"

"Yes, I talked with the family during my investigation."

Before Bill could answer further, Judge Morrow called to someone in the outer office, "Mary, is that you?"

A deputy stepped through the door, "Judge, Mary is not here. I brought in our information about the suicide last Wednesday."

"Ben, come in. This is Deputy Bill Brown from Greene County. He is here with files from the troubles over in Greensboro last week. Two murders and two suicides, we need to try harder. Bill, Ben Lannigan, one of our Taliaferro County deputies."

"Pleased to meet you, Bill, but Judge, I'm okay with our work load. I'll wait out here until y'all are done." Ben and Bill shook hands.

"Just have a seat in here, Ben. We are done unless you have any questions for me, Bill. If you see Mary DuBose again, please tell her I said hello. Her husband and I were friends for a long time."

"I will," Bill answered. "What would you like me to do with the things I brought?"

"You take them all with you. You will need them when you present your cases."

"Yes, sir. Give me a minute to pack up and I will be out of your way. Good to meet you, Judge Morrow, and you, Ben." Bill began putting his photographs and reports in their envelopes.

"What do you have for me, Ben?" asked the judge.

"This is the guy who put his head on the rail in front of the Atlanta express last Wednesday afternoon. No problem with the time of death. Exactly two-twenty pm. The train was right on time."

Bill dropped the box of envelopes he had just picked up and turned to the Judge and Ben.

Judge Morrow looked and said, "Are you okay? You are as white as a sheet." Bill fell into his chair.

Bill sat still for a moment. He asked, "Did you say this man died at two-twenty last Wednesday afternoon?"

"Yes," Ben replied.

"Do you have any idea who he is?" Bill continued.

"Not at all. Po' Boy said he'd been hanging around the depot all day. He'd show up when a train was coming and disappear until the next one came in. The two-twenty was the only one that wasn't supposed to stop."

Ben reached into his folder, "Bill, do you think you know who he was? I have a picture, but it's only his body. I would say he was lying face down, but he don't have a face anymore. It was chewed up with his head under the train." Ben pulled a five by seven print from the envelope and handed it to Bill.

It was a picture of a man's torso and legs. He was lying chest down beside a railroad track. The legs were crossed in an awkward position. His pants were up to his knees, and he had no shoes or boots. The ends of his pant legs were frayed.

As Bill studied the picture, Ben added, "The only thing we found on him was a nearly empty pack of Beech Nut tobacco and this little handkerchief." He held up a small blue patch of cloth Bill recognized immediately.

"Son of a bitch!" Bill said as he reached for the cloth. There was no doubt it was the same cloth as Annie's dress. This piece was the same shape as the one he found at the cabin but it was smaller because the edges had been folded and sewn together to make them smooth. He realized it was the second pocket for the dress. As he turned it over in his hand he saw the slit in the material. His heart was racing, and he didn't know what to say to the Judge or to Ben. He opened Annie's envelope and pulled out the dress and spread it on the Judge's desk.

Both the Judge and Ben recognized the scrap of cloth and the dress were the same material. Bill took the judge's silver letter opener and pushed it from the inside of the dress through the hole made by the knife that killed her. He threaded the letter opener through the slit in the pocket and pushed it down to the dress. It lay on the dress exactly as the pocket did in the magazine picture. He took his scrap from the envelope and lay it on the right side of the dress where it would have gone.

Ben looked at what Bill had done and said, "I see the cloth matches the dress, but what does this all mean?"

Bill answered, "It means your suicide victim had a piece of the dress my murder victim was wearing when she was killed." He let the that hang for a minute. He looked again at the picture Ben had shown him, and asked, "Does the name Tommy Coles mean anything to you?"

It was Ben's turn to blanch a little and he responded, "I'll say son of a bitch myself. Po' Boy found some stuff where somebody had been sleeping in an old shed at the depot. He brought it in this morning, and it's still sitting on my desk. I just started looking at it. Here, let me get it over here before I tell you. Judge, can I use the phone."

"Sure."

Ben picked up the receiver and dialed two numbers, "Willie, do you see the stuff Po' Boy brought over this morning, it's on my desk? ... Yeah, that's it. Bring it over to Judge Morrow's office as quick as you can .... Yes, right now. Lock the door. It will be all right." He hung up. "It will be here in a second."

Bill asked, "Who's Po' Boy?"

The judge explained, "Po' Boy is Hans de Graffinreed. He's the depot agent. He's been Po' Boy a long time because he's always complaining about not having any money. Bill, he and Du-

Bose were friends, and they were supposed to be in the rail car deal together. If they were, it looks like DuBose got the better end of it. They might not have stayed friends to the end."

Bill looked at Ben and explained, "My murder victim was wearing this dress when she was killed, but it was not finished. The bottom wasn't sewn and the pockets weren't on it. The piece your suicide guy had is a pocket, and it was probably pinned to the dress when she was stabbed. See how the hole in the pocket matches the one in her dress, right where the stab wound was on her chest." Bill looked closely at the dress where the pocket lay. He moved it a little so the patterns matched exactly. "See, look here. I bet these little picks in the dress are where the pins were and were made when the pocket was torn off."

Ben and the Judge both looked and nodded in agreement.

Judge Morrow looked at Bill, "Do you think this man might be your murderer and not Poole?"

"It sure does look like he was involved. If this guy is Tommy Coles, and I think he is, things get complicated. Coles and Poole knew each and didn't like each other, and both of them knew Annie Mattox."

Ben asked, "Bill, what did you know about Coles?"

"I didn't know Coles at all. He showed up at my car on Tuesday morning saying he knew Annie. After talking to Sheriff De-Witt, I took him by the funeral home and he said the body was Annie. Come to think of it, he suggested Poole might have killed her, and I remember him saying somebody should swing for killing her. Ben, did you say de Graffinreed said this man had been around all day?"

"That's what I remember, but I'll check for sure."

There was a polite knock on the door and a voice asking, "Ben?"

"Come in, Willie."

"Ben, is this what you wanted?" Willie said as he held up a rolled-up blanket and a canvas satchel.

"Yes, it is, Willie. Thanks."

"Yes, sir."

Excited, Bill said, "Tommy Coles had that satchel when I saw him Tuesday morning. Is there anything in it?"

"Yep," said Ben, as he opened the satchel and first pulled out an oilcloth duster.

"It was raining and Coles was wearing that duster," Bill said.

Next, Ben took out a leather belt pouch which he opened and took out a small card he handed to Bill. It was a draft registration card for Tommy Coles.

Reaching in to the pouch again, Ben said, "And this" as he passed Bill an old wooden handled dagger in a leather sheath. Bill froze, his eyes fixed on the handle. There was a rough carving there, Coles' initials, a T and a C joined together.

Bill mumbled, "It wasn't Pi, it was his initials. Annie gave us her killer's initials exactly the way they were carved on his knife. The rotten son of a bitch."

"Bill, what are you saying?" Judge Morrow asked.

"Nothing. Something a person said to me. I think Coles did it. I know he did. Tommy Coles killed her. Look." He took the dagger from the sheath and laid it beside the cut in the pocket and the width of the blade matched the cut in the dress and pocket.

21

As he walked from the outer office, Ben said, "Judge, Mary is back." He turned to Bill, "I called de Graffinreed and he said he saw the suicide victim at about eight-fifteen when he came to work. He said he would see him when a train was coming in and then he wouldn't see him. He also said whoever was behind the shed may have been there several days."

"Thanks, Ben," Bill replied.

Looking at Bill, Judge Morrow said, "Bill, I guess we've helped you today, but maybe not."

The judge turned to Ben, "Ben, as far as the inquest on your suicide, I can't think of a problem. You have two witnesses, with de Graffinreed being one of them. His testimony is likely all you'll need to get a finding of suicide."

"Thank you," Ben said.

Judge Morrow continued, "Take good care of all the things you have. I imagine Bill is going to want them for something in Greene County. I think we are done. Thanks."

"Yes, sir," said Ben. "I'm going to take this all back and get it in the books. Bill, stop by when you leave and let me know what you might do."

"Sure, and thanks, Ben. I'm real glad you mentioned the time of death. It's what started me thinking." As soon as the words left his mouth, Bill realized what he said could create questions. Why would the time some fool jumped under a train in Crawfordville, Georgia mean anything to him, even if the fool was his murderer? Maybe they won't notice.

"Ben, tell Mary, I'll see her in a few minutes. Ben and Bill, I will be glad to carry anything of Ben's evidence over to you on Wednesday when I come." Judge Morrow looked at Bill and said, "Sit down a minute. I'm going to have some coffee, would you like a cup?"

Bill understood, the offer of a seat and coffee was not an invitation, but an order, "Yes, sir, black will be fine."

Judge Morrow walked out of his office and spoke with Mary for a few minutes and came back, closing the door behind him. "Bill," he said, "you have four deaths for the inquest. Three of them are no problem as to manner of death. There is no doubt in my mind Annie Mattox was murdered, so her death is a homicide. You have it to solve. The Brunsons are a murder-suicide. As soon as we can put that one away, everyone will be better off."

Judge Morrow reached his desk, sat down and continued, "With this business of Coles, Mack Poole's death is a bit more complicated. Correct?"

Bill answered, "Yes, sir."

"If you now think Coles was Annie Mattox's murderer, why would Poole commit suicide? If Poole didn't kill himself, who hanged him? If your doctor is anywhere close to the time of death, and I suspect he is, Coles couldn't have killed Poole. So right now, I'm not convinced about Poole's death being a suicide. But, I'm not the jury either."

There was knock at the door. "Come in." A lady came in carrying a small tray with two mugs of coffee. Bill stood and the judge continued, "Mary, this is Bill Brown, the deputy from Greene County. Bill, Mary Watkins."

"Pleased to meet you, and thanks for the coffee," Bill said.

"Nice to meet you too, Deputy Brown. How is Diane? I speak with her often."

"She's well, I'll tell her you asked about her."

"Please do," and Mary looked at Judge Morrow, "anything else, Judge?"

"No, but do close the door please."

Judge Morrow sipped his coffee and looked up, "Bill, when Ben mentioned Coles' time of death, you looked like you had seen or heard a ghost. What is important about Coles dying at two-twenty?"

"I guess I did see a ghost. Judge Morrow it's real hard to explain, and it has nothing to do with anything I could use in court. You said you knew Mr. and Mrs. DuBose."

"Yes, I would say Jeff was a good friend of mine."

"What do you know about Mrs. DuBose and her, her ... "

"Gifts?" Judge Morrow completed Bill's sentence.

"Yes, sir, gifts."

"Let's say I've had some experience with her and her gifts. She sometimes knows things she has no reason to know, and there is no rational explanation for it. In my day, I've seen plenty of fortune tellers, mediums, and the like, and I know most of their tricks and scams. I suspect she does, too. But she is not like any of them. Is that what you're asking? Is she a part of this?"

"Yes, sir, she is and her younger daughter Connie is, too. There's plenty about this I don't understand, but like you said, they know things they have no reason to know." Bill told the judge of their visit to the place where Annie's body was found, and Mrs. DuBose and Connie feeling the spirit of the murderer come through at two-twenty.

The judge simply said, "Damn."

Bill continued, "When we found Poole hanging from that tree, it seemed to all add up to everyone for him to be the killer, me included. When Dr. Parker said he had to have died before noon, I wasn't going to say Poole didn't murder Annie because Mrs. DuBose said the murderer's spirit didn't come looking for Annie until two-twenty."

Judge Morrow nodded in agreement and said, "Go on."

"Judge Morrow, at first, I didn't believe her. But when I came to tell her about finding Poole and when he died, she told me again Mack Poole didn't kill Annie. She wanted to know if I wanted to ask Annie who killed her. By this time, I was curious, and I had another reason to stay in touch. So, I agreed to come to a session. I had to pay two dollars."

"I'm going to use one of my gifts, this one may be termed a gift of the flesh, and say the oldest daughter, Betty May, might have something to do with your other reason. She was a cute girl last time I saw her and by now I suspect she is quite attractive."

Bill answered, "Yes, sir, you're right. Up to now the real Elizabeth, Betty May, has been more important to me than any of the spirits."

With a chuckle, Judge Morrow said, "I think you have your priorities in order."

"Yes, sir," Bill continued "We had the session yesterday." Bill gave a recount of it up to describing the mark on the shoes. "When we looked at the shoes and the mark was there, I thought it was the Greek letter Pi. I measured it and copied it."

Bill reached for his wallet and found the drawing he had made and handed it to the judge. He turned the dagger over so the carving on the handle was up.

Judge Morrow took the paper. "You made this yesterday in Greensboro at the DuBose house?"

"Yes, sir."

"Damned if I understand." With the knife in one hand and Bill's drawing in the other, Judge Morrow's eyes went from one to the other. "I can see how it looked like Pi, but I can see the T and C, too." The judge tore the bottom off a letter on his desk and lay it over the carving on the handle of the dagger. With the side of a pencil point he rubbed the paper. An image of the carving appeared in white. He held the image he created over Bill's and Bill's over his. "They are the same, no doubt about it, and they are the same size, exactly the same." As he handed both papers to Bill, he asked, "Did you see this knife when you saw Coles on Tuesday?"

"No, sir. If he had it, it must have been in the satchel. See the scabbard is torn. It wouldn't stay on a belt."

The judge turned the knife and scabbard over and made a sound of agreement. "Well, Deputy Brown, it looks like you have a situation or two to work out. Remember your MP school and motive means opportunity?"

"Yes, Judge Morrow, I do and I will."

"Work on them and see what you come up with for Annie's

murder and perhaps Poole's murder. I'll see you on Wednesday. I would have said make it a point to see Mrs. DuBose and pass along my greetings, but after today, I have an idea you won't have to make an extra effort. Remember, too, Wednesday is an inquest not a trial. Everything can be undone if we don't get it right. Does the sheriff know about any of this, the session and the mark?"

"Not yet. Until I found out about Tommy Coles and when he died and his knife, there wasn't really anything to tell."

"In a way you're right, but I'll tell you Ben does not like surprises, and your going to a session would be a big one. The rest of this, who knows? Bill, he knows about the DuBose gift, probably a good bit more than me. And, Bill, this is personal advice. Be careful. Things seem to happen around the DuBose family. It was good to meet you. I'll see you on Wednesday."

"Thank you, and it was a pleasure to meet you."

Bill walked across the court house square to the sheriff's office where Ben was explaining to Willie what had happened in the Judge's office.

Willie looked at Bill as he came in the door. "Our guy who jumped in front of the train is the same guy who murdered your girl?"

"Looks like it, Willie," Bill said. "His knife matches the cut on the pocket of the dress he had on him and the cut in the dress she had on when she was stabbed. That's means and opportunity right there. But right now, I don't know enough about him or the girl to know what sort of motive he might have had."

"Maybe he was going to rape her and was trying to scare her with the knife."

"Rape is as good a motive as I have."

Ben agreed to send all Bill had seen in Judge Morrow's office with the judge on Wednesday. He would add a letter stating what everything was and when and where he got it, and put his mark on the pocket and the knife so he could identify them as the items he had.

22

Riding to Greensboro, Bill worked through who he would tell what. He walked into the office right at one o'clock.

Diane looked up and said, "I would have thought you would have checked in on the radio. How did things go with Judge Morrow?"

"It was interesting and a lot has changed since Sunday. Where's the sheriff?"

"He went home to eat and, I guess, take a short nap. He ought to be in here in fifteen or twenty minutes."

"Good, because I need to tell you some things before he gets here. Oh yes, and Mary said to tell you hello."

"Hello, to Mary and what the hello is going on?"

Bill explained about their deputy, Ben, talking about their suicide that occurred at two-twenty on Wednesday. Diane wasn't aware of the significance of the time so Bill had to explain about the time and why Mary Greene DuBose said it meant Poole couldn't have killed Annie Mattox. He told how he asked Ben about the dead man and he showed him a picture and pulled out the hemmed pocket to Annie's dress they had found on the dead man's body.

"You are saying their suicide victim had the matching pocket to Annie's dress on him when he died."

"Yes."

"Shit," said Diane, in one concise syllable.

"But, that's not all." and he told her about the depot agent finding the satchel and bed roll and the draft registration card. And he told her about the knife, a dagger, with the mark from the shoes carved on the handle.

"Wait a damn minute, Bill Brown. You don't expect me to believe what we saw at the DuBose house drawn on Annie's shoe was carved on the handle of the knife Tommy Coles had in his pack?"

"Do you remember how the mark looked?"

"Hell, yes I do. I'll never forget it. I was scared so bad I wet my pants. I never have been so glad to get out of a place before in my life."

Bill took his drawing out of his wallet and gave it to Diane. "I said this was the Greek letter Pi, but it's not, it's Tommy Coles initials, a "T" and a "C" put close together and the "T" has a little front tail."

"Okay, I see."

He handed her the rubbing the judge had made. "This is what the judge got from the handle of the dagger. See, they are the same."

"They are the same! I guess it proves Coles is the murderer."

"Maybe to you and me, but nothing we saw at the session, or what Mary Greene DuBose told me about the murder's time of death would ever come into court. The knife, the cut in the pocket, and the cut in the dress all match up. With his initials carved on the knife, we know it was his. All those things together can only add up to Coles being the murderer. Here comes the Sheriff. We'll talk more later."

"We will, I still have something to tell you about Mary Greene."

Bill went over nearly everything with the sheriff. He skipped over his reaction to the time of Coles' death and tied connecting their suicide victim to Annie's murder by the pocket Deputy Lannigan produced.

Sheriff DeWitt agreed the pocket and the knife with Coles' initials worked for opportunity and means and without anything else to go on rape was a reasonable motive.

"Poole's hanging doesn't make sense, does it?" the sheriff asked to no one. "Bill, go out there and talk to Moses Jackson and his boy. Get them separated if you can. I've known Moses a long time. But, he – they always keep things to themselves."

Bill said, "When I saw Travis the first time, he said something about another man who came around to Annie's cabin. He said he didn't know his name, but he said his daddy did."

With a sigh the sheriff said, "You see there. Moses could have told us about the other man. It sure would help things if it was Tommy Coles. As far as you know, does Moses still have Poole's mule?"

"Yes, sir, as far as I know. I'll find out for sure when I go talk to them. But, I need to tell you something else. Something about Mrs. DuBose."

"Just Mrs. DuBose and nothing about her daughter?"

"Mostly, it's about Mrs. DuBose." And Bill told about the two-twenty spirit. He finished with, "I didn't think much about what she said until I found out Dr. Parker said Poole had to have died before noon. When I went back …"

Sheriff DeWitt interrupted, "Going back was only about the murder and didn't have anything to do with a daughter, right? What happened when you went back?"

Bill continued, "She said if Poole died before noon, he wasn't the one who killed Annie. And she asked if I wanted to ask Annie who killed her."

"That's when she invited you to a session?"

"Yes, sir."

"What did it cost you?"

"Two dollars."

With a laugh, the sheriff said, "Two dollars! Lordy, lord, I never heard of her doing a session for less than ten dollars. Hell boy, she must think you are going to be family."

Bill was realizing Judge Morrow was right, there wasn't much in Greene County Sheriff Ben DeWitt didn't know about. "Sheriff DeWitt, I've got to be honest, I'm pretty interested in her daughter, Elizabeth."

"I didn't think you'd buy new clothes for Momma. I'm glad you got the black coat with the silver buttons. Nice tie, too. But, I'm not interested in your love life. Tell me about the session. Diane, come over here. I want to hear what you've got to say about your visit with Mrs. DuBose."

Although she had been acting like she had been uninterested in Bill's and the sheriff's conversation, Diane knew that was over and rolled her chair over to the two of them. "Yes, sir." she said.

Bill quickly got to the chalk drawing on the shoe and showed the sheriff the drawing he made and the tracing Judge Morrow had made from Tommy Coles knife.

"Either one of you see her do anything when the candles went out? Did she let go of your hand Bill?"

Both answered, "No."

"Sheriff, I need to tell you about Connie and the shoes," Bill said.

"Connie? She's the younger daughter, right?"

"Yes, sir."

Bill told the Sheriff about Connie and his arm, about Connie holding the shoes and what she said about Annie being carried and being in a wagon.

Sheriff DeWitt looked at the two of them and said, "Well children, it is scary as hell, isn't it? Who else was there, the two of you is not enough for a session and she doesn't use her children?"

"Moses Jackson and his wife."

"That's what I heard. Did Moses recognize the mark?"

"He said he didn't. But I don't know if he can read."

"He can read. Moses has more than a little education. He served with the 369th in France in World War I. I think he came out as a sergeant. He learned to play his horn in the Army. Knowing for sure Moses was there makes things a little different." Partly thinking and partly speaking, the Sheriff continued, "He doesn't know anything about what happened this morning. We'll both go out there this afternoon. I'll talk to Moses, you talk to his boy. If there's anything in what the little girl said about Mattox being in a wagon, they are the only ones on the road with a wagon. Coles sure as hell didn't have one."

Looking at Diane, he asked, "Do you have anything to add?"

"Just this. When I saw Mrs. DuBose on Sunday, something caught with me and I remembered her from fourth grade. We lived in Madison and she came in the middle of the year because most of her family had died of the Spanish Flu. She and her mother lived with a lady. I don't remember her name. I think she was her aunt, probably her great aunt, and she was an old maid. They didn't stay long and moved back to Sparta, and we moved before the year was out. I doubt she had any memory of me. Bill told me she said she had been to her sister's when Annie was killed. I don't think she had a sister. I don't remember ever hearing about her husband having any kin around here either."

"Hmm, Diane, I don't remember any relatives for either of them. Bill, is that what she told you?"

"Yes, she said they had been to her sister's and didn't get home until Monday. She often talks about people being a brother or sister. Maybe that's what she meant."

"I wouldn't lean too hard on that, Bill. The DuBose family has its secrets, and if you are going to be involved, you best be careful. Now let's go see if we can find Moses and his boy."

"Travis. Travis is his son's name."

"I ought to be able to remember Travis. Let's go."

23

"Bill, ride with me. Put your stuff in the back."

As they pulled away from the office, Bill looked at Sheriff DeWitt and said, "Sheriff, I've been to college and I've been to war. I can fly a heavy bomber loaded with four tons of bombs through anti-aircraft flak at night and put it where my bombardier can drop them on a table top. I saw my pilot die in the seat beside me when one stray round from a Zero machine gun blew a hole in his chest the size of a half dollar and his life flowed out of him like piss out of a race horse. I couldn't even reach over to touch him and tell him I loved him because I was trying to keep our plane in the air, drop our bombs, and get the nine of us still alive on the ground. I flew the son of a bitch home on two engines with a hundred fifty flak and machine gun holes in it. Except for my pilot, we all walked away from our airplane."

Bill paused a moment and looked ahead, "I had my arm crushed when I had to crash land another plane in the jungle. My copilot had his gut pierced by a tree limb that came into the cockpit when we hit the ground. He died slow, and I couldn't move. My gunner got me out after half a day of hell and pain and heat. I had my ass dragged through the jungle for three days by him and two old native women. One of them drowned getting me across a river."

Bill closed his eyes as he continued, "I spent nearly a year in hospitals in places so hot it would make Greensboro in July feel like a mountain cabin. The first week I was aware enough to know what was going on, they came three times in the night and took away a dead soldier from the bed beside me."

He turned back to the sheriff, "I'm not afraid of some woman in the middle of Georgia who claims to be able to talk to dead people in the front room of a fancy house on a hill. Hell, I've talked to plenty of dead people where they died and while they were dying. But, right now her daughter is important to me. I don't know what will come of it, but I sure as hell want to find out. I think I can deal with what I know of her mother. But if there is something you think I should know, I sure would appreciate you telling me."

Sheriff DeWitt drove slowly to the side of the street and turned his car off. Looking straight at him, he said, "Bill, the problem is I don't know what the secret of Mary Greene DuBose is. I know there is one. I told you a little about Jeff the other day. He came to work here when I was the deputy. I was maybe eight years older, but we became pretty good friends, drinking, playing cards, hunting. A couple of times a year, we'd take the train to Atlanta or Augusta for a few days. We even went to Florida for a week once."

The sheriff turned to Bill, "After he met Mary and they married, our trips stopped. I married and we didn't spend much time together, but we were still friends. My house is one of those that came in a rail car. It's not as big and nice as his, but it is a lot nicer than a deputy sheriff in Greene County, Georgia could have had."

Now the sheriff looked away, "Mary was young when they married. and Betty May came quick, maybe too quick. But even then, Mary did things Jeff didn't understand and sometimes didn't know about. He never believed she was running around, but she would go away for several days. When she came back she never had anything to say about where she'd been or what she did."

Turning back to Bill, "Jeff would take them places on the train, New York, St. Louis, New Orleans, Memphis, lots of places. He'd tell me while they were there, Mary would disappear for a day or two and show up ready to go home. Later, he said she'd send him home and she'd come home in a couple of days."

A man walking toward them from down the block, waved and headed in the direction of the car. "Let's go," Ben said as he started the car and moved into the street. Ben waved as he drove away, "A couple of years ago, they had a birthday party for the young one."

"Connie."

"Yeah, Connie. I think she was six. Everybody was outside and me and Jeff went in to have a drink. He tells me Connie is different. She knows things her mother doesn't, can see and feel things her mother doesn't understand, and is going to change her mother."

The sheriff paused a moment, chuckled. "Jeff told me he changed brokers in New York one year because Connie, who was probably three, cried when she came into the guy's office. The next guy showed Jeff how the first one was taking a double commission on trades. The next year Connie wouldn't even go into the second broker's office, so Jeff changed again. The third guy found out how the second guy was cheating him, too. I think Jeff found a lawyer Connie liked and sued both the brokers and got well." Another little laugh, "Jeff had plans to teach her how to play poker."

"Sheriff, I will pay attention and be careful. I wasn't trying to keep anything from you about the Mattox murder. I didn't think anything from Mrs. DuBose mattered in court."

"You ran into a bunch of stuff last week for someone who's only been working at this for what? Eight months? And, you did pretty good, damn good. Just remember, this is my county and my job depends on me getting re-elected and me getting re-elected depends on what I know. Now let's see what we can find out from the Jacksons."

"Sheriff, there is Travis. He usually drives that little wagon with the single mule. Moses drives a team."

"Bill, I'll let you out to question him. See if he comes up with a name for the other man. Ask him about Poole watching Annie's cabin. Don't scare him, but push some. Like I told you, they always keep something back. I'm going to do the same with Moses."

The sheriff slowed his car and continued, "Travis ought to be a little scared, but Moses won't be. After we talk some, I'll tell him about Coles if he hasn't given me his name. But remember, there is reason to think somebody carried Annie out of here in a wagon, not because of what Connie DuBose said, but because it makes sense."

Travis had stopped his wagon as close to the side of the

path as he could get it, and Sheriff DeWitt eased around it and stopped. Bill got out and called, "Travis, good evening. I want to talk to you." As soon as Bill closed the door, the sheriff drove on toward Moses' cabin.

"Evening to you, Deputy Brown," Travis said, and started to get down from the wagon.

"Don't get down. I'll walk along. We can talk while you unhitch and take care of your mule."

"Yes, sir."

"Travis, your daddy told me sometimes Mack Poole would come to Annie's cabin and not go up to it. Do you know about that?"

"Oh, yes, sir. We knowed he go visit some, but there'd be other times we'd see signs of his wagon or his mule tied out by the road. From the tracks and all, you could tell it had been there a couple of hours. Sometimes at night we'd hear the mule snort or bray. I don't know how much he come 'cause you can't see up to the cabin, and he'd come some after dark."

"When was the last time you think he was here?"

From his reaction, Bill knew immediately he had asked a question which troubled Travis, and he took the opportunity to lead his mule to the shed and pull out some hay. When he came back, he said, "I think he was here Saturday, Saturday night."

"Go on, tell me."

Travis told Bill what he and Clara had seen as they came home.

"Are you sure it was Poole?"

"I'm sure it was his wagon because of the bad wheel, and the driver didn't have no hat on, and it were a real cool evening. You know Mr. Poole never did wear a hat."

"Did he see you?"

"I don't think so, sir. My lantern had gone out and I didn't try and light it again 'cause we were close to turning off the road. And, he was going fast. Not real fast, but as fast as his little mule could pull that raggedy wagon. No, sir, I don't think he even looked our way."

"Was he by himself?"

"Yes, sir. I mean there weren't nobody else sitting up in the wagon."

"When did you find out about Annie's murder?"

"When I got home Monday evening. My woman, Clara, told me, 'cept it weren't for sure it was Miss Annie."

"You told me about another man who came around Annie. Did you ever ask your daddy what his name was?"

"Yes sir. He said the man's name was Coles. Tommy, I think he said. Yes, sir, Tommy Coles."

Moses was walking toward the car as Sheriff DeWitt stopped. "Moses," he called out, "you still have Poole's mule here eating up all your hay?"

Moses' pace slowed, and he smiled at a question he had not expected and was pleased to get. "Yes, sir, he's still here, but he don't eat much, but he ain't earning his keep neither."

"We'll have to see about that. Are you interested in buying him?"

"No, sir, I don't need another mule to feed when I ain't have work for it."

"Travis told Bill you might know the name of another man who would come to see Annie Mattox. Who was he?"

"The only otherest one I'd ever see come around Miss Annie was that nature boy. You know, he'd stay in the woods all the time and didn't have no regular house. I think they called him Tommy Coles. He weren't much for being around regular folks, let alone us coloreds. But I ain't seen him around in three or four weeks. The way he come and go, you don't always see him."

"Annie, did she have other men who came to see her, regular like?"

With an edge in his voice, "Oh, no, sir; no, sir. She weren't like that. Miss Annie was poor and all, but she was a good girl and worked hard. We were glad she worked for Mr. Brunson 'cause it made her some cash money. No, sir, Annie weren't that kind of girl at all. She were a good Christian girl. She made Travis' baby her dedication gown, and she went to church with us when the baby was dedicated. No, Annie wouldn't do nothing like that."

Without a reaction to the tone of Moses' voice the sheriff asked, "Do you think Mack Poole killed her?"

"Yes, sir, I do. He were always around bothering her. And Saturday night my boy saw him driving his wagon out of our road toward town, and he was driving fast. I think he had Annie in the wagon with him."

"Moses, why didn't you tell me about this sooner?"

"Travis ain't tell me until Monday evening late when he first found out about Miss Annie. It weren't nothing unusual for us to see Mr. Poole on this road. I could've told Deputy Brown on Wednesday but I already said how Poole had tormented Miss Annie. Sheriff, we got to be careful about what we say about white folks. After we found him where he done hung himself, well it didn't much matter. If this had gone on, I swear Sheriff

DeWitt we'd told. Miss Annie was always nice, and she had a hard time, specially with her daddy. He weren't no easy man to be around. We hoped Annie would get to Athens like she wanted to."

"What do you know about Athens, Moses?"

"Since she'd been working for Mr. Brunson she'd been saving a little money. She wanted to get to Athens and get a sewing job. Travis' Clara and Annie talked some 'bout her going."

"I know you went to Mrs. DuBose on Sunday, you and your wife."

Moses dropped his head, "Yes, sir."

"Just so you know, Deputy Brown didn't tell me, and Mrs. Weston didn't tell me."

"Yes, sir. I guess Mrs. DuBose has her ways and you got yours."

"That would be a good thing to remember, Moses, a real good thing. But what did you think about what happened on Sunday?"

"Sheriff, I couldn't hardly tell nobody but you, I don't hold much with what Mrs. DuBose do. I been two times before, once with my cousin when his wife's momma passed, and when my Liza's daddy passed. Those times, Mrs. DuBose didn't say nothing that weren't so, but none of it were a real mystery."

Moses shifted his feet, "I reckon she made my cousin feel better, I know Liza got some peace. But, sheriff, Sunday was different. It felt different in her room. My skin moved, my head sweated, and I was dizzy. I would have run 'cept my I don't think my legs would let me. Then that thing fell down. We was all holding one another's hands, so I don't know how it fell. When we could see, there was powder on the table and on those shoes and a mark was on one of them."

"Do you know what the mark was? Did you ever see it before?"

"No, sir, I never seen it before. Deputy Brown said it was some kind of Greek mark, but I never seen anything like it."

"Do you remember it."

"Surely, I do. I don't think I will ever forget it."

"Draw it on the ground there for me."

"Sheriff DeWitt, please don't make me do that. It might be of the devil."

Ben DeWitt looked directly at Moses, "Don't you think me and you are past that kind of talk now. I know you are an educated man."

Moses raised his eyes and looked at Ben DeWitt, "Yes, sheriff, I suspect we are." Moses knelt and drew a vertical line and a line with a little curve across the top.

Before he could continue, Sheriff DeWitt asked, "What does what you've drawn look like?"

"I guess I'd say it was a T, but the mark had a little tail on the front like this." And Moses added the mark he described.

"Go on," said the Sheriff.

Moses drew a half circle that just touched the top of the T on the right.

"Look at what you just drew. What is it?"

"I'd say it was a C," replied Moses.

Moses looked at what he had drawn, turned and looked up. "That is the mark that was on the shoes."

"Moses, there is something more I need to tell you." And the sheriff turned so he and Moses were both facing toward God-frey's Store Road. He spoke calmly, "Today, Deputy Brown went to Crawfordville to see the judge there. While he was there he talked to one of the deputies who told him about a man who killed himself on Wednesday afternoon by laying his head on the track in front of the Atlanta train."

"Mercy," was all Moses said before the sheriff continued.

"The man's head and face were gone, but the deputy showed Deputy Brown a picture of his body. Deputy Brown recognized the man's clothes. They talked on some and it turned out the man had a piece of Annie's blue dress in his pocket and a knife that matched the cut on Annie."

Ben DeWitt paused and turned so his back was almost to Moses and continued, "Moses, he was the man who killed Annie Mattox." Sheriff DeWitt turned to face Moses and pointed to the ground where Moses had drawn the mark. "The handle of the knife in his satchel had that mark carved on it. Moses, Annie's killer was Tommy Coles."

Moses' shoulders slumped and his head dropped to his chest. He barely raised his eyes and weakly asked, "Coles? Coles? You say Tommy Coles killed Annie because the mark was on his knife?"

"No, Moses, the mark doesn't mean nothing to the law. It's because he had a piece of her dress and the knife that killed her. The piece of cloth was a pocket for the dress and the knife cut through it, the dress and into her heart. Yes, he is the murderer."

"I just knew it was Poole after Travis saw him coming out from here on Saturday night. It don't make sense. It don't make no sense at all. Why would anyone want to hurt Annie?"

"Coles might have been trying to have his way with her."

Moses moaned an agreement and added, "Maybe Poole was watching like he do and heard something and went to the cabin and Coles ran away, and he saw Annie hurt and tried to take her for help."

"That's possible," said the sheriff.

"And maybe Coles killed Poole because he seen him kill Annie."

"No, it doesn't work. Dr. Parker says Poole died Wednesday morning. We have witnesses who say Coles was in Crawfordville on last Wednesday morning. Either Poole killed himself, or somebody else hanged him."

"Sheriff, nobody comes down here except us.

"Moses, I'm going to have to tell the judge what I think happened to Poole on Wednesday. Since I can't figure who would have killed him, I am going to say he killed himself. But, I don't know why he did it. Do you think I'm right about Poole?"

A long pause, "Yes, sir, sheriff, I do."

"I do, too, Moses. You know how it is going to be. When we have somebody who has been killed, some are going to want the sheriff to find a murderer. Now, I think we have good enough proof on Coles to show he murdered Annie. When it comes to Poole, it ain't so clear he killed himself because we don't have a good reason why he would kill himself."

"Yes, sir, I understand. If Travis said he saw Mr. Poole coming out from down here on Saturday night, they might think Travis was trying to tell a lie on Mr. Poole. Sheriff, Travis wouldn't do that. He is a good boy, and honest."

"I know he is. And I'm not concerned about Travis. When did I tell you Poole died?"

"You said he died before noon."

"You know, Moses, you are the only one I know was down here last Wednesday morning before noon."

Moses Jackson understood what Sheriff DeWitt was saying to him. It was a full minute before he replied. "Yes, sir. I can see that. My Liza, Travis' Clara and baby were at Liza's sister's, and Travis was working at my sister's. I suspect you'd say Mr. Poole was here, too. Yes sir, I'd be the only one you and me know about who might have hurt Mr. Poole. Yes, sir, I can see that."

"I don't think you hurt Mr. Poole, and I don't want anybody else to think you did."

"Yes, sir, I don't want that neither. I always try to do what's right. That's the way I raised Travis, too. Mostly, I thought Mr. Poole killed Miss Annie, but it wasn't my place…and it…" Moses' voice trailed off.

"And what, Moses?"

"And if Mr. Poole saw Travis and Clara on Saturday night, he might try and hurt them."

"Moses, this is what I am going to do. I'm going to say I think Poole killed himself like we talked about when we found him. I'm not going to arrest you because I don't have any evidence you did anything. I'm going to tell how you and Travis helped us find Poole. Mack Poole didn't have any friends or relatives I know of, so I don't think there will be anyone calling for me to find a murderer. But you never know what might happen."

"Thank you, Sheriff DeWitt, thank you so much."

"Moses, there's something else to talk about. Something else I might need your help with."

"Yes, sir?"

"I know the colored doctor from down at Columbus has been around here talking about voting, and you have been with him."

"Yes, sir, Dr. Brewer has been here and I've taken him around to churches."

"I'm up to run for sheriff again next year and I hear there's going to be somebody to run against me. I know things are going to change, and some folks aren't going to like it. There's folks who might not understand things the way you and I do. Do you know what I mean?"

"Yes, sir, I do."

"I'm not as bad as some might think. I know what you did in France and it makes a difference to me and maybe some others. I know you don't want no trouble here for you and your family. I don't want trouble either. Moses, I'm going to need your help with some votes next year. Can I count on you and Travis to help me when it comes to voting?"

"Yes, sir, you can."

Bill and Travis had not talked nearly so long as the sheriff and Moses. Bill walked to the sheriff's car and sat inside. Travis worried with a loose board on the porch. The sheriff started walking toward the car. When Bill saw him coming, he got out. The sheriff called to Travis to join them. "When are either of you coming to town?" the sheriff asked.

"Clara's has me a little list of things to buy and I was going to go on Friday when my uncle pays me," said Travis.

Moses broke in, "Sheriff, if you need me, I can come any time."

"There is no rush, Moses. I want to get the mule off your hands and on the county payroll out at the camp. I figure we owe you six-bits for boarding. Does that sound okay?"

"Yes sir, six-bits would be a gracious plenty."

"I'll pay you if you take him to the camp, or I can get somebody from the camp to come down here and get him."

"Daddy, I have a little money and with what you get for feeding the mule, I can buy what Clara needs. I'll take the mule tomorrow and go on in to town. I can pay you at the end of the week. I weren't going to work tomorrow."

"You can pick up some things for me and I won't have to go on Friday," said Moses.

"Good. That will be one more thing off my plate. When you get to the office, Mrs. Weston will have your money. Come on, Bill, we need to get to the office." From the driver's seat, Sheriff DeWitt looked to Moses, "Good talk today, Moses. I'll let you know how it goes with the judge on Wednesday."

"Goodbye, sir," Moses said as the sheriff turned around and started up the road.

"Daddy, you don't look so good. What's the matter?"

"I'll be all right. I have a lot on my mind right now. Did the deputy tell you about Tommy Coles being the one who killed Annie?"

"Coles? No sir, he didn't tell me nothing about Coles!"

"Just give me a minute and I'll tell you what Sheriff DeWitt said about him."

Travis said, "Yes, sir" and started toward the barn. He came back in a few minutes. "Daddy, where's the old rope you keep in your wagon. I was going to use it to lead the mule to the camp."

Moses turned quickly to Travis and in a sharp tone said, "I ain't studying about no old rope. If you need rope there is a new one hanging in the shed."

"Yes, sir."

24

The sheriff didn't say anything until they turned onto Godfrey's Store Road, "What did you find out from Travis?"

Bill recounted his conversation with Travis and ended by saying when he found out Annie had been killed he knew Poole had done it, and he was scared Poole had seen him."

"Did he say why he didn't tell you about Poole when he saw you on Wednesday morning?"

"Yes, and I pushed a bit on him. He said his daddy told him to let us take care of it. He said he wanted to tell so Poole would get caught, but when it looked like we were going after him he didn't think telling would make any difference."

"His story pretty much matches with what Moses said. I don't think Moses would outright lie except maybe to save his own hide, or his son's, but not telling something? Yeah, he'd not tell. Likely, we all would. But it still comes down to him being the only one we know about who was down here Wednesday morning with Poole."

They rode until the car reached the paved road. "You've had a long day, Deputy Brown. And you might be looking for a longer night. I'll drop you at the office and you can head home or somewhere."

"Suits me," Bill replied. "I'm on my own for supper."

The moon was just rising as Bill drove to the DuBose house. He walked up the stairs and reached for the bell when Mrs. Du-Bose opened the door.

"Good evening," Bill said. "I've come to tell you about my meeting with Judge Morrow, and what I found out in Crawford-ville this morning. I think you will find it all very interesting."

Mrs. DuBose answered, "Please, go ahead."

Bill repeated her response in his head and said, "There is really quite a bit of information. May I come in?"

"I think not. We are busy preparing for our trip. Perhaps after we return, we can talk further. Good evening." Mrs. DuBose closed the door and disappeared into the dark hallway.

Bill stood for a moment and started to ring the bell, but decided to regroup. He turned and walked to his truck, and stood by the door several minutes before getting in. His late meal, the busy afternoon, and the disappointment of this encounter had resulted in a considerable buildup of digestive pressure. With no need to be concerned for decorum, he rolled up on his left cheek and released the pressure in a loud rip that stung. "That felt good. And, damn it, what the hell's going on with that woman?" he said as he waved the door two or three times to vacate the fumes. He slammed the door, started the truck and pushed the shift lever into reverse. As he pulled the shift lever down to first gear, he realized he was not alone in the truck. Elizabeth was crouched in the well of the passenger side with her dark jacket over her face.

Elizabeth looked up. "Go," she said with real urgency in her voice. "Hurry, and stop when you go around the turn at the tree."

Bill started fast and his tires threw up some dirt as he did. "What's going on?"

"Just hurry and turn off the lights when you stop. I've been hiding out here since you went to the door, and now I have to pee…real bad. Go!"

Bill slammed the truck into second and sped down the hundred yards to where the drive turned hard to the right behind the big oak tree. The pickup slid into the turn. Once around, he killed the lights and the truck bumped to a stop.

Elizabeth had the door open before the truck stopped moving and rolled out the door, grabbing paper napkins from Sunday's hamburger meal. She vanished into the darkness beside the big oak.

"Me, too," Bill called out. "I'm on the left." All Bill heard was water hitting the fallen oak leaves and his heart thumping in his chest.

In what seemed like five minutes he heard the door to the truck close. Back in his truck, he turned to Elizabeth. There was enough moon light to tell she was looking at him.

Elizabeth spoke first. In a measured voice, she said, "That was the loudest fart I ever heard. It must have hurt."

Bill stammered, "No. I uh, uh, pardon…"

Before he put together a complete thought, Elizabeth giggled and said, "Waving the door back and forth didn't help, especially where I was." Her giggles became a laugh.

"If I had known you were in here, I might have closed the door and put you in a Dutch oven," Bill said with a laugh.

Elizabeth laughed harder.

When Bill realized she understood, he got tickled and was caught up.

Elizabeth held her nose with her right hand and made the door closing moves with her left as she laughed.

Bill pounded on the steering wheel and the pickup rocked gently.

Elizabeth finally got out, "Bill, stop it. Stop laughing. You're making me have to go again. Please stop."

Bill forced himself to take a big breath, "You started it."

"I do. I do have to go again." Elizabeth opened the door and vanished in the darkness by the side of the truck. Getting in, she wiped her hands on the last of the Sunday's napkins and brushed off her shirt and straightened her hair with her hands. "This is so unlady-like," she said.

"Oh, no it's not, I've known for a long time ladies peed. I'm pretty sure my momma does."

"And men pass gas." After another pause, Elizabeth turned toward him and said, "Bill, please don't hate me."

"Hate you? Elizabeth May DuBose, I love you. Your mother broke my heart when she sent me away. I was afraid it was you."

"No, no, no, Bill, it wasn't me."

Bill took Elizabeth's face in his hands and kissed her. She wrapped her arms around his neck and held tightly. When their lips separated, Elizabeth said, "Take me home with you. Take me there, right now."

"Oh, I would love to. But I can't take you, and you can't go. We can't run away."

Elizabeth looked down and said, "I know, damn it."

"But, can you please tell me what happened since last night when your mother kissed me on the cheek and left me with you and Connie?"

"Connie told Momma she saw us doing things last night."

"You mean Connie came downstairs and spied on us?"

"No, she didn't come downstairs. You know how she is. She sees things in her mind or in dreams. Sometimes real things and sometimes things I don't even understand. She saw us in her mind. And thought we were...we did...You know?"

"And, that's what your mother thinks?"

"Yes, she always believes Connie."

"Did Connie tell you what she saw...in her mind?"

"No, she wouldn't talk to me about it, and mother didn't want to talk either. They wouldn't have believed anything I said."

"Does Connie even know about...what she thinks she saw?"

"Yes, a little. After all, we live on a farm. Daddy raised pigs, and he had a horse, a mare, that he bred twice. You don't need Connie's gift when a stallion and a mare get together. Daddy always answered questions directly. And Connie always had more questions than I did. She knows some things."

Elizabeth didn't speak for a long moment. Looking at Bill, she said, "Bill, take me to Momma and Connie."

There was enough light to easily follow the drive up to the house, and Bill did not turn on the truck lights. They saw light coming from the parlor window and no light upstairs or in the front hall. Bill asked, "I want to talk to Connie, too. Do you think she will be downstairs?"

"Yes, and damn it, I am sure she knows we are coming."

"Swearing and peeing in the woods. That's the way I like my ladies. Does Connie ever keep a secret?"

"No."

Elizabeth took Bill's hand and led him into the parlor and

they stood in front of Mrs. DuBose. Elizabeth released Bill's hand, and started to speak, "Momma..."

Interrupting, Mrs. DuBose said, "Deputy Brown, at least you had the good sense to bring her back."

Looking straight at her mother, Elizabeth said, "He didn't bring me back, Momma. We came back together." Turning to Connie and in the same tone, she said, "Connie, Bill and I need to talk to you, too."

Connie looked at her mother, as Elizabeth started speaking to her. "You remember last night when Momma said the blessing and she talked about what St. Paul said about love?" Connie nodded. "Momma's told us about love before, hasn't she?" Connie nodded again. "And, you heard Paul say when he was a child, he understood and spoke as a child. And you understood you might have thought like a child when you became angry at me for kissing Bill."

Another nod by Connie and Mrs. DuBose turned to her. Elizabeth continued, "Paul was talking about all kinds of love, but one kind of love, the kind Momma and Daddy had for each other, the kind of love Bill and I have for each other, and the kind you will have for someone one day is part of it. But the love between a man and woman is the hardest to understand. We show love by kissing and touching, sharing ourselves with each other. You remember how Daddy would hug and kiss Momma." At this Connie dropped her eyes from her sister and wiped a tear away. Mary Greene closed her eyes.

Elizabeth continued, "When men and women get married, they promise each other to share their love and bodies with each other. Other than loving the Lord, this is the most important promise we ever make."

Connie shifted on the ottoman, and Mary Greene put her hand on her younger daughter's shoulder.

Elizabeth said, "Connie, what makes this really hard is you don't always know who you are supposed to make that promise to." At this, Elizabeth turned her eyes to Bill. "It is all right for girls to have boyfriends and boys to have girlfriends to find out who is right. It is all right to kiss and hug and be close. But there is some sharing that should be left to marriage."

By now Elizabeth had turned to face Bill. "I've found the one I want to share my love, life, and body with." Bill took Elizabeth's hand again, "if Bill feels the same, when the time is right, we will get married and have a life together. But Momma, Connie, we understand we are not married now."

Turning to Mary Greene, Bill said, "In less than a week, I have become a part of you. Neither you nor I can change that. I love Elizabeth. I know five days is much too short a time to say it, but the truth is I loved her from the moment she opened the door last Wednesday. I would never do anything to hurt her or her family. If we marry, and I hope we do, I know I am marrying things I don't understand. I hope Elizabeth and I can continue to see each other with your blessings."

Mary Greene looked up to Bill and then to Elizabeth and asked, "Elizabeth?"

"Momma, I love you and Connie. I know I don't understand things the way you do or anywhere close to the way Connie does, but you are my family and I don't want to lose you. I do love Bill and I want to marry him, but I know it is not the time right now. I think I loved him from the time we sat down to dinner, but we don't really know one another and I want to learn more about him. Tonight, has been a part of our learning about one another."

Mary Greene looked at Bill and said, "Bill Brown, you have your gifts, too. We don't argue with a gift of the Spirit, no matter what it is. For now, you will be a part of us. Remember, with Connie, you may not have much privacy. That doesn't bother me so much, but you two will have to deal with it. Now, I would like some wine, and perhaps Connie will fix you another whiskey, then you can tell me about what happened in Crawfordville today."

With drinks in hand, Bill related the events of the morning with Judge Morrow. Neither Mary Greene nor Connie was surprised at the time Tommy Coles laid his head on the train track, or that his knife had a carving matching the symbol on Annie's shoes.

Connie said he pulled the pocket off the dress when he pulled the knife out. It was such a matter of fact statement the gruesomeness of it seemed to pass by.

Bill told them about Travis and Clara seeing Mack Poole coming out of their road in his wagon on Saturday night. Connie added she had known whoever had carried Annie in their arms and rode her in a wagon wasn't the one who killed her.

Bill explained what he was going to do in court on Wednesday, and most likely Tommy Coles would be found as Annie's murderer, and Mack Poole's death would be ruled a suicide.

Connie asked, "Can you get me the rope that was around Mr. Poole's neck. I think I might tell something from it."

"Cornelia, we are done with all of this after tonight. I don't want you to think any more about any of this. The spirits are calm, the souls are at peace and the good Lord will sort this all out on Judgment Day."

"But, I might ..."

"No more, Cornelia, or you will be upstairs."

"Yes, ma'am."

Mary Greene was pleased Judge Morrow had asked about them and she asked Bill to remember her to him on Wednesday and to ask about his wife. "It is nearly eight-thirty and we do have much to do tomorrow. Connie, come on with me and let's get ready for bed."

"I won't be long, Momma," Elizabeth said. "I know we have a lot to do."

Bill looked to Mary Greene and asked, "I wonder if I could take all of you for supper tomorrow evening. There is a restaurant out from Greene Pointe that is open for supper, and it would save you having to fix anything before you go. But we would have to take your car."

Connie jumped in with, "Hot dogs, do they have hot dogs? That's what I want and some French-fried potatoes."

"I think a restaurant meal would be nice, but we will need to go early," Mary Greene answered.

"I'll come as soon as I can get away from work. Maybe five-thirty?"

"Yes, five-thirty would be fine."

Bill looked to Connie, "Connie, they have hot dogs and French fries and a really good milk shakes, chocolate, strawberry, and vanilla. When you get upstairs think hard about which flavor you want."

Standing beside Bill, Elizabeth punched him in the side hard enough he caught his breath.

Connie said, "Oh, I don't need to think at all, I always get chocolate."

"Nice try, Deputy Brown," Elizabeth said.

Connie added, "I want my goodnight kiss."

Bill stepped over to Connie and picked her up and gave her a quick peck on the lips, still holding Connie he kissed Mary Greene on the cheek and added, "Good night," and let Connie slide through his arms to the floor.

Mary Greene and Connie went through the kitchen to the backstairs and up.

Bill picked up his glass. There was one sip left and he finished it, and sat the glass down and took Elizabeth's two hands in his, "This has been quite an evening."

"Yes, it has," Elizabeth replied. "Let's sit down on the couch."

"No, we can't or else I would not leave. And besides Connie knows she wants chocolate. Elizabeth, I meant everything I said tonight. I love you and I want to be with you forever. But in this short week there is something very important we haven't talked about."

"Bill, I'm not sure what you are saying."

"I'm talking about the rest of our lives. I am not going to be the Greene County deputy for the rest of my life. I think you would've figured that out pretty quick. I have an education. I can fly big airplanes and I like to. And, I am very good at it. I think passenger air travel is going to be a big thing in this country and in the world, and I might want to be a part of that."

Dropping her head and closing her eyes, Elizabeth said, "And you think a little girl from Greensboro, Georgia is not smart enough or good enough to be a part of your bigtime life."

"No, a hundred times no, a thousand times no. What I am saying is I want you to be a part of a life with me. I want us, you and me, to be in this new world.

Lifting her chin, Bill said, "Elizabeth, there was no reason for me to ever come back to Greensboro and take a job as a deputy sheriff if it wasn't for me to find you and you to find me. The Army and my dad dying made me understand the rest of my life is in my hands. Now, in our hands. In this short time, we have had together there was no reason for you to think about these things. But here they are. They are a part of us now."

"Before Daddy died, I dreamed about some of the things you are talking about. Going to college, do you know I went to GSCW for two years? Daddy took me to visit Georgia last winter, and I spent the night in the dormitory and went to a social. I was accepted at Georgia, and I should have started in September."

Looking away from Bill, Elizabeth continued, "But after he died I couldn't leave Momma and Connie. With all their gifts, they can't do much when it comes to running a home, a little farm, and a conjure woman business. Connie is smart, smart enough to figure out the real world, but she is only ten years old. And Momma, despite all she can do, when it comes to money, she doesn't know baby shit from apple butter."

As Elizabeth paused, Bill said, "You have taken on a lot of responsibility since your daddy died. Your mother really does depend on you, doesn't she?"

"Yes," and Elizabeth paused. "Well, I'll be damned! I'll be goddamned. Momma finally figured it out. She wasn't mad about what Connie visioned. Hell, Momma would have been happy about anything we did on the sofa if it meant you and I would get married and stay here."

"I'm not sure what you're talking about," Bill replied.

"Momma figured out if we were married, you would take me away from her. That's why she was mad. My virtue doesn't mean anything to her. She doesn't mind running you off if it means keeping me here to take care of her."

"You mean she would split us up just so you'd stay here?"

"Hell, yes. You and anyone else that would change her world," Elizabeth said. "Daddy dying was more change than she ever considered. And, Momma doesn't like change."

"Does she, all of you, have enough money to live on?" Bill asked.

"She has enough, if she knew how to mind it. Daddy was smart and he showed me about what he did. He taught me a lot. The money is in banks and investments and, despite the talk about it, there is no rail car load of cash hidden away. If it were left to Momma, she would give it all away or forget where she put it. But I will tell you this, I think Momma still knows something I don't know. Most of the people in town think Momma is wise, and we are rich and powerful and live a high life, but the truth is we're pretty fucked up."

"I take it your daddy was profane at times, or did you learn to cuss at GSCW?"

"I'm sorry, Bill, I don't mean to talk like this. Yes, Daddy could swear with the best of them. I guess it was working with the train crews. It's just...just. I get mad sometimes."

"Mad because of your Momma and Connie? And you think you might not be able to do the things you dreamed about, the things you and your daddy talked about for you?"

With tears on her cheeks. Elizabeth gripped Bill's hands hard, "Yes, goddamn it. And now, now it is you."

"Didn't we, me and your mother, get past that tonight. Isn't everything okay with her?"

"No, Bill. It is not. Her blessing is only a truce until she decides what to do next. Remember, she knows you will take me away from her. I will have to be careful in New York. You, too. I don't know what she could do to you, but she might try something. I don't have any idea what Connie will tell her. For that matter, Connie is probably visioning this right now like it was an episode of *The Guiding Light*. And now we pause for a word from our sponsor, Lux, fucking soap. I wish I had peed in the woods, and we drove off and kept going."

"Right now, I do, too, but we both know it wouldn't have worked very long."

"I know. But I feel trapped, more trapped than ever. Bill, it is not only you. I've had some of these feelings ever since Daddy died, and it looked like my dreams died with him. I have a lot to decide. Everything was not right between me and Momma before. Now, it is really bad.

"Remember what I told you the other night. Don't try and make this only you. I am part of your life now, and I want my say in everything that happens. Do you understand? And Elizabeth, you get your say in everything that happens in my life. As much as I am going to miss you, I think the next couple of weeks will give us both time to think through some things for ourselves."

He wrapped his arms around her and pulled her close to him. "God, I'm going to miss you. No matter what you think, never consider we will not be together. Never."

Standing together in the parlor, they kissed. Finally, Bill pulled away, grabbed his jacket and let himself out the front door. Elizabeth turned off the light in the parlor and kitchen and walked slowly up the backstairs to her room.

25

So, Elizabeth had gone to college for two years. College explains a lot about her, but why hadn't I figured some of her out? High school girls from Greensboro don't kiss like she does. And Sunday night on the couch she wanted to be more than comfortable. What would Mary Greene do to split us up? What could she do? Did Connie have another vision last night? What sort of range does she have for getting visions? This vision thing could be damned inconvenient. What the hell kind of secret does Mary Greene have that Elizabeth doesn't know about? If she has a secret, does Connie know what it is, will she tell? What will Mary Greene wear to supper tonight? Will I get to drive the Packard? Will Elizabeth wear the plaid shirt and jeans?

He knew the shirt was a hope, more than a possibility. But still.

Why do I remember the girls in my life by the clothes that came open? And, why does only Elizabeth matter now?

He knew the answer.

Tuesday, Elizabeth worked hard like she had nearly every day for the past week getting everyone ready for their trip to New York.

The last two years she had come home from Milledgeville every weekend from the first of October to the week before Thanksgiving to help them pack. Her mother, father, and Connie went up a week earlier, but she didn't go until the Sunday before Thanksgiving and started back the Saturday after. Daddy stayed a week longer and Momma and Connie a week more.

The weeks before and after Thanksgiving when everyone else was in New York, and she was at school were some of the best times she remembered. She didn't do anything different those weeks. But, she felt different, free and herself. When her daddy died, she was angry. She was angry at him for dying and changing all the plans they had for her. She was angry she didn't go to Georgia, but the anger eased when she realized had she been in Athens she might never have met Bill. She was angry at her mother because of the things she couldn't or wouldn't do, and that she might try and keep her and Bill apart. She was angry at Connie, because none of this seemed to make a difference to her.

Elizabeth knew Connie and her daddy had a different relationship. It seemed he had no understanding of what she was about, but he fully accepted her. Connie pretty well considered him as one of the ungifted, but a really nice man who did nice things for her. When he died, Connie hardly shed a tear and when she did, it was only because she thought she was supposed to. Even so, Elizabeth knew Connie truly loved her father.

Bill, God, being with Bill made her feel like the week after Thanksgiving. He didn't take from her like her mother and Connie and even her father did. Bill's words, "You get a say in what happens in my life and I get a say in what happens in yours" kept coming back to her.

What about when it's like Daddy dying and it's nobody's fault? Who gets a say then? We can marry and live in Atlanta. There must be engineering jobs there, or he can be a pilot for Delta or Eastern. I'd be close enough to Momma and Connie. And I could go to school, maybe Agnes Scott. If I was accepted into Georgia, they would take me at Agnes Scott.

Elizabeth was standing in the front hall as she realized what she was thinking were her thoughts alone, and not theirs. She walked to the pocket doors and opened them and pushed open the black drapes. The picture of Jesus glowed in front of her and she stepped into the room and bowed her head.

"Momma always taught us Your will in our lives is all that is important," she said as she bowed her head. "I pray Your will is for me and Bill to have a life together. Amen." She turned to the picture of Saint Paul. "I don't think I am supposed to pray to a Saint, but before he died, Uncle Bob said the Romans did. Saint Paul when it comes to gifts of the Spirit, I didn't do so well. And I'm not complaining. If you can, help me with a gift of Bill I would appreciate it. Amen." She walked into the hall closing drapes and doors behind her. If Jesus and Paul don't work this out, I will.

Upstairs, there were four big suit cases lined up in the hall. She had hefted each of them to their place. There was one for each of them and one more for all of Momma's session material. Will Shivers, the new depot agent would send Bruce out in the station wagon at four o'clock this afternoon to pick them up. They wouldn't see them again until they were in their rooms in New York. In the morning, Bruce would come for them and their overnight bags.

The train trip took a day and a half and they would spend a night in their compartment. The train from Greensboro to Atlanta was a local which left at eight-thirty in the morning. In New York, the big suit cases would be taken by truck directly to their rooms at the Drake. The Drake's car would pick them up and deliver them to the dining room for afternoon tea while their cases were unpacked.

Their overnight bags were lying open on the bed in the front bedroom. Elizabeth checked them again and went downstairs to the parlor where her mother and Connie were listening to *Big Sister* on the radio. Under her breath, she said, "How appropriate."

Mary Greene looked up as Elizabeth came into the room, paused until the program went to an advertisement and said, "Betty May, fix us something to eat, I'm hungry. Do we have anything left over from last night?"

"I've been trying to use up everything before we go, Momma. I think there are some butter beans and one pork chop. Will that be enough? You know you can have a big supper tonight."

"I guess. Do we have any potatoes?"

"No, Momma. And, there is no time to fix potatoes."

"Make some biscuits."

"We don't have time for them either and besides there is no milk. We have some biscuits left from last night. I will split them and toast them. They will be good."

"No milk?" Connie whined. "I wanted some more corn flakes. But I was really going to save up for supper and my hot dog."

"Connie, a toasted biscuit with butter and jelly will be good. It will last until supper time. Besides, Bill is coming early."

"Hurry up, Betty May. I'm hungry," said her mother.

"Yes, Momma." Elizabeth said as she walked into the kitchen muttering, "*Big Sister,* Ruth Evans searches Glen Falls for food for her starving family." Elizabeth never sat down while her mother and Connie ate. When Connie finished her biscuit, she disappeared up the stairs to the bathroom. Her mother said she was going to take a nap because she was still a little hungry. And, she went up.

Elizabeth looked at her mother's plate. You couldn't be too hungry, you left half a pork chop and a biscuit. It's a good thing, too, because what's left is my dinner. I hadn't planned to save up.

She picked up the pork chop and gnawed the meat off the bone like her daddy. The toasted biscuit was cold now, but it and the fresh butter felt good in her mouth. There was nothing to scrape from the dishes so she stacked them at the sink. Connie will get a chance to earn her supper when she washes these. After wiping up, Elizabeth went into the parlor and turned the radio off and sat down on the sofa where she and Bill were on Sunday night. She enjoyed the silence and her memories of the two of them on the little sofa.

"Betty May…Betty May, wake up. It is three o'clock and the truck from the depot could be here anytime. Are you going to sleep the day away?"

Elizabeth opened her eyes in a start at the sound of her name. From the sofa, she saw her mother in a robe standing at the kitchen door. Connie was behind her looking around her into the parlor.

"Did you hear me? It is three o'clock."

"Yes, Momma, I heard. I guess I nodded off."

"Yes, for two hours."

Elizabeth knew there was no use in pointing out they, too, had had two-hour naps. As she stood she said, "I'll go up and check on the cases. They should be ready unless there is something else to go in them. Connie, I left the dinner dishes by the sink for you to wash and put up. Go ahead and get started on them, please."

Her mother said, "Oh, Connie will break something. There's not many, you can do them when you get done upstairs. And there are a few more things on my bed to go into the sessions case."

"Betty May, did you pack my blue jumper in the big suitcase? I want to wear it tonight."

Looking at Connie, Elizabeth said, "Yes, it is packed. You will have to wear something else."

"I want to wear my jumper," Connie whined. "You can get it out. Please."

"Connie, if I take it out, you won't be able to take it to New York. Besides, everything is all folded and arranged in the big suit cases. It will be too much trouble. Remember this is not a fancy place we are going to eat. What if you spilled mustard on it."

"Elizabeth, go on and get Connie's jumper out. You can pack it in the overnight case. You'll be careful tonight at supper won't you, Connie?"

"Yes'm," Connie answered.

"No, Momma. I am not going to unpack Connie's suitcase. I don't have time, especially if I have to pack some more things for you. Connie, I will help you find something for tonight.

Momma, you need to think about getting dressed, too. Bill may be here as early five-fifteen." Before either answered, Elizabeth went into the hall and up the front stairs with her fists clinched tightly and anger caught in her throat. *Those damn dishes will wait until I'm good and ready to do something with them.*

Fortunately, what Momma had to add to the sessions case didn't take much work to get in. After she closed the case, Elizabeth decided she would stay upstairs as long as Connie and Momma were down, or at least until the truck came. She heard Connie start up the back stairs, and the anger came back. *Vision this, Connie.* And for some reason, Connie stopped and went down. She said out loud, "I'm a big sister, but I'm not Ruth Evans and Greensboro is not Glen Falls, by God."

Elizabeth didn't know if she were in a standoff, or if everyone was happy where they were, but no one left their respective positions until the truck from the depot came right on time at four o'clock. Bruce brought another with him and they loaded the big cases quickly and returned.

Elizabeth came down the back stairs through the kitchen and noticed the dinner dishes had been done and put up. In the parlor, she looked at Connie and said, "Come on, let's go upstairs and decide what we are going to wear tonight. Momma you need to go ahead and get dressed, too."

Connie jumped up from her usual place on the ottoman and started for the kitchen. Mary Greene said, "I'm still tired, I don't think I'll go this evening. Connie, do you want to stay home with me?"

"No, no!" Connie said without thinking about her manners. "No, ma'am, I would like to go to the restaurant with Elizabeth and Bill. Please!"

"Momma, you were so hungry at dinner time and there is nothing here to eat. Get dressed. We will go early and be back early."

In a distant and weak voice, their mother said, "I don't think so. Connie and I will stay here."

In no mood to argue and frankly satisfied with her mother's decision, Elizabeth simply said, "No. There is nothing here for Connie's supper. She will go with us. I will bring you something back. Think about what you want. Come on, Connie."

Connie raced up the stairs ahead of Elizabeth and went into her room. When Elizabeth came in, Connie asked, "Do you hate me, Betty May?"

"Connie, I love you. You are my sister."

"I know," said Connie, "but a little while ago I felt, I don't know exactly, you didn't love me."

"Connie, I got mad, not at you, not at Momma, but mad because of the way things were happening. Sometimes, we get angry. Didn't you get a little mad because you thought Momma was going to make you stay home tonight."

"I did. I was scared she wouldn't let me go with you and Bill. I washed the dishes, put them all up and didn't break anything, and Momma didn't tell me to."

"I know you did and thank you. Did Momma say anything to you when you washed them?"

"No, she looked at me funny when I went into the kitchen."

Holding it up, Elizabeth said, "You can wear this green skirt and a white long sleeve shirt. I have a leather vest. It will look good with them. The vest will be a good accessory, and put your cross and gold chain on, too."

"Thank you, Betty May, I like the vest."

"Now, I have to look and see what I have to wear. Take a quick bath and don't get your hair wet. And dry off good. When you get dressed come to my room, and we will find the vest."

Elizabeth found a skirt and sweater among her school clothes from last year that would work for Edna's. Connie dressed and Elizabeth brushed her hair and put a touch of rouge on her cheeks. Connie went downstairs and sat in the parlor with her mother while Elizabeth went to the front bedroom to watch for Bill. She wanted to meet him on the porch to tell him her mother wasn't going with them. She would tell him, too, Momma was in a mood. It wouldn't be long before she told Bill these moods happened with some regularity.

Elizabeth saw Bill's pickup on the road before it reached the turn for the drive up to the house. She went down the front stairs and stood in the entry until the truck rounded the turn at the oak tree. Now, out on the porch, she waved to Bill and walked toward his truck as it stopped. She had never considered they wouldn't kiss hello, but when he stepped out of the truck everything from the day welled up in her. She ran the last few steps and wrapped her arms around him sobbing. Bill hugged back, he realized she was crying.

"Elizabeth, what's the matter? Why are you crying?"

"Just hold me. Everything is okay now you're here. I don't ever want to be away from you again."

"Something must be wrong. What is it? Has Connie had another vision? I've been real careful about what I thought today. Your plaid shirt came up once, but it wasn't my fault."

Elizabeth pushed away, turned her face up to his and smiled.

"I needed to hear that," she said and kissed him, not with passion, but with a promise. "We can talk after supper. We'll have plenty of time."

"But your mother will want you to get to bed early," Bill said.

"Don't worry about Momma. She's out of this now. She is not going to eat with us. I might bring her something. Let's go, I need to be away from here."

"Sure, if it's us and Connie, we can go in my truck."

"I will get Connie."

Connie was as ready to go as Elizabeth, and she was excited to ride in the pickup truck. Another trip in the big and soft leather back seat of the Packard held little attraction for her. As they started down the drive, Bill said, "I kind of wanted to drive the Packard."

Looking at Connie, Bill said, "I like the leather vest you have on. It makes you look grown up. Do you still want a hot dog and French fries?"

"Yes. I didn't eat much dinner today. Betty May says we saved up, but we really didn't have much food."

"We had plenty of food. I didn't want to cook and have to throw away leftovers."

Connie asked, "Bill, what are you going to have?"

"Well, I had a hamburger on Sunday, but the sign said they had full meals inside where we are going to eat. I want to see what else they have."

"Me, too," said Elizabeth.

Bill didn't speak as they drove out Godfrey's Store Road and he passed the landmarks of the events of the last week, places he would remember for the rest of his life. In a few minutes, they passed the now dark Brunson farm and Bill sighed and sped up. The little truck seemed to ride better with three, especially if one was Elizabeth.

They reached Edna's a little before six and Elizabeth seemed to have put the day behind her. They were excited to eat in a restaurant, even though Edna's was nothing like some of the places Elizabeth, Connie, and even Bill had eaten in during their travels.

There were booths around the walls and tables in the middle. A few of both were occupied by families and some older couples. A woman's voice called out, "Sit anywhere, I'll be with you in a minute." They headed for a booth across from the door. Connie jumped in and moved to the wall.

Bill looked at the empty seat beside Connie. "Sit with Connie. I think we'll have more room. Besides, I want to look at you."

Two menus were wedged behind the sugar jar and wall at the end of the booth. Bill took them and handed one to Connie and the other to Elizabeth.

Connie said, "I don't need this. I want a hot dog and French fries."

"Hello, love," Bill looked up to see the woman in the window from Sunday standing at the end of the table with a pad in her hand. "Glad you came back. What can I get y'all to drink?"

Bill looked at Elizabeth, who said, "I'll have tea."

"Me, too," said Connie, "No, I want a Coca-Cola."

"Sweetie, do you want in a glass with ice or a cold bottle?"

Connie answered, "Just a bottle, please."

"You, honey?"

"I'll have tea."

"Two teas and a Coca-Cola in a bottle. Be right back with those. The special tonight is the meatloaf, and the greens are good. We have fried green tomatoes tonight."

"Those sound good," said Elizabeth.

Bill agreed, "I like fried green tomatoes. I think I'll get those."

"Bill," Connie asked as the waitress walked away, "Do you know the lady?"

"No."

"Well, why does she keep calling you 'love' and 'honey' like you were her boyfriend, and why did she call me 'sweetie'?"

Elizabeth answered, "She is being friendly and wants us to like her and her restaurant."

The waitress returned with their drinks and looked at Connie. "I'll start with you. Dear, what will you have?"

"I want a hot dog and French fries."

"Onions or chili on your hot dog, hon?"

"No thanks, darling, mustard and ketchup," answered Connie.

"Okay, a hot dog, plain, and fries. There's your mustard and ketchup." The waitress pointed to the end of the table where there was a bottle of ketchup and a jar of yellow mustard.

"You, ma'am?"

Both Bill and Elizabeth decided on the meatloaf special with mashed potatoes and fried green tomatoes. Elizabeth choose the collards, but Bill chose butter beans.

The waitress returned with a big tray holding their plates. The food was hot and the plates were piled high. Connie's fries must have been made from two big potatoes and they were steaming. She added a basket with biscuits and corn bread and a little plate of butter. Bill picked up his fork when he looked across and saw Connie's hand and Elizabeth's hand extended to him. He took both and said a short blessing.

The food was good and they ate without talking for a time. The waitress stopped by with more tea and Elizabeth asked her to add a chicken salad sandwich and potato salad for them to take with them.

When the plates were being cleared, Connie decided on a piece of chocolate pie for desert. Bill and Elizabeth had a cup of coffee. The waitress brought the bill and laid it on the table. "They have your sandwich and potato salad at the register. Thanks for coming in, and come to see us again."

As Connie followed Elizabeth from the booth, she waved to the waitress and called out, "Bye, honey." Bill increased his tip from forty cents to two quarters and headed for the register.

Elizabeth and Connie stood beside him while he paid. They looked at the cake and doughnuts in the glass case by the register.

"I'm going to get some donuts for our breakfast tomorrow and to take with us." Elizabeth opened her purse and said, "A dozen, please."

The ride back was almost silent. Connie was full. Bill and Elizabeth unhappily anticipated their being apart. When they stopped in the front, Connie jumped out and ran into the house.

"Should I come in?" Bill asked.

"Certainly, and plan to stay a while," Elizabeth answered.

"Good, otherwise I was going to need to stop at the oak tree." They both laughed.

Inside, Elizabeth saw her mother was not in the parlor.

She said to Bill, "I'll be a few minutes. I'm going to take this to Momma. Don't worry, I won't be too long."

Bill turned to the bathroom under the stairs and Elizabeth headed through the parlor to the kitchen. The kitchen was a mess. It looked like her mother had tried to cook everything in the pantry and refrigerator, and put nothing up and washed nothing.

Elizabeth understood and went up the back stairs with the afternoon's same tight feeling in her throat. There was a light showing under her mother's closed door, she knocked. "Momma, I brought you a chicken salad sandwich and some potato salad. Would you like it?" No sound came from the room. "Momma?"

A weary, "Yes, Elizabeth, bring them in and go get me some tea."

Elizabeth entered and placed the sandwich and salad on her bedside table and added a doughnut from the bag. "I'll bring with some tea."

She went down the front stairs and told Bill to sit and have a drink if he wanted. She said she would be a few more minutes.

Connie was in her mother's room telling her all about the restaurant, what they ate, and how much fun she had. Elizabeth gave her mother the tea and asked if there was anything else she needed. Her mother, surprisingly, said no and she was going to bed and they should, too.

"Momma, it will be a while before I come up to bed. I have work to do downstairs, and I need to talk to Bill. Connie, go get ready for bed and I will tuck you in. We have a big day tomorrow."

"Can I say goodnight to Bill?"

"Yes. Thank him for your supper and come right up." Connie ran down the back stairs to the parlor.

"Good night, Momma. I will get you up at six tomorrow."

Mary Greene took a sip of tea and covered up. "Turn out the light as you go," she said.

When Elizabeth stepped into the hall, she met Connie. They went into Connie's room where Connie undressed, put on her pajamas and crawled into bed. Elizabeth kissed her and turned out her light. "Sleep tight and don't dream," she instructed.

"Huh?"

"Never mind, go to sleep."

Elizabeth went to the bathroom and to her room. She came down the front stairs. In the hall she called, "Bill, come out here."

"Elizabeth? Where?"

"In the hall."

When he entered the hall from the parlor, Bill saw Elizabeth standing by the front door in her plaid shirt and jeans with her hand on the door knob.

"You are not sending me home now?" he asked.

"No," she said as she opened the door and walked out. "You said you wanted to see the Packard, and I want to show it to you. Come on, it is in the car shed."

She walked down the stairs and around the house to the back, staying a few steps ahead of Bill. Both had to watch their footing in the dark. He caught up to her when they reached the car.

Elizabeth opened the driver's door and a yellow glow came from lights on the dash and overhead. "It has a clutch, but you only have to use it to start. After starting you can shift without it. It is nice to drive." She closed the driver's door and moved her hand the few inches to the handle for the back door and opened it.

"This car has a lot of room. Get in and see," she said. Bill climbed in and stretched his legs out. "Move over so I can get in. You can't tell how much room there is if there is only one person in the back seat." Bill slid over and Elizabeth got in, holding the door open so the dome light still glowed.

"Bill, I do want to talk to you. I have some important things to tell you, but they can wait until later. Right now," Elizabeth pulled the door closed and the dome light went dark. "right now," her hands found his face and she pulled him to her.

26

It was after two when Bill started home. They were in the back seat of the Packard for nearly four hours and would have stayed longer if the oak tree had been closer than the house. Most of the time they talked, they laughed some, and Elizabeth cried twice. When they didn't talk, they kissed and touched. Neither held back, but neither pushed. Sometimes they laughed at what they were doing. Neither was an experienced lover, and both knew it. They were having fun and knew this wasn't the time. Even so, Elizabeth fulfilled the promise of her kiss, and her plaid flannel shirt on the floor board of the Packard was proof.

In the kitchen, Elizabeth looked around. She said to Bill, "All Momma did was make a mess, and that is all she wanted to do. There was nothing to cook. The closest thing she had to cook was some bacon. I guess that's why the frying pan is out, but you don't need to put grease in the frying pan to cook bacon. You put grease in a frying pan so you can have a greasy frying pan."

Bill said, "Elizabeth sit down, or better yet, go to the parlor and pour yourself a little whiskey, *The Glenfidditch*, about this much in a short glass," and he held out one finger. "Add a few drops of water and take one sip and let it sit in your mouth. Meanwhile I'm going to show you something I should not."

"Bill, I've never tried whiskey."

"This may be the night for new things. Have you ever seen me clean up my girlfriend's kitchen?" Bill started water running in the sink.

"Girlfriend's kitchen?"

"No, that's not right. It is not your kitchen and you are much more than my girlfriend."

Elizabeth went into the parlor and opened the bar. She called, "Should I fix you one?"

"Yes," Bill replied, "but make mine two fingers, no three. Your fingers are little."

In a minute, Elizabeth came into the kitchen with two glasses. She held out one to Bill who wiped his hand on the dish towel he had stuffed into his belt and took the drink. He touched his glass to hers and said, "To us."

Elizabeth added, "To us," as she touched Bill's glass with hers, took a big sip and made a face. "It's …it's …it's nasty."

"Just hold a little in your mouth and breath in. You'll smell smoke and cool and taste sweetness. But don't worry. I didn't like it the first time either." Bill took a big sip, breathed in, closed his eyes and let the whiskey ease down his throat. "Sit down, Elizabeth, and let me finish."

"You don't know where things go," she replied and stood beside him at the sink drying and putting things up.

Bill looked at Elizabeth standing in the kitchen with her drink in one hand and a dish towel in the other. "Elizabeth, this is what I would like for us one day. A home where we do things together."

"We can have those things, Bill," and Elizabeth drained the

last part of her drink, made a face, and banged the glass on the table.

"We can," Bill answered and finished his drink and banged the glass down beside hers. "I hope we didn't wake anyone."

"Bill, my love, it doesn't matter anymore. Kiss me good night and goodbye. Don't come to the depot in the morning. I don't think I could take seeing you tomorrow."

They kissed and Bill walked out the front door, and headed for home. Godfrey's Store Road was dark, and the lights from his truck only penetrated the edge of the black. Before he reached the pavement, those lights found two rabbits and a skunk running into the safety of the darkness. In Greensboro, nothing moved at two-thirty in the morning. The few street lights pointed out corners with circles of white. The pale-yellow light from his truck connected them as he worked his way to his apartment.

The McLean's had gone to Tybee Island with the Robertson's. He was glad they were gone. He wouldn't bother them when he came in, and he was glad he wouldn't have to explain his late return to Mrs. McLean.

In his room, he made sure the alarm was set for six and the time on the clock was right, two-forty a.m. As he crawled into bed, he had a lot to think about. But the only thing on his mind was holding Elizabeth.

In her room, Elizabeth undressed and put on an old cotton gown. She set her alarm for five. Standing at the sink brushing her teeth she looked in the mirror and said, "Betty May … Elizabeth May, or perhaps just Mae, with an "e," you are not the same person who brushed her teeth here this morning. Mary Greene DuBose, I've changed your life forever this week." When she lay down and closed her eyes, she was asleep; an instant later her alarm sounded.

By five-thirty, Elizabeth had bathed, dressed and closed her overnight bag. She was ready. She woke Connie who stumbled into the bathroom rubbing her eyes and complaining.

Elizabeth had Connie's travel outfit laid out on her bed, but when Connie came into her room she decided she wanted to wear what she had on at supper. She really liked the vest. It wasn't a battle Elizabeth wanted or even cared about. The skirt and shirt were clean and comfortable. The first travel outfit was packed, and Elizabeth went to wake her mother.

It was nearly six. Elizabeth knocked at the door, "Momma, it is time to get up and get dressed." No sound came from the room. Elizabeth knocked harder, and Connie came from her room. "Momma, Momma!" Elizabeth added a sharper rap on the door. "Momma! Get up. It is time to get ready."

This time there were sounds from the room. A weak, "I'm awake," came from within.

"Momma, you have a lot to do to get ready and it is already six o'clock," called Elizabeth through the door.

"Elizabeth, maybe we won't go this year. I'm really tired."

Connie looked up at Elizabeth and shook her head. "Don't worry, Betty May," she said. "Momma's going."

Elizabeth mouthed, "I know" to Connie and said out loud, "Okay with me. I'll call the depot at seven and cancel our ride and get them to send our suitcases."

Connie started to say something, then she realized what her

big sister had done. She smiled at the trick, but decided she had to think about Betty May tricking her mother. It was different.

Hans de Graffinreed rose at six. The local to Atlanta didn't get into to the Crawfordville depot until 7:50. He would be traveling with only one small bag and would ride in the caboose. After the train left Greensboro, he would go to the baggage car and find their suitcases so he would know for sure what they looked like. He knew they had been picked up yesterday. He would have to be first off in New York to get to the three baggage cars in time to see them off-loaded and follow them to the hotel's truck. He expected it would still be the Drake. Jeff always stayed there, but Mary Greene does some strange things sometimes. Following the bags would let him make sure.

Bill woke with a start at the first sound of the alarm. He punched it off and lay back, letting his mind fill with the memories of the last night. Most mornings the whistle of the mail train coming through at 6:05 never registered, but this morning it brought him back from his memories. He reluctantly put both feet on the floor. Court today. Some things will be decided so I need to be sharp.

He headed for the shower. At Geer's, no one was much interested in the day's court proceedings. Why Georgia always had to play Auburn in Columbus in a stadium half the size of Sanford seemed much more important. Tomorrow, after they found out about Tommy Coles, things might be different. For today, the football conversation suited him. Even taking his time, he was at the office at quarter to eight. The station wagon should be on its way to Elizabeth's by now.

Sheriff DeWitt came in at quarter after eight, early for him. He and Bill went over all four cases. They asked each other questions they thought might come up. Both felt good about the Brunsons and Annie Mattox.

At 8:35, Bill heard the whistle of the local pulling out for Atlanta. He was sure the Sheriff and Diane heard it, too, but like most mornings it meant nothing.

Sheriff DeWitt said, "If they don't go along with a ruling of suicide for Mack Poole, I'm still done with the case. We don't have any evidence pointing to another person being there when the damn fool hanged himself. We don't have anything else to investigate."

Bill nodded his agreement.

Sheriff DeWitt continued, "Moses Jackson is the only possible suspect. I suppose we could bring him in and question him for a couple of days and make him to admit to hanging Poole, or damned near anything else I wanted."

Bill asked, "Do you think Moses killed Poole?"

"It don't matter what I think, and it don't much matter what he did or didn't do. But, no. If they want somebody to pay for Mack Poole, Moses is the only one in play. With the election coming up next year and more coloreds voting, I sure would rather have Moses on my side and helping me than him sitting in jail, or worse."

After a short pause, "Bill, all the measuring stuff you did from the picture is good. Talk about what you did to figure out how far he fell. It might make it in the newspaper. And, while you're at it, tell them you are a Georgia Tech engineer. Yeah, get that in when you talk about Poole's hanging himself. We'll do the Brunson's first and get them over with, then Mattox. Talk about Coles as much as you want. They'll all want to hear about the new stuff. It may keep their minds off Poole."

Sheriff DeWitt locked the office at quarter to ten. Carrying their files and notes, he, Bill, and Diane walked across the yard to the court house. The Sheriff was dead right. Everyone wanted the Brunsons over and done. Next, Bill provided the evidence for Tommy Coles being Annie's murderer. Judge Morrow confirmed what had happened in his office. After hearing his testimony, all the jurors were ready to get to outside with their new information especially since spectators started leaving to get a head start. Mack Poole's death was ruled a suicide without a single question, and court was adjourned at eleven-thirty. It didn't appear Bill's calculations were going to make the *Herald-Journal*.

After dropping everything at the office, the Sheriff and Diane went to their homes for dinner. Bill locked the office door and stretched out on the bunk in the holding cell and napped until Diane returned at one.

"Late night?" she asked.

"Yes, but I will rest tonight and for a while. They left this morning for New York and won't be back for three weeks."

"It looks like you are pretty serious about Elizabeth. No wonder; she is beautiful, movie star beautiful."

"Yes, she is, but she's smart and funny, too. Did you know she'd gone to school in Milledgeville for two years and was supposed to go to Georgia this year?"

"How about her family? Her mother? You know there is another state institution in Milledgeville."

"I know her mother is different, but she's not insane." Remembering their last two meetings, "At least, I don't think she is. You know, I'm not going to be here a lot longer."

A little surprised, Diane asked, "What are you talking about? Where are you going?"

"I don't know yet, but it is time for me to start planning a future based on my education and flying. I didn't realize how much I missed flying. It is really fun when there aren't a bunch of Jap assholes shooting at you."

"Would you go back into the Army?"

"I've thought about it, but I don't think so. I want to do something with my degree. I liked what I studied at Tech, and I did pretty good in school. I don't think I'd get much of a chance to use my education in the Army. A family Is tough in the Army, even if there is no war."

"I'll miss you, Bill."

"Diane, I'm not going anywhere right away. When Elizabeth gets back, we'll talk and work some things out, I'll start looking at possibilities after the first of the year."

After a few minutes, he looked at Diane and said, "This afternoon, I'm going to do something I haven't done in nearly two weeks. I'm going on patrol. I'm going to drive all over Greene County and not find a damn thing, not a felony, not a misdemeanor, not even a dead dog. Hell, I'd even drive past a still if I saw one. I think I'll head down to White Plains and go by my daddy's grave. He would have been interested in all the goings on this week. After what we learned this week, I think

I'll have a seat by his grave and tell him about Elizabeth and all the rest."

Bill grabbed his hat and night stick and walked out to his car.

As soon as the train stopped at Terminal Station, Hans stepped from the caboose and walked quickly into the grand lobby and up the stairs to the Trainmen's Dining Room. After he ate, he went to his compartment before the regular passengers boarded. Following the stop at Richmond the train went to a siding for four hours to make an 8:00 a.m. arrival in Washington.

27

Elizabeth, her mother, and Connie went to the dining car as the train rolled toward Union Station in Washington, DC. The food was always good, and breakfast could be special on a train. Mary Greene and Elizabeth asked for coffee and to wait a few minutes before they ordered. Connie decided she could wait too, if she had hot cocoa. As they moved slowly through the city, Connie and Elizabeth caught sight of the top of the Washington Monument, and as they neared Union Station, they saw the dome of the capitol.

After their coffee and cocoa, they ordered. Mary Greene had scrambled eggs, bacon, toast, and potatoes, no grits in Washington. Elizabeth ordered Eggs Benedict because it sounded like a dish suited for the new Mae. Connie stuck with her traditional train breakfast, pancakes.

The stop at Union Station was scheduled for fifteen minutes instead of the five minutes at other places, but it ran to twenty. The train started with a little lurch just as Connie was pouring syrup from the pitcher onto her last bite of pancake. Syrup splashed from the plate onto her hand. She finished the last bite while holding her sticky left hand up in the air.

Mary Greene said, "Connie, there is a restroom where we came into the dining car. Go and wash your hands before you mess up your dress. I don't want you to have to change clothes this morning. Betty May, go with her."

"I can go by myself, Momma," and Connie was up and heading down the aisle for the restroom holding her left hand up and away from her.

Hans stepped into the dining car and stood by the restroom door as he looked over the diners. He saw Mary Greene about halfway down on the left with her back to him, and Elizabeth was in the seat facing her, but he didn't see Connie.

"Excuse me, please."

Hans looked down and there was Connie standing right in front of him with her raised hand.

"I need to go in and wash my hands," Connie said as she pointed with her good hand at the door Hans was blocking.

"So sorry, my dear. Please excuse me," Hans said with a remnant of his Austrian accent. He stepped sideways and more into the car to give Connie a path to the door. Hans touched Connie gently on the shoulder as she passed by him. Hans left the dining car.

At his touch, Connie stifled a scream, quickly pushed the door open, slammed it closed and locked it. She stood in the middle of the little room, trembling. The trembles turned to muffled crying. Connie didn't move.

At the table, Mary Greene said, "Betty May, go see about your sister. She's been in there a long time."

"I guess she has, Momma," Elizabeth said as she headed down the aisle. At the restroom door, Elizabeth said, "Connie, are you all right?" Listening, Elizabeth heard crying. Knocking on the door, she said, "Connie, this Is Betty May. Open the door. Open the door, please."

From inside, "Betty May?"

"Yes, I'm here. Please open the door."

"Is he gone?"

Leaning down, Elizabeth asked, "Who? Connie, there is no one here but me."

The lock clicked and the handle turned and a small crack appeared, backed by Connie's red, teary eye. When she saw no other person there, she pulled the door full open and jumped the step to Elizabeth and wrapped one good arm and one still sticky arm around Elizabeth's waist and began to cry loudly. Her crying attracted the attention of all in the dining car, and two waiters hurried to Elizabeth and Connie. Mary Greene did not need to turn to know it was Connie. She took her pocket book and Elizabeth's and followed the waiters to the end of the car.

"Ma'am, is she hurt?" asked the first waiter.

"Are you hurt, Connie?" Elizabeth echoed.

Without stopping her wails, Connie moved her head back and forth against Elizabeth's body.

"She's not hurt," Elizabeth translated. "I think something must have scared her."

Connie made a move of affirmation and hugged Elizabeth even tighter and let out another loud wail.

Mary Greene arrived, "Go to our compartment. She will be all right." Not waiting for any response but obedience, Mary Greene pushed passed Connie and Elizabeth and opened the door to the next car. Elizabeth followed with Connie holding tightly to her.

In their compartment, Connie was nearly composed and said, "That man wanted to hurt us, hurt you, Momma. He hurt me when he touched me."

"Did he hit you?" Elizabeth asked.

"No, he touched my shoulder when I walked past him, but all I felt was hate and cold. It hurt. Momma, let's go home. I'm scared."

Elizabeth asked, "Did you know the man? Would you know him if you saw him again?"

"I'll never forget him, but I never saw him before," Connie answered.

"What did he look like?" Elizabeth asked.

"He was kind of fat in the belly like Daddy, but he had a lot of black shiny hair. It was wavy, and a big black mustache. His skin looked shiny, too. Momma, I want to go home."

Mary Greene asked, "Did he say anything?"

"When I told him, I needed to get in the bathroom he said he was sorry, and when he moved he touched me."

Mary Greene continued, "Was there anything strange about the way he talked? Did he sound like everybody else?"

"Momma, he did sound kind of different. Not like the people in Greensboro, and not like colored people. It was different. I don't know how to explain it, but if I heard him again I would know. Can we go home?"

"No, Connie, we can't go home right now. We will be all right. We will watch out for him. And, we must take care of each other. Betty May, help Connie get cleaned up. We can stay in here until we get to New York. And, we can order our dinner served in here. We will be fine." Mary Greene put her suitcase on the little sofa and dug around in a corner, found something, and put it in her pocket book.

Hans heard about the commotion in the dining car after he left, and he determined to stay in his compartment until the train arrived in New York. He was first off the train in New York and confirmed the DuBose's luggage was going to the Drake. He took a taxi to a small hotel a block away from the Drake.

Bill's Wednesday afternoon patrol was entirely successful. He found nothing of interest to the sheriff's office. He enjoyed his talk with his dad. They always had good conversations. When he was young they mostly talked baseball and how to treat people, and their conversation never changed. Bill knew his Dad's spirit was at peace and he hoped maybe his Dad's spirit would find Annie's and he'd talk to her about baseball. Bill understood now, it was the talking that was important, baseball happened to be the subject.

Bill's Thursday morning at Geer's went much as expected. Everybody wanted to know more about how he figured out Coles was the murderer. "It was pretty simple," he said. "I was packing up as the other deputy was presenting his information to the judge. When he took out the piece of cloth, I recognized it right away. I identified the dead man from his clothes and we confirmed his name with the things the depot agent found. When Coles' knife matched the cut in the dress and the pocket, everything was pretty well wrapped up."

As the regulars and everyday regulars came and went, he told the story several times several ways, but he always stuck to matching the cloth in Coles pocket to the dress and his knife to the cut. There were a few questions about Poole and why it was a suicide. Bill kept to the litany he and Sheriff DeWitt crafted, hands not tied, no evidence of a struggle, the way the rope was wrapped to the tree, and no evidence of anyone else at the hanging site.

No one in Geer's Grand Jury suggested the Jackson's might be involved. Sheriff DeWitt was pleased with Bill's report on the mornings proceedings.

The DuBose ladies didn't have their usual four rooms this year. There were only three, a bedroom, a sitting room and a smaller adjoining bedroom that had been prepared for the sessions. The Drake staff had moved the bed from the small room into the larger bedroom. It was a bit cramped, but it saved the cost of a room. Elizabeth and Connie shared a bed. The session room had a bathroom, so they had two. After two days and a night on the train all three were ready for a bath. They unpacked their overnight bags, bathed, and had supper in their room. No one was up late. In the same bed, Elizabeth knew Connie was restless all night and cried several times.

Friday morning, Hans watched as the doorman whistled for a taxi from the line parked on the street. When it pulled up the doorman opened the door for the DuBose ladies and gave the driver the address. As they moved into the street, Hans saw Connie leaning up from the middle of the seat and searching the sidewalk. He turned his head to the building and waited long enough for the taxi to be well past him. "She'll go out alone tomorrow," Hans said to himself.

At Jefferson's broker. Elizabeth spent the afternoon with an associate going over his, now her mother's, portfolio and account. Mary Greene and Connie shopped, but Connie didn't enjoy it because she was watching for the man she had seen on the train. They returned to the hotel early so Mary Greene could prepare for her evening's session.

Her clients were an upstate New York couple who were trying to contact their sixteen-year-old daughter. She had been killed in an automobile accident on a night when she should have been in her room at boarding school. When Elizabeth returned, Mary Greene sent her to the concierge to pick up the envelope left by tonight's clients, and have it put in the hotel's safe.

Colonel Holland rapped sharply on the door of General Lovejoy's Pentagon office. An order, "Enter," came from the general.

Carrying a small stack of file folders, Colonel Holland approached the General's desk. "Sit down, Duke," General Lovejoy said.

"Thank you, sir," Duke Holland replied as he placed the stack of folders on the corner of the general's desk and took a seat.

"These are the top ten candidates," he said as he touched the stack of folders. "Cal-Tech, Stanford, M.I.T. and the University of Washington have approved all the candidates for admission to their master's programs in aeronautical engineering."

The general picked up the top folder, but didn't open it, "That's what we expected. We found the top minds among our pilots, right?"

"Yes, sir."

General Lovejoy continued, "When we become the Air Force, and I get ready to buy a new airplane, I don't want to have to rely on the engineers from Boeing or Douglas or whoever to tell us what we are getting. I want some Air Force engineers and pilots who can evaluate what they tell us and fly the damn airplanes, too."

"Yes, sir," Colonel Holland replied.

"This program ought to stay under the radar for now. Hell, all we're doing is sending some good officers off for some advanced training. The whole business won't cost half what a small-bomber costs. Duke, tell me about our candidates."

"Sir, we have ten pilots, all with engineering degrees, mechanical, civil, and electrical. Five are fighter pilots, three are bomber pilots, one transport, and one helicopter. Eight are regular Army and are still on active duty, two of those look like career men. The other two are reservists, ROTC. One is still active, and one was released in January. The file you have in your hand is the reservist who was released in January. He had the best academic record in the group."

The General opened the file and read, "William McKinley Brown, Major."

"Yes, sir. Major Brown was the top graduate in his class at Georgia Tech. He flew B-17's and B-24's in the Pacific. He is the one who tested the A-26 for General Kenney and was hit by Japanese fire because the engines blocked the view of the ground."

"Yes, I remember. Kenney wouldn't take any A-26s after that," said General Lovejoy.

Colonel Holland continued, "Brown brought the plane to an island, but crashed and messed up his arm. General Kenney was impressed by the report he wrote from the hospital. The report is why Kenney didn't want the A-26s."

"What about his arm? Can he fly?" asked the General.

"Some hotshot surgeon rebuilt his right arm. The first doctors said he was going to lose it. Anyway, after he got out of the hospital, we sent him to MP school," explained Colonel Holland.

"MP school?"

"Nobody gave him a chance of flying again, but somebody wanted to keep him in. When he completed the school, he passed the MP physical. General Kenney found out and had him reassigned."

"What is he doing now? Is he married?"

"He's not married and is working in his hometown as a deputy sheriff. It is only a small county, I think he is the only full-time deputy. General Lovejoy, I think he's marking time until he decides what he's going to do next."

"Let's see if living like a civilian for two years on a major's pay and attending one of our finest schools is what he wants to do next. I think it is. If he takes the deal, he ends up with a master's degree and gives us four more years, right? When does he come in?"

Colonel Holland replied, "Yes, sir. Brown is scheduled to be here at thirteen hundred on Monday. He is the only one we will see on Monday. With his time in grade, he'll be up for lieutenant colonel a year after he graduates. I think we'd have a career man."

"Thank you, colonel."

28

"I swear I don't know how we won the war with some of the people we have in our government. Just damn stupid."

Diane looked up, not surprised someone was, she asked, "Sheriff, who is stupid now?"

Clearly frustrated, the sheriff continued, "Our idiot postmaster, Donald whatever his name is." Holding up an official looking envelope, "This came from the United States Army last week. It is addressed to Major W. M. Brown, Sheriff's Department, Greene County Court House, Greensboro, Georgia. Hell, it was eight days ago, and the dumb son of a bitch didn't deliver it because he didn't know who Major W. M. Brown was. Where is Bill?"

"He cleaned up the camera and went to buy some more film. He said he wanted to be ready for the next mayhem we have. He should be here any second."

"Go ahead and call him on the radio and tell him to come on now." They both turned to the door as Bill came in.

Surprised to see both looking at him, Bill said, "Good afternoon all, what the hell did I do?"

"Nothing, Bill. Our crackerjack postmaster held this because he didn't know, damn it, never mind. But this looks important, or at least official," Sheriff DeWitt said as he handed Bill the envelope.

Bill turned it over in his hands and said, "It looks like orders." He sat down at his desk and opened the envelope. The sheriff and Diane watched as Bill unfolded the papers inside, read and reread them. "Sheriff, I've been recalled to active duty for twenty-one months. I'm supposed to report to a Captain Belvin at Bush Field by sixteen hundred hours on fifteen November."

"Today!" Diane said.

"At four o'clock this afternoon," Sheriff DeWitt added. "Is that all it says, report?"

"No, it says report for further instructions and travel arrangements. I can make it to Bush Field by sixteen hundred hours, but I don't have a uniform with me. And if I did, it wouldn't fit, not the pants anyway. Too much Geer's. Sheriff, I guess I resign, effective immediately. It's been nice, Diane. I'm glad we had our conversation on Wednesday."

Bill stood and said, "You mind if I try and get this Captain Belvin on the phone? I guess I can get a number for Bush Field and start from there."

Diane looked at Bill and said, "Stand down, Major Brown." She picked up the receiver and clicked the button, "Hey Sally, this is Diane at the sheriff's office." After a short pause, "Yes, I'm fine, but I need a long-distance operator right away." Listening, "I'll tell you later, get me a long-distance operator right now, please." After a few seconds, "Operator, this is Agent Diane Weston with the Greene County Sheriff's Department in Greensboro, Georgia, and I need to place a person to person call to Captain Belvin at Bush Field, Augusta, Georgia. This is an urgent military matter." Diane asked Bill, "Do you have Belvin's first name or initials?"

Bill answered, "David B."

Diane continued on the phone, "Captain David B, bravo, Belvin. Yes, the Greene County Georgia Sheriff's Department and again this is an urgent military matter. And operator,…Marjorie, thank you, Marjorie I will hold."

The sheriff and Bill watched and listened to Diane in wonder. Three minutes later, Diane spoke into the telephone again, "Good, and thank you very much, Marjorie. When Captain Belvin is on the line I will connect him with Major Brown." Holding her hand over the mouth piece of the phone, she looked at Bill and said, "Billy Boy, put your major's hat on and talk to this captain when I give you the telephone."

Removing her hand, Diane said, "Yes, Captain Belvin, please hold for Major Brown." Diane held the phone long enough that Bill started reaching for it. She stood and pointed to her chair, indicating for Bill to sit down. When he was seated, she handed Bill the receiver.

"Captain Belvin, this is Major William M. Brown. I need your help," Bill said into the phone.

The sheriff looked at Major Brown on the telephone and at Agent Weston standing behind him, and he shook his head. "Agent Weston? Who the hell is running this place?" he asked to no one.

Agent Weston looked at Sheriff DeWitt and said with a smile, "Don't worry about your job, sheriff, it's something we do."

Deputy Brown became Major Brown to talk to Captain Belvin. After ten minutes, he held the receiver against his chest and said, "He's gone to talk to the colonel about me coming in tomorrow afternoon. If the colonel says okay, I have time to drive to my sister's, pick up all my stuff and get to Bush tomorrow. Belvin seems like a good guy. He said he would get me new pants if I gave him my sizes. Belvin says their only orders for me were to get me to Washington by Sunday, and they have me a seat on a commercial flight leaving on Sunday morning."

Wanting to take charge, Sheriff DeWitt said, "Get a telephone number for Belvin. As soon as you get done with him, I'll call Jack Breeden in Athens and get your sizes. He keeps a card on all his clients. Correction, Agent Weston will contact Mr. Breeden for the required information."

"I might as well sign over my pay for the week to cover the long-distance telephone charges," Bill said to the sheriff. Then speaking into the receiver, "Yes, Captain Belvin and thank you." After not speaking for a minute or more, Bill said, "I understand, I will report to the BOQ at Bush midafternoon Saturday and contact you. I will not be in uniform." Another short pause, "Please give me telephone numbers to reach you today and tomorrow. Di…Agent Weston will call you shortly with my sizes." Bill wrote down the telephone numbers and looked up at Diane and the Sheriff, asking with his expression is there anything else? When they nodded no, he said to Captain Belvin, "Thank you for your help and I look forward to meeting you. Please give the colonel my thanks as well. Goodbye."

Bill hung up the phone and looked at Diane and the sheriff, "This whole thing is really strange. Belvin knew who I was and he acted like my coming there was a big deal, and it was real important for me to get to Washington on time. At least, I don't think I am in trouble. Now what?"

Diane looked at Bill and said, "What is you must get your butt on the road to your sister's. You know you may not get back here for a while. Is there anything here of yours? And how much do you have at your place?"

"Nothing here," Bill said as he rummaged through his desk drawer. "The only things at the apartment are my clothes, two bottles of whiskey, and my one good glass. Everything else belongs to the McLeans. I can get all my stuff into my duffle bag. My rent is paid to the end of the month. Oh, I need to stop at the bank and close my account. I reckon I might need the cash."

Taking charge again, Sheriff DeWitt said, "Diane, Agent Weston, go ahead and call Jack Breeden and get Bill's pants sizes and call Belvin. Bill, we'll go by the court house and get you paid out, and go to the bank. I'll drop you at your place and help you get your stuff in the truck."

"Okay and thanks," said Bill and he stood and took a small framed snapshot of his mother and dad from his desk. He gave Jack Breeden's card to Diane.

As he started for the door, Diane said, "Wait a damn minute." She stepped to him and hugged him tightly. "Major, Deputy Brown, I will truly miss you. You must let us know what's going on. I know you'll come to see Elizabeth, but remember we are important, too."

In an hour, Bill was on the road to his sister's.

29

Mary Greene was still asleep at nearly eleven o'clock on Saturday morning. It was not unusual for her to sleep late after a session.

Elizabeth and Connie had dressed and gone down before nine. They ate breakfast in the small dining room and explored the lobby to see what had changed from the year before. Neither wanted to go out. It was cold with a drizzle, the doorman said it would clear up at lunch time. Connie asked Elizabeth, "Why do they always call it lunch when we are here and not dinner? I only had lunch at school."

Elizabeth had no answer and offered nothing.

When they made the second pass by the concierge, he looked and asked Elizabeth, "Do you have plans for the afternoon?"

"Not yet," Elizabeth replied.

The concierge continued, "A great new movie premiered in Atlanta last week, and it is here now. It's called *Song of the South*. Have you heard about it? Aren't you from Georgia?"

"Yes, we are from Georgia, and no, I haven't heard about the movie. Is it about Georgia?" said Elizabeth.

"It is about Georgia, Uncle Remus, and Brother Rabbit. Do you know about them?"

"Oh, yes!" said Connie, "Daddy read me stories. The man who wrote them was born near us."

Elizabeth looked at Connie with surprise, "Well, he did Betty May. He read them to me when Momma wasn't around. Daddy said they taught lessons like the Bible."

The concierge jumped back into the conversation, "It is a Walt Disney movie with part of it in cartoons, and there are good songs. If you want to go, I have a few tickets for the two o'clock matinee. They are fifty cents each. The theater is in the next block. It is close enough to walk."

"Thank you," said Elizabeth.

"Betty May, I want to go see Bre'r Rabbit and Uncle Remus. Momma won't know it's about Uncle Remus if we say it is a Walt Disney movie named *Song of the South*."

"Cornelia Irene DuBose, I do believe you are trying to trick your momma. You better be careful," chided Elizabeth.

"Well you did the morning we left. Besides, I really want to go."

"Connie, I would like to see it, too. Let's see what Momma has planned. If we don't go today, we can go another day. New York is not like Greensboro. This picture show will probably be on the whole time we are here."

Mary Greene was having coffee and toast in the room. She looked up when Connie and Elizabeth came in. "Have you been out? is it cold?"

Connie answered, "We didn't go out except to put our heads out. It is cold and raining a little. The doorman says it's going to clear up after lunch."

"After 'lunch'? Connie, you are in New York one day and you are already talking like a Yankee. Elizabeth, I am going to dress and go out for a time at 'lunch'. Do you think you and Connie can find something to do? Maybe you can go to a movie, there's a movie theater in the next block. See if the concierge has tickets and you can charge them to our room. Oh, and tell him to add a quarter for himself."

"I will go and see him right now," said Elizabeth. She returned in a moment with the tickets. "He said the movie started at two, but we should be there early to get a good seat. Connie, we can get a hot dog at the theater for our 'lunch'. Oh, and it has stopped raining, but it is still chilly. Do you want to go now and window shop? Is it all right, Momma, for us to go now?"

"If you want," Mary Greene replied.

"I'm ready," said Connie.

Mary Greene handed Elizabeth a dollar. "This is for 'lunch'. Things are so expensive in New York. I should be back by three o'clock. I'll see you then."

"No, Momma," Elizabeth answered. "The movie doesn't start until two and won't be over until at least four or maybe after. We will be here before five o'clock."

Mary Greene simply said, "Oh."

From across the street, Hans watched the two girls leave the hotel and walk south. "Good, Mary will be out soon, and alone," he said to himself.

Elizabeth and Connie took their time walking the two half blocks to the theater. Connie relaxed some, and didn't look at every man they passed. They didn't go in until one o'clock. They bought hot dogs, Coca-Colas, and potato chips and ate standing at a high table on the edge of the big lobby.

"This is a good lunch, isn't it, Betty May?" said Connie.

"It is a good lunch," Elizabeth answered. "Connie, I want you to do something for me. You know how you and Momma call me Betty May, and Bill calls me Elizabeth?"

"Uh huh."

"I think I want everyone to call me Mae, not Betty May, but just Mae. How would that be?"

"It would be okay. What should people call me, Betty May? I mean Mae," Connie asked.

"We will have to think about what to call you, Connie."

Connie and Elizabeth heard music coming from inside the theater, and people started to go in. Elizabeth said, "Let's get some popcorn and go inside."

They found seats they liked. On stage, a lady was singing and trying to get everyone in the theater to sing with her. Connie and Elizabeth didn't know many of the songs, but it was fun to listen. When she left, the theater darkened and the big curtain opened.

First, there was a news reel with some airplanes. Elizabeth whispered to Connie the airplanes were the kind Bill had flown.

There was a Mickey Mouse cartoon, and the movie started. It was a real movie, in color, but when Uncle Remus would tell a story about Br'er Fox or Br'er Rabbit, it would be a cartoon and they both liked the cartoons.

30

Thirty-five minutes after Elizabeth and Connie left the hotel, Mary Greene DuBose walked out of the front door of the Drake Hotel and turned north toward Central Park. Hans de Graffinreed followed her from his side of Park Avenue.

At the next corner, 57th Street, she crossed to his side of the street and Hans stepped into the doorway of the building at the corner. She never noticed him, and he fell in behind her as she crossed Madison Avenue, 5th Avenue, and 6th Avenue. After crossing 6th, Mary Greene slowed her pace, stopped, and looked at her watch and moved close to the building and stood still. Hans had not crossed 6th Avenue. He looked at his watch. It was 12:50. He was cold standing there. I wish she would start moving again. But he had no choice but to stay where he was.

After what seemed to be a very long time, she looked at her watch again. Hans looked at his. It was now 12:58 and Mary Greene started up the block toward 7th Avenue. As soon as the light changed, Hans crossed and moved up the block behind her.

She slowed again as she came to the Russian Tea Room. The door to the restaurant was opened for her. Rather than enter, she turned toward the street and a man, a well-dressed gentleman in an overcoat, exited a taxi. He crossed the sidewalk quickly and greeted her with kisses on both cheeks. Together, they entered the Tea Room.

Hans realized how cold he was and how badly he needed to find a restroom. Twenty minutes later he was across the street from the Tea Room watching the door and shivering. At nearly 2:30, Mary Greene and the gentleman came out of the restaurant. They clasped hands in a warm goodbye. He turned toward 7th Avenue, and she turned toward 6th. At the corner, she turned toward Central Park. Again, Hans had to duck into a doorway as she crossed to his side of the street.

Mary Greene walked two blocks and went into the park at Center Drive. Hans closed the distance between them. With the cold and the earlier rain, there were only a few people in the park this Saturday afternoon. Hans didn't think Mary Greene would spend much time in the park, but if she did, he would have a hard time not being noticed. He watched from the sidewalk as she moved down the path toward the zoo and passed the big rock.

It might be now or never. He started to follow her until he realized she had stopped just beyond the rock.

She didn't look toward him, but in the other direction down the path. In less than a minute, a young man in what looked like a doorman's uniform came up the path, spoke and handed her an envelope. He bowed slightly and turned down the path. Mary Greene opened her purse, put the envelope in it, and started toward the park entrance.

Hans stepped over a low fence which separated the path from plantings and crossed an old flower bed and stepped into her path. In a few more steps he was directly in front of her, but she had not looked up to notice.

She stopped short when Hans said, "Mrs. DuBose, please turn and walk down the path with me." As he spoke, his hand went into his jacket pocket and he raised his coat tail slightly and pointed it at her.

Mary Greene didn't turn or move. She looked directly at Hans and said, "Hans de Graffinreed, I thought it might be you. You scared my little girl. I didn't like that. What do you want?"

Hans answered, "You know what I want. I want the money your husband stole from me. Now walk."

"You got your share, Hans. As much as Jefferson did. He took better care of it than you, and he didn't waste it. He stole nothing from you or anyone. There is no money for you, you miserable little kraut."

"Kraut! You lie again. You know I am Austrian, not German. I will shoot you if you don't tell me where the money is hidden."

"Shoot me?" Mary Greene said, "You don't have a gun. If you did kill me, you would never find out."

Hans smiled, knowing Mary Greene might have said too much. He answered, "Never find out? What would I never find out? If I don't find out from you, then from your girls. And, I have a gun." He slipped his hand from his pocket. In it was a small silver revolver. "Now walk." He pointed with the revolver toward the path and returned it to his coat pocket.

Mary Greene turned, and the unlatched purse fell open in front of her. She walked a few steps down the path. As she walked, her hand found the double-barreled .22 caliber derringer she had put in her purse on the train. She stopped with Hans right behind her. "Hans," she said, "there is something I should tell you."

"Ja," he said, "go ahead."

Mary Greene turned slowly to her left, keeping her right hand and the derringer behind her. When she was nearly facing him, she screamed at the top of her voice, "I'll tell you!" She brought the little gun up toward his face and fired one barrel and then the other.

Surprised by the scream, Hans never saw the gun. He only heard one little pop of the .22 caliber short cartridge and saw a flash.

Fired from just above her waist, the bullet was traveling upward when it struck Hans between the eyes an inch above the bridge of the nose. It penetrated the skin but flattened against the frontal plate of his skull and slid along it to the top of his forehead. The energy his head absorbed knocked him backward.

Without realizing it, he fired his .32 revolver through his coat. The bullet hit Mary Greene directly in the chest and tore through her aorta. She hit the ground and bled to death within a minute.

They both liked the songs, especially "Zip a-Dee-Doo-Dah." Everybody laughed when Uncle Remus told about Br'er Rabbit and his "Laughing Place." As the scene ended, Connie screamed. When she caught her breath, she cried out, "He hurt my momma, Betty May he hurt Momma bad!" Connie was up and climbing over people to get to the aisle. "Come on, Betty May, we have to help Momma! Hurry, Betty May, hurry!"

Elizabeth caught Connie in the lobby. "Wait, Connie, tell me what you saw, what you felt."

"It was the man, the man on the train. Oh, he shot Momma with a gun and she fell down. She fell down beside Indian Rock. Betty May, we have to go. We have to help Momma!"

An usher came over, "Ma'am, is she, all right? Can I help with something? Do you need a taxi?"

Connie looked up at the usher and said calmly, "The man from the train killed my momma, and she's lying in the cold by Indian Rock. We have to go there." She started to cry.

"We are staying at the Drake. I need to go there," said Elizabeth.

The usher said, "It's close, I'll go with you." He picked up Connie, who didn't resist and the three of them walked quickly to the hotel.

Connie continued to cry as they went up to their rooms. Elizabeth had too much faith in Connie to believe her mother would be in the room when they returned, but she hoped.

Hans reeled several feet, but he never fell. He couldn't see clearly, his ears were ringing, and the ringing was all he heard. His head hurt like it was being squeezed in a vice. He felt warmth on his nose, and he reached up and touched wet. He looked at his hand and saw blood. He reached up to his head again and found the small hole between his eyes. How am I not dead? He reached for the handkerchief in his pocket and pressed it against his forehead.

Neither gun was loud, and against the sounds of the city, no one had noticed the shots. But now, a couple of passers-by saw Mary Greene lying on the path, and Hans standing there with a bloody handkerchief held to his head. An older man walked over. Hans said to him, "Help her. She has been shot, me too, but help her."

A young couple heard him and went directly to Mary Greene's body. The older man followed. The young man shouted about needing an ambulance. Hans head was clearing and he knew he needed to get away. He turned and walked toward 59th Street, holding the handkerchief on his head.

More people now were heading toward Mary Greene's body. Some were running. At the street, he turned toward Park Avenue and walked purposely but not fast. At 5th Avenue he crossed 59th Street and kept moving toward Park Avenue. By now, if anyone noticed him, he was only another man with a cold and a handkerchief to his face, but in New York, no one noticed.

In twenty minutes, he was in his hotel room. He undressed completely and stood in front of the big mirror in the bathroom. The only wound he saw was the now black spot directly between his eyes. There was dark, dried blood in the creases on either side of his nose. When he touched the spot, he could feel a hard clot. He noticed the little ridge running up his forehead from the spot. It looked like a lawn when a mole pushes up the sod. He touched it. It didn't hurt, at least no more than the rest of his head. He moved his finger slowly up the ridge to his hairline. There he felt something hard. He moved his fingers around the lump. The bullet, the bullet is just under my skin. That's why I am not dead.

Hans pinched the skin above the lump and could feel it move

down the ridge. Maybe I can get it out. He pinched and pushed and the lump moved down the path it had made going in. Fresh blood started to ooze from around the clot. It ran down either side of his nose. He reached for a towel, but realized a he couldn't leave a bloody towel in the room. He went to his case in the bedroom and found his clean undershirt.

In the bathroom, holding his head over the lavatory he pushed the lump down to the clot. He started picking at the clot with his fingers. It hurt when he tore away dried blood from raw skin. As pieces were removed more blood began to flow down his face.

The lump felt like it was in the hole. He looked in the mirror and dabbed away blood with his undershirt. Sitting there in the hole in his forehead was the mis-shapened bullet. He pinched, but it wouldn't come out. The pinching brought more blood. Holding the shirt over his face, he found his pocket knife in his pants in the bedroom.

Back in the bathroom, Hans opened the knife's smallest blade and held it under running water. He pressed hard on his forehead to keep the bullet from moving up its path. He worked the blade into the hole, under and behind the bullet. Surprisingly, there was little pain from the knife, but he felt the blade scraping against bone. When it felt like the blade was completely behind the bullet, he paused for a second and quickly pushed the blade hard against the bullet and out. There was a sharp pain as bullet and knife tore more skin. More warm blood ran down his face, and he heard a very satisfying plink and plink as the bullet hit the back of the lavatory and fell into its bowl. He stumbled back and sat down hard on the toilet with his bloody shirt pressed to his face. Hans didn't move for twenty minutes.

31

Bill had arrived at his sister's home in the late afternoon. Everyone was glad to see him on this unexpected visit. His mother's excitement and pleasure quickly turned to concern when she found he was being returned to active duty. Even though there was no combat, she never did like for Bill to fly.

Bill spent the time before supper getting his uniforms and paper work together. After they ate, he told them all about Annie Mattox.

His mother knew of Mary Greene and Jefferson Davis DuBose and all the stories around them. Telling his mother Elizabeth DuBose was somebody special to him only added to her concern, but like most mothers she hid her feelings because she understood how excited Bill was about both the return to flying and Elizabeth DuBose.

Saturday morning, shortly after nine and following what he had learned from Diane, Bill placed a person to person call to Elizabeth at the Drake in New York City. He heard the hotel operator tell the long-distance operator there was no answer in the DuBose suite. Mary Greene's sleep was not affected by the ringing telephone in the sitting room.

He would try again when he stopped for dinner. To make sure he could complete the call at a pay telephone, Bill swapped bills for coins and left with nearly five dollars in change in his pocket. He called again after one o'clock when he stopped to eat outside Athens, but again no one answered.

As the theater usher left, there was a knock at the open door. "Miss DuBose?" Elizabeth looked to the door from Connie who was standing in the middle of the room with her fists clinched tight and her eyes closed.

"Miss DuBose, I am Michael Hart, the hotel manager, and this is Miss Browner, my assistant. How can we help you?"

"Mr. Hart, do you know where my mother is?" Elizabeth asked.

"No, we haven't seen her since she went out. Alex, the doorman said she walked up toward the park. Do you think something is wrong?"

"Mr. Hart, you do know about my family and my mother's gifts?"

"Yes, ma'am. I do."

Elizabeth continued, "At the movie, Connie had a vision of someone hurting our mother, shooting her. Mr. Hart, I know for some it is hard to accept, but my sister's visions are often very accurate. We are … we are … " and for the first time Elizabeth understood her mother might be dead, and she and Connie might be alone. She broke down in tears and went to Connie and the two of them stood together in the middle of the room. Elizabeth was crying and Connie still standing like a statue.

"Miss Browner, please go downstairs and call Detective Reagan at Mid-Town North. Tell him we are concerned about Mrs. DuBose and ask him if he has any information. Tell the switchboard to route all my calls to this room and you come back here as soon as you can."

"Yes, sir, Mr. Hart," Miss Browner said as she left.

As soon as the door closed, Mr. Hart wished he had gone to make the call to the police, and he had left Miss Browner to deal with the DuBose girls. "Might I get you anything to eat or drink?" he asked, and there was no real reply. He stood for a moment longer and took the chair near the telephone.

In a time, longer than he had wanted to wait, there was a knock at the door followed by the sound of a key in the lock. All three in the room looked toward the door as Miss Browner pushed it open about halfway.

"Mr. Hart," she said, "may I see you out here a moment?" When he was in the hall with her, Miss Browner said, "Detective Reagan is on his way here. Mrs. DuBose was shot and killed at the 59th Street entrance to Central Park. According to him, it happened right before the girls came from the theater. Mr. Hart, from what they said, it happened exactly like the little girl said it did."

"Damn, how do they know it was her," Mr. Hart asked.

"Her pocketbook was under her body with her papers. And Detective Reagan asked me to describe Mrs. DuBose, and he said it had to be her. He wants to talk to the girls."

"Should we tell them about their mother?"

"Detective Reagan said not to say anything to them except he was coming and had some information."

Speaking to Elizabeth, Mr. Hart said, "Miss DuBose, the police are coming here. My friend, Detective Reagan, wants to talk with you."

Connie looked at Mr. Hart and said, "He's going to tell us my momma is dead, shot through the heart by the man on the train." Looking at Elizabeth, "She's right there by Indian Rock."

Miss Browner caught her breath and whispered to Mr. Hart, "My God, Reagan said she was right by the big rock off Center Drive."

When Detective Reagan arrived, he was accompanied by two uniformed officers. He greeted Mr. Hart and Miss Browner. "Please stay while I speak with Miss DuBose," he said. Turning to Elizabeth, "Miss DuBose I must tell you a woman matching your mother's description has been found dead in Central Park. She has been shot."

Elizabeth acknowledged this with a nod.

"The papers in her pocketbook identified her as Mary Greene DuBose," Reagan continued.

Elizabeth closed her eyes and let her head drop. She pulled Connie close. Connie never took her eyes from Reagan.

"Would you come with me to Bellevue Hospital to make a positive identification. It will only take a few minutes, and the little girl won't have to come."

Connie said, "I'm going to see my momma."

Elizabeth answered, "We will both go."

At the hospital, they waited in a small room with a large window which looked into a short, brightly lighted hall. Detective Reagan picked up a telephone receiver and tapped the button. "We're here," he said. "Yes, from this afternoon."

The door at one end opened, and a man in a white coat, hospital mask, and cap pushed a cart with a covered body into the hall. He looked up at Detective Reagan through the window. Detective Reagan asked, "Elizabeth, Connie are you ready?" Elizabeth and Connie never moved.

After a short pause, Elizabeth said, "Go ahead."

The detective nodded to the man and he pulled the cover from the face. The red hair left no doubt it was Mary Greene DuBose.

Elizabeth choked out, "That's her, that is our mother."

Reagan nodded again to the man, and he started to pull the cover over Mary Greene's face.

Connie said loudly, "No! Don't cover her. I have to see her. I have to touch her. She has things to tell me."

At the sound of Connie's voice, the man stopped.

Detective Reagan looked at Connie, "Young lady, you don't want to go there, do you?"

Connie cried out a long, "Take me to my mother!"

Elizabeth looked at Detective Reagan and said, "Detective Reagan, we are going to see our mother." She took Connie's hand and opened the door. "Now, take us."

"This way," Reagan said, and he led them into the short hall.

The man in white moved to the wall, and Reagan closed the door and stood beside it. Elizabeth stood at her mother's head and Connie walked to the side and stood there looking at her mother's face.

She bowed her head and closed her eyes and started to pray. Connie spoke softly at first and her words made sense, but she became louder and louder and sounds ceased to be words until she screamed "Amen, Shalom!" The man in white crossed himself.

Connie put her hands on her mother's face and held them there without a sound for at least two minutes, she leaned in and kissed her mother on the cheek. She looked up to Elizabeth and said, "It's okay now, we can go. The man on the train is the one who shot her. It didn't hurt much and was over quick. She shot him, too. In the head, but he's not dead. I don't know his name, but it is a funny name. If I see him, I will know it's him. Betty May, I'm hungry. When can we go home?"

Elizabeth answered, "Soon, Connie. We will go home as soon as we can. Detective, please take us to the hotel."

"I have some more questions for you and Connie. Then we can go to the hotel," Detective Reagan said.

Elizabeth turned to him and said, "No more questions today. Please take us to our hotel right now."

In the hall with a policeman and Miss Browner, Detective Reagan said to the policeman, "Please take them all to the hotel. Miss DuBose, I will call in the morning before I come. I will also send someone who can help with arrangements to have your mother returned home. Thank you." He walked out of the hospital.

By the time they returned to the room it was nearly six o'clock. Miss Browner ordered supper for them and waited until it arrived. She gave Elizabeth the name of her counterpart who would be on duty during the night and she left. Connie ate a big meal, but Elizabeth only picked at her food. Connie decided to take a bath, a shower, something she couldn't do at home.

Now alone in the sitting room, Elizabeth rose from the table set up for them to eat and sat down on the little sofa like the one in their parlor at home. She pulled her knees up to her chest, wrapped her arms around them and pulled them as close to her as she could. She called out quietly, "Bill Brown, I wish you were here, I need you." Elizabeth jumped at the sound of the telephone ringing. She picked it up and answered, "Hello?"

"Miss Elizabeth DuBose?" the hotel operator asked.

"Yes," Elizabeth replied.

"The long-distance operator has a person to person call for you from Major William Brown, can you take this call?"

"Yes, oh, yes, please put him on."

"One moment," and Elizabeth heard a click.

"Bill," Elizabeth cried into the phone.

"Ma'am, I'm the long-distance operator. Is this Elizabeth DuBose?"

"Yes."

The operator said, "One moment, please."

Elizabeth heard clicking and a hissing sound followed by, "Elizabeth, is it you?"

"Bill, thank God it's you. This is all so terrible," Elizabeth broke down in tears. For a minute, Bill tried to get Elizabeth to stop so he could find out what was terrible. She finally calmed and all that had happened poured out.

"Elizabeth, I wish I were with you right now."

"Oh, I wish you were here, too. I need you. I need to hold you. I need you to hold me."

"Elizabeth, this is going to be hard for me to say and harder for you to hear, but no matter what, remember I love you."

The operator broke in and told Bill he had to put more money in the payphone to continue. As Bill dropped in the coins, one by one each chimed the amount until he was paid for the next three minutes. Bill continued, "I have been recalled to active duty."

"What are you saying, Bill? I don't understand."

"I'm back in the Army. I had orders to report to Bush Field, and I have to fly to Washington tomorrow. I am supposed to report to a general at the Pentagon on Monday. I'm not in Greensboro and I don't know when I can get there."

Bill spent the rest of his three minutes explaining what he had done since Friday afternoon and how little he knew of what was to come. The operator asked for more money and he deposited enough for another three minutes.

"I'll call you from Washington tomorrow night, when I see General Lovejoy. I will tell him about us. I'm going to tell him you are my fiancé. I hope it's okay with you because, I don't tell lies to generals. Tomorrow, call Diane Weston. Do you have something to write down her number?" After a short pause, Bill said, "Her number is 14 -72 and he repeated 1 – 4 – 7 – 2. Tell her everything. She will know how to help. Ask her to get in touch with Fred Thompson. He will know how to help getting your momma home."

Bill heard the telltale noise of the operator getting ready to break in for another payment. "Our time is gone, Elizabeth, I love you."

Bill didn't hear her answer, but he knew. He had a little change left. Maybe it was enough to call Diane since it was in-state and he wouldn't have to call person to person. She answered on the second ring, and he told her everything he knew and asked her to tell Sheriff DeWitt. Their time was running out and Diane told him not to worry. If Elizabeth didn't call tomorrow, she would call her.

32

Hans was up moving around his room. Another hard-black clot had formed in the hole in his forehead and the bleeding had stopped. He knew he wasn't dead. He knew, too, his fate depended on Mary Greene's. If she were alive or lived long enough to tell who shot her, he would spend the rest of his life in a New York jail. If she were dead, all he needed to do was get home without drawing any attention to himself. He needed to get out in the morning to get newspapers. And he knew for sure there was money.

Saturday night, Bill had slept little. He wanted to be with Elizabeth. At some point in the night it occurred to him whoever killed Mary Greene might want to kill Elizabeth and Connie, too. He knew he had to see Elizabeth. He cycled these thoughts all night long and was glad when the alarm went off at six.

Captain Belvin had done well for him. With what he brought from his sister's and what Belvin had gotten for him, he had acceptable uniforms with the correct ranks, ribbons, and insignia. Unless he heard otherwise, he would save the dress uniform for meeting General Lovejoy. Neither Belvin nor his colonel had any idea of what was next for Bill. They had nothing to tell him about whether to carry his gear to Washington or not. It really wasn't much, only enough for Monday and maybe Tuesday. He didn't have a return ticket to Bush Field. With the hope of getting to New York or to Greensboro, he packed everything. Belvin sent a car to drive him across the base to the civilian terminal.

The Piedmont DC-3 flew to Charlotte. The same plane went on to Washington, but it stopped long enough for a meal. When he arrived at Washington National he was met by a Lieutenant Tolson who drove him to the BOQ at Fort McNair. On the way, Bill asked the Lieutenant if he would take him somewhere to get change for the payphone. Bill explained a little about his situation.

"Major Brown, we were told to give you every courtesy. My office is directly across from the BOQ and it is manned at all times. I don't know who is on duty tonight, but I will stop by and tell them you will come over to use the phone in my office. They will show you. Just dial 0 to get the base operator. Ask him to connect you with a long-distance operator. Don't worry about the time and charges, it's my job to review the telephone log."

"Thank you, Lieutenant. Thank you very much."

"My pleasure, sir, and I hope it helps," he replied as he stopped in front of the BOQ. "Corporal Sharpe has your room ready. I'll meet you at here at 1100 tomorrow. We'll drive over to the Pentagon and eat there."

In ten minutes, Bill was on the phone with Elizabeth. This time they had time to talk. Elizabeth told him about Detective Reagan coming over to question Connie. Bill remembered how he felt the first time he met Connie. He knew the detective was in way over his head. In the end, Elizabeth explained how Reagan listened to Connie and wrote down what she told him about the killer.

Elizabeth told how Reagan came with their mother's pocket book, gold cross, and wedding ring, and he showed both the derringer the police found in their mother's hand. He said one barrel had fired, and it looked like the other had been a misfire. She said Connie wanted to hold the gun and Reagan reluctantly handed it to her. She held the little gun in both hands, not really looking at it. When she gave it back, Connie touched a spot on her forehead saying it was where the bullet hit the man who killed her mother. She repeated he was not dead.

Elizabeth said Reagan just shook his head. "I think he was glad to leave."

Bill lacked none of Detective Reagan's doubt about what Connie said and asked, "Just what does Connie know about this man?"

Elizabeth related Connie's encounter in the dining car at breakfast in Washington. Both agreed the man likely had been on the train since Atlanta. Elizabeth concluded she was sure Connie would know him when she saw him, but her identification wouldn't mean anything to the police.

"Bill, I am not sure I understood what's happening to you. I guess you are in the Army. Will you have to go overseas? Are you still going to be a pilot? And, how long?"

Bill explained, "I don't know all of those answers yet. Maybe I will after I meet General Lovejoy. Elizabeth, it is very unusual for me to have to see a general, especially this general, just because I have been recalled. Something else is going on. I don't have any idea where I would go. I don't think overseas, but I think I would still fly. The Army spent a lot of money to teach me to fly. I think they want to get it out of me. My orders say I have been recalled for twenty-one months. When I get done with my meeting tomorrow, I will try to call you."

"We are going to start home tomorrow. When Diane called, I gave her the name of the man at the hospital who has mother's body and she had Fred Thompson to call him and they made all the arrangements."

"Good, I'm glad Diane could help."

"Thank you for Diane, she helped so much and she was somebody good for me to talk to. I needed her. Our train leaves at 11:00 and we'll get to Greensboro at 3:30 Tuesday afternoon. Diane says we can have a service at her church on Wednesday afternoon. With all of Momma's Bible reading, she never was one much for church. I guess this is the thing to do."

"I think it is too, Elizabeth. I'll find a way to be in touch with you on Tuesday. I love you."

"I love you too, Bill, and I need to see you."

Hans de Graffinreed was hungry. He had not eaten since Saturday morning. His head still hurt, but not as bad as yesterday. The ringing in his ears was still there, but not as loud. He looked out the window of his small room. There was not much traffic. He remembered it was Sunday morning. A truck moved away from the curb across the street and for the first time he noticed a newsstand.

The truck had dropped off papers, and a man was moving them onto their places in the stand. He had on a heavy coat and a stocking cap pulled down over his ears. Clouds of white came from his mouth as he lifted the big bundles of Sunday papers. When he turned to the street to get the next bundle, he paused, put his hands on the small of his back and stretched. His eyes looked closed, but he was facing Hans' window. His cap was pulled down over his ears and across his forehead above his eyebrows.

Hans' mind raced, "Da's it. Dat kinda cap will cover my wound and no one will notice. Where to get one on Sunday?"

Hans inspected his own face. His wound was one black spot, but some blood had leaked out during the night. He washed his face well but decided not to shave. The man at the newsstand had a scruffy beard and it looked right with the stocking cap. He dressed quickly, putting on a sweater under his much too light coat. He had a scarf he wrapped around his neck and pulled his fedora down low on his forehead. He looked in the mirror, "If I keep my head down, the black spot on my forehead is hard to see."

When he walked out, he felt the cold immediately. His coat was no match for the Manhattan temperature and the wind funneled down the streets by the tall buildings. At the stand, he moved down the row of papers until he reached the *New York Post*. The headline in inch high letters read: "Ga. Women Killed in Broad Daylight." Below the headline was a big picture of the path and rock where Mary Greene fell.

Hans reached out to pick up the paper and the man said, "That'll be a dime, Mack."

"Yes," Hans answered and folded the paper under his arm, pulled two nickels from his pocket and handed them to the man without looking up. He raised his head slightly and said, "Do you know where I could get a cap like yours?"

"Like this, Mack?" and he touched his head.

"Yes."

The man stepped behind the table of papers and pushed a canvas curtain revealing a variety of candy, snacks, cigarettes, cigars. Held on by clothes pins to a wire strung across the stand were caps like the man's. "Take your pick, Mack. Thirty cent. They are all the same size."

"The black one on the end, please."

"Sure, Mack."

Hans crossed quickly to his hotel and to his room and read the *Post* story twice and searched the paper for anything else. The story said the victim was dead when police arrived and an interview with one of the first witnesses said she was unconscious when he reached her.

Hans felt some relief in reading this. Another witness said there was another man who was hurt, but he left. He was described as an older man in a suit. There was nothing in this story to suggest this other man had been shot.

Hans knew now he needed to get another paper to see if the stories were the same, and now he really was hungry.

He wanted to get in someplace and have a big breakfast. The stocking cap worked well enough to cover his wound, but it rubbed, and he was afraid it would bleed again. If I can go to breakfast, I can go to a drug store and get something to make a bandage. He rubbed his hand over the dark stubble of his beard.

With this beard and a big sweater or heavy coat, I might be a dock worker. I wouldn't look anything like an older man in a suit.

In an hour, he returned from Walgreens with a good breakfast under his belt, gauze, tape, the *New York Times* and *The Sun*. Both papers confirmed the *Post* story. Hans made plans to go home on Monday.

For Elizabeth and Connie, Monday began early and was busy. The Drake sent two maids to help with packing. Connie was unusually helpful because she wanted to go home. At nine, bellmen picked up all their luggage except for one bag Elizabeth packed for the two of them for the train. They ate a small breakfast in their room and at ten, they were taken to Penn Station. At ten-thirty, they boarded and went directly to their compartment.

Hans slept until seven, late for him. When he awoke, his head was much better except the wound itched. He bathed but did not shave. His heavy beard made his face almost black. He looked in the mirror. "Good. no one will recognize me." He made a new bandage for his wound and covered it with his cap. He ate breakfast at Walgreens again and bought copies of the *Post* and *Sun*. There was nothing new in either paper.

He decided to arrive as late as possible to board. As he left his hotel, he dropped the Sunday papers in the garbage can by the newsstand. Wrapped inside them were his bloody shirts. He had a taxi drop him on 8th Avenue and he wandered slowly to the main entrance. At quarter to eleven, he went directly to the platform and into his compartment. He didn't plan to come out until the train arrived at Terminal Station on Tuesday.

For Bill, Monday morning dragged. He woke early, dressed in his class B uniform. He tried to take his time over breakfast at the officers' mess. After breakfast, he had absolutely nothing to do and no one to do it with.

Back in his room, he started to dress and decided his shoes needed attention. He asked the sergeant on duty for some shoe polish and the sergeant simply asked for his shoes and said he would return them in twenty minutes. He repacked, leaving his dress uniform out. There was a knock at the door, followed by, "Major Brown, I have your shoes." He opened the door and a corporal handed him his shoes with a blinding spit shine on them. He thanked the corporal who saluted, did an about face, and marched down the hall.

This is interesting. I've never been an officer during peace time on a big base full of enlisted men. It sure is a lot different to have a sergeant look after your shoes than to cover your six as the tail gunner in a B-17. I'm not sure I'm cut out to be this kind of officer, but some of it is okay. He dressed and was pleased with the way he looked. If I didn't have to sit down, I wouldn't mess up the crease in these pants. I sure as hell need to be careful when I eat. At 1055 hours there was another knock.

"Major Brown, Lieutenant Tolson is here. He asked me to bring your pack. He doesn't know where you will go from here. May I come in?"

Bill opened the door, "Yes, thank you, corporal," and they

walked out to the lieutenant's car. He was standing at attention beside the car. He saluted and Bill returned the salute, and Tolson opened the back door. Bill paused a moment, expecting to ride in the front with him.

"We are going to the Pentagon, sir," expecting that was enough explanation of the protocol. After accompanying Major Brown to the officers' mess, Lieutenant Tolson gave him a short tour of the Pentagon lobby and they headed inside and up. At precisely 1300 hours they reached a polished oak door with gold letters announcing, "Major General Francis Lovejoy, United States Army Air Force" and at the bottom "Colonel Ernst Holland, Adjutant."

Lieutenant Tolson rapped sharply on the door and a voice from within called "Enter."

Inside, Lieutenant Tolson and Major Brown both saluted Colonel Holland who had risen to meet them. Tolson said, "Colonel Holland, this is Major William M. Brown."

Colonel Holland dismissed Lieutenant Tolson and the colonel and Bill shook hands. He asked Bill to sit. Bill removed his hat and sat on the edge of the chair opposite the colonel's desk.

"Major Brown, do you have any questions about this program you are being considered for?" the colonel asked.

Bill answered by explaining about the delayed orders and no one at Bush Field seemed to have any idea about what was going on except Bill was to go to the Pentagon to meet the Army Air Force's highest-ranking officer.

Taken aback, Holland repeated the question.

"Sir," Bill said, "last Friday morning I was a deputy sheriff in Greene County, Georgia. My last thought about the Army was the Notre Dame game."

"Sit there, major," and Holland stood and knocked on the door to General Lovejoy's office.

"Enter."

Colonel Holland entered and remained several minutes. He returned, leaving the door open. Bill stood. From within he heard General Lovejoy call, "Major William Brown, please come in. I have something to discuss with you that you will find very interesting."

Interesting was an understatement. For Bill, this was the most exciting opportunity imaginable. Except for Elizabeth, it put everything together Bill cared about. He knew now, no matter what he did, making things work for him and Elizabeth, and now, Connie, was going to be difficult. But, with this, he had options and resources.

Right away, he knew he wanted to be a part of what the general explained, and he had no choice about being in the Army for at least twenty-one months.

General Lovejoy ended his explanation and asked, "What do you think?"

Bill took a deep breath and said, "Sir, I think this is an astounding opportunity and challenge. One I am ready to accept. To which school will I be assigned?"

"Major, you are our first-choice candidate and as such you have the option of choosing whichever school you wish. All of them have accepted you based on the information we have submitted. Do you know now, where you would like to go?"

"Yes, sir, M.I.T."

"Done. Colonel Holland will help you with the details. Welcome to the program. Major Brown, you should realize shortly you will be an officer in the United States Air Force."

Bill stood. "Yes, sir, General Lovejoy. I look forward to it," and he saluted his general.

In Colonel Holland's office, Bill explained what happened to his fiancé's mother.

"All of the program candidates who accept the offer are going for orientation at Alamogordo Army Air Field, starting next Monday." Looking at Bill's file, the colonel continued, "It hasn't been a year since you have flown, so all you will need to do is get checked out on the program's aircraft. The checkout will keep you at Triple A Field until thirteen December. I was going to send you straight to Triple A from Bush tomorrow, but since you don't need to be there until Monday, how about I give you travel time until we get you a flight on Saturday from Bush?"

"That would be great. Would flying from Atlanta be a problem?"

"Hell, no, much easier. Okay, I'll get you on something out of Atlanta on Saturday, 23 November. Until then you are on travel status. Sorry to hear about your problems, I hope this helps. How can I get in touch?"

"It all helps. You can call me at this number. It is my sister's home. I will be at her home by Friday. Thank you very much, Colonel Holland."

33

Connie's attitude about her mother's death confounded Elizabeth. Connie was not sad. Elizabeth knew she had been much more distressed when their father died. This morning she was excited about going home. In their compartment, she put away her heavy coat, inspected and claimed the rear facing seat by the window. But at quarter to eleven, she changed, "Elizabeth, the man who killed Momma is close by. Something is wrong about him, but he is close to us. We have to be careful."

"Connie, we will be all right in here. The door is locked and this button will call the conductor. Rest a little; we've been busy a long time this morning. When the train gets started, we will have dinner brought in. Think about what you want to eat."

Elizabeth checked the lock on the door and adjusted the curtain so no one could see in. She was beginning to realize how much their lives had changed. With or without Bill, her whole world would never be the same. "Connie," she said as she knelt in front of her chair, "come pray with me."

Connie joined her and Elizabeth put her arm around her little sister's shoulder. Elizabeth prayed in the same conversational manner as her mother. Connie added some of the words only she understood. They never said a final "Amen." Kneeling on the floor of their compartment and holding each other, they cried together until the train was well into New Jersey. Later, they ordered ice cream sodas and cookies.

Both were feeling better by supper time and enjoyed supper in the compartment. The long day had worn on both and they asked the porter to make their beds early. The sun was up when they woke and its light glistened off a heavy frost on the fields they passed. Elizabeth guessed they must be in North Carolina by now, maybe even South Carolina. It was Tuesday and they were getting close to home. Bill! What had he found out yesterday?

"Elizabeth," Connie asked, "Can we eat in the dining car this morning?"

"Are you sure you want to?"

"Yes, it will be all right. Last night, something happened to the man, and he is not going to bother us. Let's go to the dining car."

"Yes, Connie. We will eat breakfast in the dining car. Get dressed."

The train from New York arrived at Terminal Station in Atlanta at 12:20 p.m., right on time. The conductor stopped at their compartment a few minutes before they arrived in Atlanta and told them if they would stay in their compartment he would return with a porter to get them to their connection to Greensboro. When he returned, he assured them the rest of their luggage and their mother's body were ready to be put on the train to Greensboro.

Hans de Graffinreed did not leave his compartment when the train stopped at Atlanta. While Mary Greene's bullet did not penetrate his skull, it did cause a bruise to his brain directly behind the point of impact. Over the past fifty-seven hours there was increased bleeding in his head. By supper time on Monday, Hans hurt terribly, and he ate little of what he had ordered. At eleven o'clock Monday night a clot formed and he suffered a stroke. He was not found until early Wednesday morning when maids were making up the train for a return trip to New York. Barely alive and unconscious, he was taken to Grady Hospital.

Diane had planned to ask her pastor at the First Presbyterian Church to perform Mrs. DuBose's funeral until Sheriff DeWitt told her Jefferson DuBose had been a member of First Baptist, so she called their pastor. Reverend Massey declined. He said Mary Greene DuBose had never joined his church, and he didn't know if she had been properly baptized. Diane told the sheriff what Reverend Massey said. "I am going to call my pastor," she said.

"Wait a little while before you call," Sheriff DeWitt answered. And he went out.

In about twenty minutes, the sheriff came back to the office and began reading some old files. At least he had old files open on his desk. Diane answered a phone call and talked a few minutes. She hung up and turned her chair to face the sheriff. "That was Reverend Massey. He said he would be happy to perform Mrs. DuBose's funeral tomorrow, either in his church or at graveside."

"Well, that is helpful, isn't it? What service and what time did you decide?" Ben asked.

"Graveside at eleven. You didn't have anything to do with him changing his mind, did you?"

"Don't worry about it, Diane. It is something we do."

Bill's flight from Washington to Charlotte left early Tuesday. The flight from Charlotte landed at Bush Field at two o'clock. He drove from Bush directly to the DuBose home and arrived there shortly after Elizabeth and Connie. By five o'clock, Diane and Fred Thompson were there as well.

The Jacksons were the first to bring food, and Liza and Clara generally took charge of the house without being asked and almost without being seen. Food continued to come and by six o'clock the refrigerator was full, and the dining room table was piled with dishes. The outpouring of food was less a function of the DuBose family's standing in the community and more one of curiosity. But, of course, it was what was done.

Neither Elizabeth nor Connie wanted their mother brought to the house for a viewing, and told Fred to use the same type of coffin their daddy had, and to keep it closed. Fred said he would send one car at ten to pick up Elizabeth and Connie. Elizabeth explained Bill would be riding with them and asked Diane to ride with them as well. Diane agreed.

Reverend Massey came after Fred left. Elizabeth led the group into the parlor. Reverend Massey said he wanted to pray, so they all bowed and he started. After a few invocations and pleas, Bill noticed Connie rise from her usual kneeling position at her mother's ottoman. He watched her as she stood with her hands by her side, her eyes wide open and looking at the preacher.

Reverend Massey sensed the change and raised his eyes to see Connie staring at him with a puzzled look on her face. He caught her gaze, and closed his eyes and bowed his head again to indicate to Connie she should do the same. Connie didn't change her posture or expression. Clearly bothered, Reverend Massey dropped in a quick "Amen" at his next breath and ended his prayer. Connie turned and walked to the sofa and sat down beside Elizabeth and Bill.

The preacher quickly listed the scripture he would read and asked if there was any other scripture he should read. Connie whispered something to Elizabeth who whispered to Bill. Bill nodded affirmatively and Elizabeth said, "We will have a passage Bill will read."

With some relief, Reverend Massey said, "That will be fine. Do you want to have a hymn or any music?"

Again, Connie and Elizabeth conferred and Elizabeth answered, "We are going to ask our friend Moses Jackson to play "Taps" for my mother at the end of the service."

"Taps" is a little unusual for a civilian," replied Reverend Massey as his voice drifted, "but "Taps" will be fine. And I really must go. I will meet you at the cemetery tomorrow. Shall we pray again?"

Connie stood and answered him, "No, thank you. Good evening."

They all walked with the reverend to the front door. When it closed, Elizabeth asked, "Connie, what do you want Bill to read?"

"It's the part about the gifts of the Spirit, but I don't know where it is."

Diane answered, "I think it is First Corinthians, Chapter Twelve, right at the beginning."

"Agent Weston strikes again," Bill said. "I'm going to get the Bible."

Connie looked out and said, "Here comes Moses in his wagon. Elizabeth, you can ask him about playing for Momma."

Moses brought his wagon to the back door, and Liza and Clara started out to meet him. Elizabeth called to them, "Miss Liza, Clara, please take some food. It is only us, and no one else is coming. It will go to waste if you don't take some. Take lots. I want to ask Moses something." Bill, Diane, Elizabeth, and Connie walked out to the wagon. Moses climbed down and removed his hat.

Miss Elizabeth, Miss Connie, we are so sorry about your momma. She was always good to us. We be praying for her."

"Good." said Connie, "and it's better praying than old Reverend Brassy."

"Connie!" Elizabeth admonished. "Mr. Moses, will you play "Taps" for my mother like you did for Annie? Will you play for us?"

"Oh, yes ma'am, I'd be proud to do play. I carry my old bugle for calls and signals and such. But at home I have a regular horn I can play tunes on, you know, hymns and songs. Could I bring it and play something? Maybe "Closer Walk?"

"Momma would like that very much," said Connie.

Diane spoke to Elizabeth. Elizabeth asked, "Mr. Moses, can Miss Weston come pick you up at your home tomorrow? She will drive our car and all of you can follow us to the cemetery?"

"Yes'm, that will be good, very good." Moses helped load the wagon with the food Liza and Clara brought out. The Jacksons started down the drive in near darkness.

Diane said, "I'm going home, too. I will be out about nine unless you want me earlier."

"No, nine is good. Diane, thank you so much for everything you've done," Elizabeth said, as she and Connie hugged her.

They turned to the house. "Bill, I need to hear about what happened on Monday. And, I think I would like a glass of wine," Elizabeth said.

"I wouldn't mind a drink, myself," Bill replied. "We'll talk a while, and I'll head to town. I can still get into my place."

"The hell you will, Bill Brown!" Elizabeth answered. "I am not about to let you leave me alone tonight. We have two spare bedrooms and a whole downstairs, and there are no neighbors to see your old truck parked here. Besides, we're both too tired to do anything if we were a mind to."

As Connie opened the door she asked, "What are you too tired to do? I'm hungry."

Elizabeth answered, "Connie, get a plate and help yourself to anything on the table or in the refrigerator. No rules, no limits, eat what you want and as much as you want. But remember, we have a big day tomorrow."

"There are cakes and pies and other deserts. Can I have two?"

"Tonight, anything you would like."

With a whiskey and a glass of wine, Bill and Elizabeth sat on their sofa. At first Elizabeth did not understand why Bill had no choice about going in the Army for at least twenty-one months. Understanding the choices he had, and knowing he was going to be in Boston and not overseas, she said, "You made the right decision for you and perhaps for us."

They were happy to be together again. But the day, the time, and the travel caught up with both and they followed Connie to bed shortly after she rose from her feast. Bill took the front bedroom and everyone slept until nearly seven o'clock when the march to the funeral began.

For a mid-day and mid-week service, curiosity and funeral regulars made for a good turnout. Bill wore his dress uniform. Elizabeth and Diane told him how nice he looked in it. Connie said it was pretty and she would like one.

At the service, Bill and Elizabeth were glad for the scripture readings because that was all Reverend Massey had. While he prayed the last prayer, Connie added some of her own comments the preacher didn't understand, but some of the mourners apparently did, and they added their 'Amens' and 'Hallelujahs'.

At the end of the prayer, Elizabeth and Connie walked up and put their hands on the polished pine coffin. Connie leaned in and kissed it. Moses Jackson, standing away from the grave, brought his trumpet to his lips.

He stretched the first note of "Just a Closer Walk with Thee" into a prelude. Clear, sweet and at a tempo suitable for a funeral, the first verse brought a reverent stillness over the assembly. As the last note of the refrain faded, Reverend Massey closed his Bible and raised his head to speak. Moses was two beats ahead, and started the second verse still smooth and easy but with a little more pace. When he came to the second refrain, the notes seemed to dance and bounce from the granite headstones to the trees. Some mourners, especially the ones who had understood Connie's prayer, began to sing the words of the refrain.

The preacher knew not to move when the second refrain ended. The third time through, Moses made the notes alive; It was no longer a funeral march, but a celebration song. Most sang, swayed, or clapped time to the music. Reverend Massey walked away as Moses stretched the last note. Massey had the good sense to "let it be."

Bill stepped to the coffin and took Elizabeth and Connie by their hands and walked them to the Thompson Funeral Home car. The mourners evaporated in the noon sunshine. Thompson's car started for the DuBose house, and Diane followed in the Packard with the Jacksons.

Pete Moss and the two gravediggers lowered Mary Greene DuBose's coffin into the red Georgia soil and began to fill her grave. At Grady Hospital, Hans de Graffinreed's body passed over. His spirit searched fruitlessly for the spirit of Mary Greene DuBose in Central Park, New York, New York.

By two o'clock, the few who had come to the DuBose home after the funeral had all gone home. Liza and Clara brought dishes from home and repacked most of the remaining food into their dishes and loaded Moses' wagon. They were gone by two-thirty. There would be a nice supper and memorial service for Mary Greene at their church this evening, compliments of the people of Greensboro. Connie and Elizabeth napped and Bill toured the house.

When Elizabeth woke, they talked. They were sure now they would marry. Not now, but maybe when Bill finished at M.I.T. Elizabeth assured Bill money was not a problem for them for the foreseeable future. With a major's pay and a quarter's allowance money was not a problem for him.

Bill suggested Elizabeth and Connie might move to Athens so Connie could go to school there and she could go to Georgia. With summer schools, Elizabeth could have her degree when Bill finished M.I.T. and Connie would be out of elementary school. Elizabeth thought there was enough money for living in Athens and going to school. Maybe the three of them could spend holidays in Greensboro or even in Boston.

Though no one was hungry, Bill, Elizabeth, and Connie fixed a plate from the food left in the kitchen. They sat at the metal table, and Bill said a blessing.

After supper, the three of them sat in the parlor. Bill told Connie about his leaving and going to school and being in the Army for four more years. In typical Connie style, she sensed the peace Elizabeth, Mae, had with this and let them know it was okay with her.

Connie said school was good and she liked the idea of going to school and living in another town. Connie was pleased to know they were going to drive to Bill's sister's home the next day, but she was sorry Bill was going to be gone for a while, maybe a long time.

Connie went to bed on her own. Bill and Elizabeth talked a little more, kissed some, but not with the passion of other times on the sofa or in the Packard. Elizabeth fell asleep in Bill's lap. Bill closed his eyes and let the past week catch up with him and he slept.

About two-thirty, Elizabeth turned and nearly fell from the sofa. They both roused and walked up the back stairs. Elizabeth kissed Bill goodnight at the door to her room. Both understood this might be their last real kiss for a long time. Bill walked on to the front bedroom and undressed. The house was warm but he slipped on the robe Elizabeth had given him from her daddy's closet. He started to go to the bathroom when he heard Elizabeth's door open and her walk down the hall to the bathroom.

When she returned and he heard her door close, he made his trip. As he passed her closed door he saw a band of light beneath it. He leaned to the door, tapped once and said, "Good night."

"I love you," came from the closed door and the band of light beneath the door went black.

The hall was dark when he came out of the bathroom. He kept the light on with his hand on the switch to get his bearings. He switched off the light and darkness filled the hall. In his last few steps, he slowed as he searched for the knob. Instead of the hard glass door knob his hand found something soft…the plaid flannel shirt was hanging from the knob. He took it and held it against his cheek and pushed into the room and closed the door.

When Bill woke, his bed was empty. He switched on the lamp beside the bed and looked at his watch. It was five-thirty and time to start Army life. In the stillness of the big house in the country, he heard sounds from the kitchen, good sounds, the sounds of a home and of a family. He stood and picked up his boxers from the floor and tossed them on the bed before putting on the robe. Barefooted, he padded down to the bathroom by the back stairs and breathed in the aroma of bacon and coffee and biscuits. Had I a choice, today, I could spend my life as the Chief

Deputy of Greene County. When he came out of the bathroom, he stood for a second at the top of the stairs.

Elizabeth called out, "Bill, are you up and stirring?"

"Yes," he answered. "Do I have time to bathe?"

"Yes," Elizabeth called back. "Would you like some coffee?"

"Yes."

"I'll bring it up when you get out of the tub."

"I won't be long," he called. For him a tub was nothing more than sitting in an inch of warm water and giving himself a sponge bath. If I'm going to spend any time here, I will have a proper shower. He retrieved his shaving kit and ran a little water in the tub and washed quickly. Standing at the sink and working a lather on his face, Bill heard a bump at the door.

The door swung in and Connie said, "You don't have any clothes on!"

"I thought you were…"and he ended his answer. "Connie, you are right, as usual. Now, please close the door while I finish shaving."

The door closed and he heard Connie say, "Betty May, you can't go in there now. Bill is shaving, and he is naked. Do men always shave with no clothes on?"

"Connie, you are up early this morning. Why?"

"I don't know, but I have to go to the bathroom."

"Just go downstairs." Speaking to the closed door, Elizabeth said, "Bill, I'll put your coffee in your room."

Connie looked up at her sister, "You were going to take his coffee in the bathroom, and you knew he was shaving naked. You only have on your old shirt and no underpants! Even if Saint Paul said, 'love thinks no evil', Momma might think some evil if she were here. I might, too. I don't know, Betty May, I mean Mae, this love thing is hard. I'm going to think as a child for right now, but you better be careful. I do know some grownup things."

Elizabeth put the cup of coffee down on a table in the hall. She was standing behind Connie and she wrapped her arms around her sister. "Connie," she said, "today is going to be the beginning of a big adventure for you and me. We will learn many things, and we will put away childish things. But, we might do some childish things, too. We will have fun and love and each other."

And Connie said, "And Bill?"

Elizabeth answered, "Yes, we will have and love Bill. I love you, my little sister."

When they were all dressed, Elizabeth scrambled eggs and they sat down to breakfast. After they ate, all three helped clean up.

Bill put his duffle in the trunk of the Packard. Connie rode with him to Jim's station, and Elizabeth followed in the Packard.

As they entered town, Connie asked, "Bill, you call Betty May, 'Elizabeth'. She asked me to call her 'Mae'. What you are going to call her? Did she ask you to call her Mae, too?"

"Not yet, but if she does, I will. Or maybe I'll call her 'hon' or 'love' or 'sweetie pie' or 'darling'. What do you think?"

"I don't think Mae wants to have a restaurant," Connie answered.

At the station, the Packard stopped at the gas pump. Bill parked the truck on the side and found Jim. "Jim, fill up Elizabeth's car. She is taking me to Sandy Springs to my sister's. I have been recalled to active duty and will go to school in Boston for the next year and a half and I have to do four more years."

"When did you find out? You hadn't said anything about it. Will you still be a pilot?" Jim asked.

"I didn't know anything about any of it until last Friday. My orders were held up at the post office. Oh, yes, I will fly. And maybe I'll get to fly some new planes. Between school and the Air Corps, the next few years ought to be exciting."

"What about Elizabeth?"

"Jim, we will make it work somehow, some way. I love her."

"I know you do. Let me know if I can help."

"Well, you can sell my truck. I can't take it with me to Boston. I want $85 for it, but I will take $75 and pay you $10 to sell it. Would you sell it for me?"

"You will take $65 net for it, right? I will give it to you now!"

"No, that won't work. From you it would have to be $60. Deal?" Jim nodded in agreement. "I'll sign the title and you take the gas out of the $60. Jim, I will miss you. The next time I see you, you and Bec might be married and have a passel of young'uns."

Jim smiled sheepishly and said, "Well, married and maybe one. The gas is on me." They shook hands and Jim gave Bill a small salute. "Be careful, Major Brown. I will look after Elizabeth and Connie."

As Bill walked to the big Packard, Elizabeth slid out and walked to the passenger door and got in. Bill got in, pulled the big door closed with a solid and satisfying thump, started the engine and dropped the shift lever into first and looked at Elizabeth. "Sweetie pie, are you ready to start?"

"When you are, hon."

Connie looked at Bill and at her sister and said, "You two are being childish."

Acknowledgments

There are a number of people who helped me make this book possible. In the dedication, I mentioned my wife, Sandra Bloodworth, who did not discourage me from working those early morning hours, and encouraged me after reading what I had written. Without her, none of this would have happened. Others were my first readers. Those were the ones who ordered a Kindle version and plowed through typos, punctuation errors, double words, and at least ten thousand too many words, and still told me they liked the story and the characters. I have a long list of names. Too many for here, but I think they know. However, there are two I should mention by name. Both are newspaper guys and both have been tremendously supportive and helpful: Dick Huguley, retired from the *Atlanta Journal Constitution,* and Gary Ward of *The State* in Columbia, SC and the Trinity Book Club.

About the Author

We Southerners are more a product of our place and time, than other aspects of our being," said Johnny Bloodworth. "I am a story teller, and when I tell a story about us, I need to connect the narrative to place and time."

Johnny has roots in Georgia, but South Carolina has been his home for more than sixty years. His places are Columbia where he worked and the Cedar Creek community near Blythewood where he and his wife Sandra have lived for 45 years. He says he could keep a job, but his work life has included teaching, coaching football and track, government service, and mortgage banking.

He says, "Before *Gift*, my story telling was oral and consisted of turning an incident or a joke into a tale about friends or family. *Gift* added discipline to the creative process. But it paid off. *Gift* has been extremely well received.

CPSIA information can be obtained
at www.ICGtesting.com
Printed in the USA
FFHW02n0114210818
47944289-51628FF